Magnolia Storms

A Coastal Hearts Novel

Janet W. Ferguson

Copyright © 2017 Janet W. Ferguson

Southern Sun Press LLC

Southern
Sun Press

ISBN-10: 0-9976587-6-2
ISBN-13: 978-0-9976587-6-7

Acknowledgments

My thanks go out to:

The Lord who holds me through the storms of life.

My husband, Bruce, for supporting me.

Charles DeMetz, a ship pilot and long-time friend, who answered hundreds of questions and supplied videos and pictures of pilot transfers to large vessels through treacherous waters. Dedicated ship pilots like Charles love the water, but they risk danger on a daily basis to guide travelers from around the world into safe harbor.

Dr. Benjamin Kerr, neurosurgeon, who answered more injury questions for me. I really appreciate his valuable time.

Lisa Donitz from the U.S. Merchant Marine Academy Alumni Association and Foundation who answered questions.

Chip Henderson, Pinelake pastor, for an inspiring sermon which helped shape the faith elements of this story.

Meteorologist Barbie Bassett for reading through the early draft and checking the weather data.

All the staff at the National Weather Service Forecast Office in Jackson who did their best to explain a bit of weather terminology to a spacy author.

My fabulous ACFW critique partners and my street team.

Editor Robin Patchen, mentor author Misty Beller, and cover artist Paper & Sage.

When you pass through the waters, I will be with you...

Foreword

There are a few monumental days that divide our lives. Some are happy—a marriage or the birth of a child. Others are horrifying—that knock on the door or that phone call with bad news—the death of a spouse, child, or parent. There are days when we remember exactly where we were when something horrific happened—September 11, the Challenger explosion, a president being shot.

August 29, 2005.

Hurricane Katrina was a horrifying day that divided the lives of most Mississippians. The destruction and loss was staggering.

Though my home is three hours inland, Katrina's storm winds still howled and moaned for hours, uprooting trees in every yard in my neighborhood, many of them crashing on rooftops. We had no power or phone service for a week, which was nothing compared to what happened south of us. I had dear friends from the Coast, and for weeks on weeks, I had no idea whether they were safe, due to the damage to communications infrastructure. The storm hit in August and caused the Gulf to surge up to twenty-seven feet in places.

Six months later, I traveled with a rebuilding team to hang sheetrock. The surreal mutilation of the landscape I witnessed, even months afterward, is forever branded onto my mind. No street signs, no landmarks, food still being served by members of churches under tents, because there was nowhere else to get it. I've done my best to honor the people who lost so much in this disaster.

This book is dedicated to my friends and all the Mississippians who went through the devastation that was Hurricane Katrina.

Janet W. Ferguson

Chapter 1

Fear and loss snaked around Magnolia Marovich's heart like they always did when she studied the satellite images on the three computer screens in front of her. *Not again.* The waters should be calming down in November, not churning up a monster.

Maggie twirled one of her untamable, dark curls around her finger and blew out a shaky breath. The mid-morning hurricane hotline conference call had left her stomach roiling like the spinning air mass out there in the atmosphere.

Sure, they'd had an unseasonably hot year—okay, a sweltering year—which fueled the tropical weather, but why couldn't God keep the seas calm a little longer? They'd been so close to the end of the season. Yet here it was almost Thanksgiving, and the Mississippi National Weather Service office hummed with activity. The storm had hammered Haiti and Cuba before barreling into the mouth of the Gulf overnight. Already a category two in the warmer waters, the long-term forecast placed the trajectory cone over the Mississippi and Alabama Coasts.

Though Maggie's current house and office in Jackson were located three hours north of the Coast, memories of Hurricane Katrina's wrath pounded on the doors of her mind. The fury of the wind, the fierceness of the rain, and finally the savage cruelty of the tidal surge that ripped away so much of her beloved hometown.

And her heart.

Another email notification popped up, pulling her from the recurrent nightmare of emotions. She clicked on the forecast track. More data on the storm. She needed to live in the present and stay on top of the computer models, so she could warn others to get out of harm's way.

Others…like the few left of her own family.

Would her stubborn sister come inland or wait until the last minute as usual? She pictured Cammie working in the quaint antique store in downtown Ocean Springs—much too near the coastline. She imagined Cammie's daughter, Dahlia, drawing pictures or doing homework behind the checkout counter while her mom worked. Familiar nausea swept through Maggie's midsection. Cammie didn't have to stay and endanger her little girl. Their great aunt's store could close for good this time, and Cammie could find a job here in Jackson, where she'd have help with Dahlia and Aunt Ruth.

Maggie rolled her shoulders to loosen the building tension. There was plenty of room in her empty house for her family. If only they'd come.

"You look like you could use a neck rub." Her co-worker Jane's voice chirped as she leaned over the cubicle's half-wall. "Your tendons are poking out like the spokes on my bike, and Steve hasn't taken his eyes off you all morning. I'm sure he'd love to oblige."

With a vehement shake of her head, Maggie scowled. "If he touched my neck, he might find my latest lukewarm cup of coffee splashed across his expensive loafers." The weight-lifting womanizer had made her his target for months now, despite her continued refusals.

Her petite blonde friend offered a compassionate smile. "Staring at those screens won't change anything, Maggie. You can't control the weather."

A fact she knew well…which partly explained her stale life. "But I can prepare for what's coming and warn others to do the same." And save some of them from enduring the heartbreak and grief she'd suffered.

"I'll be praying the storm passes and your family stays safe." Jane patted the laminate at the edge of the desk. "Come eat dinner with us after work. There's always enough for one more at the table with the latest Crock-Pot creation I've devised, and it'll save you from pacing around your place all night. At least for an hour or two."

Jane was sweet, her blue-eyed children adorable, and her husband a kind man. Maggie's fingers ran across a scratch in the coating of her desk. Being with Jane's happy family underscored Maggie's own shipwrecked life. Isolated and alone. The ancient debris from her relationship with Josh always muddied her odds for finding someone who could measure up.

Josh. Maggie's heart still pinched as she dredged up his memory. The last person she wanted to think about during a hurricane.

"Earth to Maggie." Jane touched her hand.

"I don't know."

"The kids will be excited if you come."

"Sure. Thanks."

Not like she had anything else planned. Playing preschool-level board games would be a good distraction. "I'll pick up cookie dough ice cream for dessert." Might as well stress-eat with a crowd…or else she'd devour the whole carton herself.

Maggie managed a small smile and turned back to her monitors. The swirling form waiting there mocked her. She'd gotten too comfortable, too secure that Mississippi would make it through another year without mass destruction.

Sinking into the deep pain of the past, her mind conjured up the eerie roar of wind, the crack of splintering trees, and the earth-shaking boom as they fell to the ground, rattling the walls. Her father kissing her forehead before he disappeared through the door. The last she'd ever seen of him.

Maggie mashed her eyes shut. No. Stop.

Please, Lord, let me forget.

Her phone's vibration on the desk jerked her back to the present. Cammie's number. Maggie grabbed it. Maybe she could talk some sense into her sister this time.

"Hello."

"Aunt Maggie?" Her precious niece's voice quivered.

"Is something wrong, Dahlia?"

No answer except a sniffle and a quiet sob that wrenched Maggie's insides. "Sweetie, are you having a bad day? You can tell me anything, you know."

"I need you to come to Aunt Ruth's house. Mama's been in an accident." Another sniffle and a hiccup. "Hit by a truck. They took her in an ambulance."

"Hit by a truck?" Her voice came out way too loud. In an instant, Jane and Steve hovered by her workspace with anxious expressions clouding their faces.

Maggie pressed her burning eyes closed as she tried to make sense of her niece's words. A truck. An ambulance. The hospital.

No, Lord. Don't take my sister, too. Let Cammie be okay.

She needed to help her family.

Her mouth dried as she tried to swallow the lump of panic strangling her.

Not down to the Coast.

Not in this weather.

"I'll be there in three hours." For Cammie. And for Dahlia.

Jane kneeled near the swivel chair and rested her hand on Maggie's. "What's happened? What can I do?"

"It's my sister. She's in the hospital…" Her stupid voice quivered.

God, help me do what I have to do.

Determination rose in her chest, ran down to her fists. "I have to go home and help my family."

"Maybe I can go with you." Her friend's eyes welled with tears. "I know the storm has you upset already."

Steve slipped closer. "I can take her."

Maggie shot up. "No." Again her voice came out louder than she'd intended. A few other heads in the office rotated her way. "I need you both here keeping an eye on the hurricane."

~~~

Wind whipped Josh Bergeron's face, and the spray of salt water filled his eyes as his boat battled the swells rocking the Gulf of Mexico. Most days he loved his job as a river bar pilot, gulping in the sun and briny air. The tides and the marsh and the sandbars had been a part of him for as long as he could remember. But stormy days like this made him wonder whether he was crazy after all. Like Magnolia Marovich had insisted so many years ago.

Maggie. Much like a storm herself, she'd been on his mind during this hurricane season. And every season since Katrina. With the new storm moving into the Gulf overnight, he couldn't help but wonder what she was doing right now. Stocking up on supplies and advising everyone who'd listen to scurry inland, no doubt. Staring at some computer screen to monitor the storm. She'd never gotten over her father's death.

Josh pictured his own son back home. Those innocent eyes that hung on his every word.

11

Lord, take care of J.D. if anything should happen to me.

Enough. Nothing was going to happen.

Mr. Marovich's death was a rarity in this industry. Pilots and their crews took precautions, but an attempted rescue during a monster hurricane like Katrina…too many variables, too much devastation.

The pilot of Josh's vessel maneuvered close, and the massive tanker alongside them slowed, preparing for him to make the swap so he could board and pilot the larger ship up the mouth of the Mississippi. The chain on his waist clamped him to the rail system surrounding the pilot boat while he waited. The ladder from the tanker undulated as even the enormous vessel pitched in the waves. If visibility and winds hadn't been so bad, they could've used a helicopter to get to here. His partner edged their boat ever closer. Josh took a deep breath and prepared for the switch.

The two vessels seesawed in the whitecaps. It had been a long time since he'd seen the waves this brutal. He'd have to time the transfer carefully. A stumble in this weather, and he'd be swept out, lost to the sea's wrath despite his rescue beacon.

The ladder neared. Josh unclipped his harness and reached for the closest rung. He caught hold and held on with fingers tightly clenched. The other ship rocked away and left only the ladder keeping him from the churning waves below. Rain bludgeoned him, cold and blinding. He pushed one foot and then another up the rungs, counting his steps as he ascended. Almost there. Near the top, his shoe slipped, and he lost his footing. Dangling with white knuckles, he grappled to catch the step with his toe.

A gale force wind whipped up, challenging his grip. A rush of adrenaline heightened his senses and gave him a burst of strength.

"Are you kidding me?" He fought to swing closer and, finally, his right ankle made contact with metal. After wrenching his leg around the rails, he stood and scrambled the rest of the way up by sheer will—and determination to see his son again. At last, he made his way to the captain's bridge and assumed control of the ship.

The orders he gave the helmsman would deliver the tanker around the underwater obstructions in the mouth of the Mississippi River. The routes, depths, and current flows were etched in his mind, like everything Mr. Marovich had taught him. Bittersweet memories stirred an ache in Josh's chest. Once the deliveries were wrapped up, he'd return home tomorrow for his two weeks off. If he hadn't promised to help Cammie at the store, he'd grab J.D. and go inland until the hurricane passed. But he'd keep his promise. He wouldn't bail out.

Unlike his own father.

The thought of the skirt-chasing deserter tightened Josh's fists. He'd never let his son down like that.

Other than his faith in God, being a pilot and being a good father to J.D. were everything to him.

Maybe because they were *all* he had.

Chapter 2

After a stop at her house, where she'd packed quickly and flung a wadded heap of clothes onto the backseat, Maggie took off down the highway. The drive was calm, but the battle in her mind was colossal. She hated leaving her meteorology team in a crisis, especially heading into a storm she should be monitoring.

Fear engulfed her. Scars, pitted and deep in her heart, gashed open, raining tears down her cheeks, sending prickly shivers across her shoulders and down her arms.

Lord, give me strength. I have to make this trip.

Maggie took a deep gulp of air then blew it out. Trepidation gave way to resignation. What else could she do? She had to go. Cammie was injured. Their great aunt was too elderly to manage, and Dahlia too young to stay alone.

An hour into the trip, Maggie glanced in the rearview mirror to find a pickup truck on her tail.

Sorry, mister.

She accelerated to the speed limit. Yes, her speed had been erratic. Somewhere between mashing the gas pedal almost to the floor and barely coasting along Highway 49, wishing she could turn back north.

Growing up along the Mississippi Sound, she'd savored home, been proud to live in the area where those stately antebellum houses had stood facing the deceptively gentle Gulf waters. But she sickened at the thought of those lots that still stood vacant and deserted more than a decade after the storm. The sidewalks and steps that led to bare concrete slabs—empty foundations that used to be someone's home or business. Memories flooded her mind. Streets and bridges, buckled and broken. Debris piled high in surreal mounds like something from a Salvador Dali painting. The stench of rotting meat swept out from the bellies of containers at the port competing with the smells of mildew, mold, and death.

Whole towns obliterated.

The seeming stability of her life, crushed like a fragile eggshell under the heel of a beast.

Maggie neared the cutoff toward Ocean Springs and stared at the cumulus clouds. Windy, but no evidence of the huge storm entering the Gulf. What must life have been like before modern prediction systems? How awful it must've been to have no warning before a storm hit. She'd read historical accounts of coastal areas being completely wiped out. Another shiver ran across her shoulders.

Palms slick, Maggie wound her way around the low-lying, flat streets of her historic hometown. Vibrant landscaping and trees with long overhanging branches nestled around the charming cottages. The gnarled limbs and trunks of the ancient live oaks had struggled to make their comeback since the deluge. So many of the beautiful trees had been lost in Katrina.

Katrina.

No matter how hard she tried to control herself, she always shuddered at the horror that name brought to mind. The damage and devastation of homes and lives—her home. Her father's life.

She'd rarely returned since she'd finally made her getaway to Mississippi State University to earn her master's in meteorology. Knowledge and preparation provided security…safety. Her degree had been a place to dump all her froth of emotions and find a way to take a small measure of control. Too bad her sister hadn't followed suit. Instead, beautiful Cammie had found comfort in the arms of a sweet-talking boy at Tulane. The sorry fellow left her high and dry once he found out about the baby. But Dahlia had been a joy and a blessing for them all. Named after their mother, the darling girl had eased the blow as Mama had battled breast cancer. A battle they'd lost three years ago.

The child owned a piece of Maggie's heart, either despite the fact Dahlia looked like she could be her younger twin or because of it. Except, fortunately, the child hadn't inherited the uncontrollable, curly mane.

"Okay, world, I'm back in Ocean Springs." She parked her Acura in the drive of the old Greek revival home and steeled herself for what she was about to face.

When she stepped out of the car, a muggy gust of wind attacked, slapping her hair across her cheeks. She glanced up at the tottering trees' creaky branches. Nice welcome. It figured.

Not much had changed at Aunt Ruth's. White wooden panels, green shutters, and a black roof. Always the same, though it had all been remodeled a few times over the years. How the old home had weathered so many hurricanes didn't compute. Especially when Mama and Daddy's home a few blocks away had been ripped from its foundation and strewn in the piles of debris that stretched and littered the earth for miles in every direction.

The front door flew open, and Dahlia ran onto the wooden porch.

Poor baby. Maggie's heart lurched, and she took quick steps toward her niece. The ten-year-old had grown taller and slimmer since their last visit a few months ago. Hair still hung straight like her mother's. Luckily. And she was holding…a smaller child? Maggie blinked hard to confirm what she was seeing. Why would Dahlia have what looked to be a three-year-old boy?

"Hey, sweetie." Maggie climbed the four steps to the porch and wrapped Dahlia in an embrace. "I've missed you. Who's this?" Maggie studied the boy's enormous blue eyes gazing up at her.

Oddly familiar blue eyes.

"His name's J.D., and he's getting heavy." Dahlia held him toward Maggie, and his freckled cheeks spread in a tentative smile.

She scooped the child into her arms and onto her hip, studying him closer.

"That's why I needed your help." Dahlia coughed and wiped her dimpled cheeks, her eyes red from crying. "I should be able to stay by myself, even though Mama never lets me, but he's a handful. Usually the three of us tag team, but when Mama…" Her niece's voice quivered.

"Come on. Let's go inside." Maggie laced her free arm across Dahlia's thin shoulders. "I'll take care of everything." Or die trying.

"What's wrong with your hair?" J.D. grabbed a chunk of her curls into his fist. "It's all bent up."

The question she'd asked her entire life. "I inherited these unruly coils from my Cajun grandmother, Delphine Boudreaux." Too bad she'd inherited her hips from Grandma Marovich. She followed Dahlia through the entrance hall into the living room, which was more like an antique store itself, and they took a seat on the red camelback couch. So many memories surrounded her. The Flow Blue china collection on every flat surface. Ornate gold frames displaying pictures of her and Cammie, more of Mom and Dad. She breathed in the smell of home and let it settle deep inside her chest, where it wound through shadows and emotions she'd bound up over a decade ago.

"What's 'herited?" The boy's voice reeled her back as he twirled her hair round and round on his index finger.

"It's when you look like your mom or dad."

His big eyes widened. "I look like Daddy."

Talking to the boy was sweet, but she needed to get the scoop on her sister's accident and take action. Maggie glanced at her niece. "Speaking of, where are J.D.'s parents, and what's happened to your mom? Where's Aunt Ruth? Why were you out of school so early?"

Tears welled up and leaked out onto Dahlia's cheeks. "Mama checked me out of school to watch J.D.'s Thanksgiving play. She let us come back to the store with her afterward. We were doing a puzzle behind the counter while she went to the delivery entrance. A truck backed into Mama outside the store. An ambulance came, and Aunt Ruth sent me home so she could follow them in the car. I put the *Closed* sign in the window and walked here with J.D."

Aunt Ruth drove? The eighty-five-year old couldn't see a yacht in a baby pool. And she let Dahlia walk home with a three-year old? Ten wasn't old enough to stay alone in the first place, despite Dahlia's ideas to the contrary. Of course, her little family didn't have anyone else nearby—all of their cousins lived in Louisiana. But a customer or friend might've helped. Aunt Ruth couldn't have been thinking clearly.

Maggie sighed. At least the house was only two blocks from the store.

"What hospital? Have you heard anything?"

"Mama might need surgery on her back. I...I can't

18

remember…"

Cold fear rooted and took hold in Maggie's chest. Back injuries could be serious. Would she be able to evacuate them all with Cammie injured? Another tug on her hair brought her gaze down to J.D. Who'd take care of this child? And why were they keeping him in the first place?

Maggie pasted on a calm expression. "Don't worry. I'll find her." But Aunt Ruth must've had her phone on silent again. Maggie had tried to get her a dozen times since Dahlia first called. "What time does J.D. get picked up?"

"Not until Mr. Josh comes in from the ship."

Josh?

J.D.

Not as in Joshua David Bergeron?

Maggie's pulse throbbed in her ears as she stared at J.D. No wonder she recognized those eyes. They were the exact sky-blue color eyes of the boy she'd grown up with, fallen in love with…and tried to forget. The stubborn man had insisted on following in her father's footsteps to become a river bar pilot, even after the storm. Nothing would change his mind. And she wouldn't change her mind about being with someone she'd likely lose to the Gulf. She refused to relive that agony.

"How long have you been babysitting J.D.?" Cammie hadn't bothered to mention this new development the last time they'd talked.

"Since they moved in next door…like six months ago. We keep him every two weeks. Mama was gonna tell you, but she kept putting it off. Aunt Ruth said she needed to hurry up."

A rather huge omission. And next door? "Next door, as in they live in the house beside this one?"

"Duh, Aunt Maggie. That's what next door is."

Already a smart aleck at ten. She and her niece grew more

and more alike.

But where was J.D.'s mother? And why wasn't she keeping her own child? Maggie's chest tightened. Now she'd be forced to call him. So maddening. They hadn't spoken since their breakup. And she'd hoped to keep it that way.

First she'd check on Cammie, though. She stared at the little boy beside her.

Lord, help me if I have to see Josh. Seeing his child is tough enough.

Despite over a decade of trying to forget the man, Josh still haunted the vacant corners of her heart.

~~~

Once he'd finished the delivery of the ship and made it safely back to his own boat, Josh sank into a seat in the center of the passenger area and closed his eyes while his partner, Graham, piloted them back to base. The waves still rocked the smaller vessel, but not nearly as much as they had earlier in the day. He'd had a close call.

Thank you, Lord, for keeping me safe.

His hand slipped to his pocket, and he switched his phone back on. It chirped over and over. He stared at it. Cammie's number. Tendrils of anxiety roped around his midsection. Was something wrong with J.D.? She rarely called him until the evenings when she let J.D. talk to him. Josh touched the contact number to call back.

"Hello, Josh." The voice slammed him like a punch to his stomach. Not Cammie.

This tone was low and strong, yet sultry. The slight Cajun accent. *Maggie.* That voice that could gut him from miles away, even after all this time.

Words froze in his throat.

"Are you going to say anything?"

"Why do you have Cammie's phone?"

"We're in a crisis, and you need to get back here ASAP."

Fear clawed at him now, shredding his composure. "Is J.D. okay? What's happened?" His voice cracked.

"Your son is fine." Her tone softened for half a second. "Cammie's injured her vertebrae. Some delivery guy wasn't paying attention and hit reverse instead of drive. Knocked into her hard."

"Oh, Maggie. I'm sorry." Though thankful J.D was safe, his stomach still sank. Maggie's family had been through too much already. Lost so much already. His gaze traveled to the window, past the American flag whipping in the wind, to the gales rocking the murky water before them. Somewhere in the depths, her father had been buried.

"Yeah. Me, too." A wistfulness carried over the distance, snagging his heart. "Is there someone else here who could pick up J.D.?"

Apparently she didn't keep up with his personal life. Which, given the way his ex-wife had dumped him, maybe was best. It was embarrassing enough looking like a failure to the people who knew. "I'll leave as soon as we reach Venice." Too bad they weren't already back.

"Really?" The sharpness returned. "They've still got y'all out in this wind? And there's a hurricane entering the Gulf as we speak."

"We're fine, Maggie. That storm's days away." He could picture the fire in those chocolate eyes framed with the longest black lashes he'd ever seen, wild curls falling down her shoulders.

"Right." A dramatic sigh crossed the airwaves. "So, a few hours?"

As fast as he could. Did the woman want him to jump ship and start swimming that way? He shook his head and held in the sarcasm. He wouldn't dare say something like that to *her.* "Yes, ma'am. See you in a few. Promise."

"Don't make promises you can't keep, Joshua Bergeron."

Abruptly, the call ended. A lot like the way their relationship had ended years before.

Chapter 3

Maggie checked the weather on her cell. Again.

No change.

She shifted her gaze to J.D. Three-year-old boys and waiting rooms went together about as well as an ice storm at the beach, but she'd had little choice.

It had only taken her a minute at Aunt Ruth's house to unload, and they'd raced to the hospital. Of course, with Josh driving in from Louisiana, she'd had to bring the boy. She'd corralled him with a coloring book from the gift shop—the third trip they'd made since arriving at the hospital. Frustration had already claimed a huge chunk of her minuscule patience when she'd had to figure out how to get the booster contraption into her car and J.D. fastened in it. Snarky comments from a ten-year-old girl hadn't helped. When had her sweet Dahlia turned into a sassy preteen? Add a few more hormones, and her niece might refuse to be seen in public with any of them. And that might be okay for a while.

"I can't hear this thing." Aunt Ruth ambled over to the television positioned in the corner of the brightly-lit room and adjusted the volume. It blasted out an old episode of *Walker, Texas Ranger*. Obviously, more than her aunt's sight was dwindling. Explained the missed phone calls. They might need to bring earplugs for the other families in the waiting area.

The hospital's smell of antiseptic and something stale reawakened a sense of sorrow. She'd spent many days and nights with her mother in the Jackson hospital and the cancer

23

center. Had even flown to a couple of other medical clinics for second opinions. In the end...

No. She couldn't retrace that journey. This was different. It had to be.

But, they'd waited hours already. And Cammie had been in surgery before their arrival. Couldn't be good news.

Lord, be with her, heal her. Don't take her.

"Miss Maggie?" The little voice summoned her attention.

"Yes, J.D." She ran her fingers through his silky hair the color of sand. A bit lighter, but almost the same shade as Josh's had been the last time she'd seen him.

"I gotta go potty."

"Sure. You remember, the bathroom's right here." She pointed at the door straight in front of them. They'd picked these specific seats strategically. "You went earlier, and we left the light on."

"Not like that. My tummy hurts, and I need help."

"Wait. What?" Josh would have a good laugh if he heard about this. He always did love to tease her...get her riled up. Then sweet talk her into laughing, too. A laugh she'd missed. She held in a groan and pushed the thought away.

Amusement crinkled Dahlia's nose as she snorted. "Go, Aunt Maggie." Dahlia would, no doubt, love to tell Josh all about her blunders today. "You're supposed to be tough, right?"

"Who said that?" Maggie frowned. A tad feisty, but that had nothing to do with this situation. She liked breathing fresh air.

J.D.'s bottom lip poked out. "Miss Cammie always helps me."

"If Cammie can do it, I can. Let's go." Cammie owed her big-time when she got well. Josh, too, but she'd rather not collect any favors from him. Other than him moving and staying away from them all.

What seemed like an hour later, Maggie escaped the small bathroom. If the kid wasn't so stinkin' cute, she'd swear off children forever. Although the probability of having any of her own was slim to none.

That familiar vacant gnawing clawed at her throat. All of her college friends had married and moved on with their lives, but she'd never found that someone to make her feel like…home.

Apparently Josh had. But where was the woman?

"I'm hungry." J.D. again.

Of course he was hungry now. Maggie glanced at Aunt Ruth and Dahlia. They'd forgotten to eat a real supper with all the chaos—only snacking from the vending machines. "As soon as the doctor comes in, we'll go for dinner. I have more Hot Tamales in my purse until then." Not that giving candy to a kid stuck in a small area was a good idea. She didn't know much about kids, but that's what she'd heard from her coworker, Jane. The dropping barometric pressure must've been muddling her judgement, but she handed him the box of candy anyway.

The door swung open. Some maternal instinct took over, and she swept J.D. up in her arms.

A thirtyish dark-haired man in blue scrubs entered. "Family of Camelia Marovich?"

Maggie stood. Was he the doctor? He hardly looked old enough to be a specialist. "I'm her sister, Maggie. What's the news on Cammie's back?"

The doctor's gaze flitted to Dahlia and Aunt Ruth. "And they are?"

"Oh, this is Cammie's daughter, Dahlia, and our great aunt,

Ruth."

He eyed each one of them…seemingly contemplating.

Was that a bad sign? Had to be. Tingles crawled down her scalp.

"I'm Dr. Castro." He stepped further into the room and studied Dahlia. "Can your great aunt Ruth take you and your brother to the nurse's desk? Tell them I said to give you some of my ice cream sandwiches to eat in the break room."

"He's not my brother." Dahlia's face screwed into a frown. "And I'm ten. You can give me the bad news."

Maggie let her eyes shut for a long moment, then opened them and shot her niece a stern but compassionate look. "Dahlia." She stood J.D. on his feet.

Her niece let out a long dramatic sigh. "Yes, sir." Dahlia trudged over and took the boy by the hand. "Let's go get a treat." She motioned to Aunt Ruth, speaking loudly and with exacting lip movements. "Come with me and J.D. They think I'm too young to do anything alone."

Once they'd cleared the area, Dr. Castro shook his head. "Starts early these days. I've got one at home. Let's go into the conference room."

She followed him into the small, bland area, and he shut the door. He offered her a chair and took a deep breath as if dreading what he was about to say. "Cammie took a hard hit, and her lower spine was injured." He held out pictures and lifted some x-rays over a light. He spoke of vertebrae and lumbar and sacral areas, scores on some tests that were named with abbreviations she'd never heard of…fractures and fragments.

Staring at the pictures of Cammie's spine, Maggie's brain fogged. Her eyes burned.

"She's awake, and right now," the doctor continued, "she

has no feeling below the waist, but with time, we hope the swelling will lessen and movement will be restored."

That popped her eyes open. "No feeling? As in paralyzed? For how long?"

"We don't know how long yet. She's in the ICU. I'll take you back to see her for a few minutes, but visiting hours are limited, and I don't think it's a good idea for the others to come right away. Do you have any questions?"

The constriction in Maggie's throat made it difficult to breathe, much less think or speak. Cammie paralyzed? She shook her head and stood, willed her feet to follow him from the room. The doctor pressed a code at the entrance to the ICU.

Once the door opened, they traversed a hall of windowed rooms. Dread and curiosity drew her gaze. She couldn't help peeking into a few of them. Some of the patients had pictures and drawings taped to the walls. How long had those families been waiting for healing?

Maggie's feet grew heavier. Each footfall sounded like a clap of thunder in her ears. At last, they entered a room filled with machines. All attached to her sister. Angry red scrapes carved across the right side of Cammie's face. Dark purple bruises, too. Her straight, honey-brown hair spread, tangled and matted, on the small pillow.

Icy terror encased Maggie's heart. "Oh, God, help us." She breathed out the whispered prayer.

The doctor stood near but didn't speak.

Cammie's eyes fluttered open. "Maggie?"

"I'm here." Maggie moved quickly to the bedside.

"Dahlia? J.D.?" The words came out raspy.

"They're fine." She kept her tone strong and much more confident than she felt. "I'm taking good care of them."

"The store? We have to stay open." Cammie's brows knitted together. "Christmas inventory… Thanksgiving sale."

Always so worried about Aunt Ruth's business. Maggie's lips pinched. Probably what got her into this mess in the first place. If only they'd move to Jackson, she could help more with Aunt Ruth and Dahlia. Cammie could work normal office hours.

"I need this." Cammie's eyes pleaded.

Like she would say no to her only sister while she lay in a hospital bed. "I have plenty of leave, and it's almost Thanksgiving anyway, so don't fret about the store. I'll handle it." Or sell the place and get all five of them out of here before another storm hit.

Not five.

J.D. was Josh's problem.

Okay, not a problem, but a responsibility. An adorable, blue-eyed responsibility.

The relief on Cammie's face made the promise to stay longer almost worth the cost, but dread remained in the pit of Maggie's stomach. The storm still brewed in the Gulf. And Cammie was paralyzed.

The young doctor patted Cammie's hand and explained what he'd already told Maggie. "Best case scenario will be the return of leg strength to functional level with no limitations, and possibly some mild residual numbness or tingling in the legs." He paused and glanced back and forth between Maggie and Cammie.

Spit it out, already. The not-knowing needled at Maggie's composure, but she had to be strong for the family.

"Worst case scenario?" Cammie managed to squeak out.

"We've already avoided the worst case because you're alive." His words were slow and calm. "No extensive internal injuries. But you could possibly have to adjust to life in a wheelchair."

A whimper came from Cammie, but she blinked and kept her face expressionless.

"There are advances being made in research and technology." His voice was kind and full of hope. Did they teach that in medical school? Most doctors she knew weren't this good at it. "Meanwhile, my patients in wheelchairs get around well, some even drive. They live good, productive lives." He stared into Cammie's eyes, which flooded with tears. "Today, focus on healing, keeping still. Let the swelling go down, then we'll work on the rest."

At least the doctor had a good bedside manner while delivering the blow. Cammie needed to focus on the positive. Maggie took her sister's other hand. "We'll pray for the best and prepare for the worst."

If their past held any indication, they could expect the worst.

The cogs of Maggie's mind whirred, returning to the storm. How long before she could get them all out of here and safely inland? The storm surge had reached the first floor of this hospital during Katrina. She turned to look at the doctor again. "What about the hurricane? Can we evacuate her?"

"The hurricane's still pretty far out." His fingers slid across the dark stubble on his chin. "I don't think we need to worry about the storm right now. The hospital has protocol set up for that kind of thing."

Not worry about the storm? She might need to check into his academic credentials. Had he not lived here during Katrina?

"I'm keeping her in ICU for at least five days so we can keep tight control of her blood pressure and to make sure we salvage as much spinal cord tissue as possible. Staff will check her every hour." His gaze turned to Cammie. "Buzz the nurse and have her call me if you feel a sensation in your legs. Tingling, pins-and-needles sensations. Anything of that nature."

A tiny nod seemed to be all her sister could summon.

"I want to stay here with her."

"Visiting hours are limited so the patients can rest. Staff will keep a close eye on her, and I'm on call. You may as well go home with your niece. As a parent of a ten-year-old daughter myself, I would suggest waiting a few days before bringing her in." He took a step toward the door. "I'll leave you two alone for a minute."

"Thank you." Cammie mustered a tired smile, and he nodded and stepped out.

The weight of the situation crashed into Maggie's heart, ramming against the old scars of grief and loss residing there. She swallowed hard against the emotion thickening her raw throat. She had to be strong for Cammie. For Dahlia and Aunt Ruth. "What do you want me to tell Dahlia and Aunt Ruth?"

"Nothing." Cammie sniffled. "I need to process."

Didn't they all? "I'll feed everyone, get Dahlia ready for bed, and come back to spend the night in the waiting room. See if they'll let me in."

"You don't need to."

"Not negotiable." If there was a way to get back here and check on things, she'd find it.

Her sister's eyes fluttered again. "Josh will have to make other arrangements."

"How in the world—?"

"Not now."

"Okay." But she would like to know how the current *arrangement* came about.

"Talk to Josh, and get it over with." Cammie took a slow

breath and let her chestnut-colored eyes close all the way. "There are bigger issues to deal with than who hurt who when you were eighteen. Time to be adults."

Whoa. That stung. Cammie definitely needed some space. "I'll tell him to make other arrangements." And when Cammie was better, she could explain how she ended up becoming a nanny for Josh Bergeron's kid.

~~~

On the way home, Josh alternated between fear, sadness, worry, and another emotion that caused him a sea of guilt. Anticipation. He was going to see Maggie again.

He tried to ignore the way his pulse ramped at the thought. What would she look like in person? Since his divorce, he'd looked her up a time or two on social media. She still had those beautiful dark curls. His chest expanded at the thought.

He was an awful human being for being the slightest bit happy that Magnolia Marovich had been forced to come back to the Coast because of an accident.

In the hospital parking lot, he glanced in the mirror, lifted his baseball cap, and ran his fingers through his hair. He was a mess from the inside out. Oh well. He'd gotten here as fast as he could. That should count for something.

He jogged toward the entrance. Of course, Maggie had texted exact instructions on where to find them. Once inside, he went straight to the elevator and pressed the button to get to the floor with the ICU waiting room. His heart knocked against his chest when the doors opened. How would Maggie take it if something terrible happened to Cammie? Of course, something terrible had already happened, but if… He couldn't let himself go there. This family always meant so much to him, and they'd been through too much sadness already.

God, please heal Cammie.

He started at a quick pace down the hall.

"Josh Bergeron?" A redheaded nurse caught hold of Josh's arm. "You made it back fast. Is my husband with you?"

Josh turned and focused on the nurse's face. His coworker's wife. "Hey, Angie. Only me. Graham should be home soon, but I hauled it." Angie and Graham had been good friends to him and J.D. after the divorce. She'd taken his son on a number of outings with their boy Conrad and often invited them both to dinner. "How's Conrad?"

She craned her neck, scoping out the area. "Conrad's fine—still a handful, but what are you doing here? Is J.D. okay?"

"Yeah." Of course, she'd be worried. "My babysitter was injured, so I hightailed it back to get J.D."

"Oh, no. Cammie's a patient here?" Her green eyes widened with concern. "What happened?"

"Right, you two graduated together." Where was his mind? Stuck on Maggie, of course. He hated being the bearer of bad news. Especially about the Marovich family. "She was hit by a truck."

Angie's hand went to her heart. "I pray God helps that poor girl. She never catches a break. Who's watching J.D. and Dahlia? Her aunt Ruth can't do it."

"Maggie's here." Just saying the words unearthed the raw emotions he'd worked so hard to bury.

"Ah, Maggie." Angie clucked her tongue and bobbed her head. "Y'all were a pretty hot item back in the day."

He wasn't touching that one. Josh shuffled his feet. Why did everyone feel the need to bring up their disastrous past?

"Are the kids here with Maggie? I can take J.D. home. Dahlia and Ruth, too, if they want. My shift's over in fifteen minutes. Conrad would love to have J.D. over to play as long as you need."

"I couldn't put you out, plus I just got home. J.D. probably won't let me leave his sight, and I can't speak for the others." And Maggie would likely send him packing.

"You won't put me out." Determination set her angled chin. "I'll follow you, and we can see." Angie touched his forearm. "You know I hate what Trisha did to you and J.D. It wasn't right. How any mother could—"

"Water under the bridge." He didn't want to throw thoughts of his wayward ex-wife into the tempest already forming.

"So, Maggie's here now, taking care of everyone?" Angie's eyes fished for more information. "A lot like her grandmother. The woman could cook a mean batch of fried oysters, but her temper and that evil eye she could give when we got out of line intimidated me."

He chuckled at the memory of the sturdy Cajun woman. "Yeah, her grandmother scared me, too." And now, so did Maggie.

They wound around the halls until they neared the waiting room. Josh's pulse accelerated. More than it had during the tanker exchange on high seas. Long dark curls came into view by the doorway. Maggie held J.D. in her arms. A swell of emotion tore through him, blasting open tender wounds he'd worked so hard to heal. Something about that picture of his son on Maggie's hip looked so right, yet swamped him with regrets. If only…

"Daddy!" J.D.'s shout jerked Maggie's head his way.

Her eyes spoke volumes. The depths of the sorrow there crushed his throat, suffocating, submerging him in the past. Then those eyes blazed, and she gently let J.D. down.

Prying his gaze from her, Josh bent to scoop up the little

form running to him. He swung J.D. around. "Ahoy, mate. Give your daddy a kiss."

Slobbery lips pressed against Josh's cheek. "Daddy, we're going to eat supper at Chick-fil-A. Wanna come?"

"I do like their chicken." Josh's eyes bounced from Maggie to Angie standing beside him. "I bumped into Angie in the hall."

Angie greeted Ruth and Dahlia with side hugs. "I hated to hear about the accident." She turned to Maggie and took a cautious step. "Hi, stranger." She hugged Maggie, then stepped away. "Long time no see. I'm so sorry about Cammie. Let me take everyone to eat, and then J.D. can come home with me for a while to play with Conrad. I'll drop off Ruth and Dahlia at their house, too." She held out her arms to J.D. "Want to?"

"Can me and Conrad play ships?"

His son was sure quick to abandon him.

"Of course you can, buddy." With a broad grin, Angie tweaked J.D.'s nose. "I think we've bought some new ones since you were over last."

Maggie shook her head, dark curls bouncing. "You don't need to do all that. I can take Aunt Ruth and Dahlia home and come back to spend the night with Cammie." An edge of steel laced her measured answer.

"I insist." One of Angie's thin eyebrows raised. "You and Josh need to talk."

Oh right. Josh held in a chuckle. Angie'd always been a bit of a firecracker, too, but she was no match for a Marovich.

A harsh laugh came from Maggie. More like flames whooshing from a dragon. "No. We do not."

"Yes. You do." She nodded toward J.D. "About Cammie's condition and what'll happen when Josh goes back out in two weeks."

Josh watched the exchange. It was like two warships preparing for battle. Should he get involved? Keeping his mouth sealed might be the smartest approach. And the safest.

Chapter 4

Maggie's hands fisted. If she weren't in a hospital and standing near children, the sick, and the elderly, she'd scream at the top of her lungs. A few times. Or twenty. She did *not* want to talk to Josh Bergeron. Why didn't anyone understand that the man reminded her of everything she'd lost? Her dreams of love, marriage, and a family? Her love of home on the Coast, her childhood on sea and shore? And with Josh working as a pilot like her father...plus the fact he hadn't been there for her when she needed him most. He hadn't even left school in New York to come to her father's memorial service.

Yet, there he stood with his hair the color of sand and his stupid big eyes with alternating shades of blue sky and water. Melting her heart again.

No. She wouldn't let him.

Angie's mere mention of his job shredded through Maggie's raw emotions like broken shells under bare feet. The reckless career of piloting ships had ripped her father from her life. Ripped away her sense of security and peace. Almost ripped away her faith.

Josh was brilliant. He could've picked any profession—any place in the world. Not that piloting ships from all over the world didn't take brains. But her father had taken Josh in like the son he'd never had. He'd taught him about the tides, the winds, the obstructions in the water. Passed on his passion for the sea. Then Daddy had disappeared into the Gulf he loved so much, leaving her family heartbroken smack dab in the middle of the most destructive natural disaster in the history of the United States.

Though exhausted with the heaviness of the day's emotions, she summoned her strength to continue the battle of wills with Angie. "We can talk later. There are too many variables. No one has to decide the future right now. Besides, I heard Josh lives next door, for goodness' sakes." She couldn't stop the eye roll or the scoff.

Dahlia pressed her hands to her hips. "Let's eat already. I'm starving." The attitude again.

"Me, too." J.D.'s small voice battered against Maggie's resolve.

"Let me help out, Maggie. You can't do it all by yourself." Angie made a dramatic wave.

Maggie bit her tongue. Who did that Angie think she was? Some kind of matchmaking counselor? The girl hadn't seemed like such a meddler in high school.

Her gaze skimmed from Angie to J.D.

Angie, she could tell no, but not the children. "Y'all go on and eat. I'll see you in a little while." Maggie lowered her voice and turned back to Angie. "And if you really want to help, someone can figure out how to get Aunt Ruth's car home…" Aunt Ruth sure didn't need to drive after dark.

"Graham and my dad can do it." Angie gave an understanding nod. "No problem."

Maybe Josh would take the hint and leave with them. But she had promised Cammie she'd speak with the man. She might as well get *the talk* over with. Groaning inside, Maggie stepped toward him.

Years ago, she'd begged Josh to shift his dream away from piloting. In turn, he'd begged her to accept his career choice. They'd both refused to budge. Hoping the other would finally give. Neither did. He'd clung to his beloved Merchant Marine Academy in New York, discarding her, while she'd grieved the loss of her father. The last thing she wanted to do was relive that misery.

~~~

The others disappeared around the corner, and Josh battened down his emotions. *Hurricane Maggie*. Blowing back into his life. The storm that swept him up and capsized him every single time he thought of her.

Suddenly, she was beside him, smelling like the sweet Southern flower that was her namesake. After over a decade, she looked even more beautiful than she had before, if that were possible. More like a woman than a teen. But where once she'd been a spirit so alive, so strong, sadness now shrouded her eyes, her posture. The image cut deep into his heart. He'd failed her when she'd needed him. Hurt her almost as brutally as Katrina had.

"Everyone wants us to talk. Let's get it over with." She avoided looking directly at him.

Lord, help me be a comfort rather than a burden. "Can we get a bite of supper downstairs?" As soon as she got some food in her, he'd ask about Cammie. But it was clear Maggie was barely upright. She needed fuel and rest first. "Neither of us have eaten. From what I remember, you got..." Why had he started that sentence?

"I got what?" Her eyes seared him.

Might as well dive into shark-infested water. "You got cranky when you were hungry."

"Me? Cranky?" Her hands went to her hips in a movement exactly like Dahlia's had done moments earlier. "You were the grumpy one."

He dared a partial smile. "Okay, I was, too. We were a lot

alike. Stubborn. Tenacious. Neither willing to bend."

"I was willing to bend." She scoffed. "I asked one thing of you. Give up the idea of piloting. Choose any other career somewhere away from the Coast and be with me."

"And I asked one thing of you. Support my dream and wait for me." And her answer still rammed against a tender scar.

She blew out a long breath. "Good grief. It's over and done with. No need to relive it." Maggie mashed her palm to her forehead as if pressing out tension forming there.

Yep. It had been many years ago. But the pain surging through his chest hurt exactly like it had before. Looking at her standing there, probably going through the same kind of anguish, twisted his judgment, and he rested a hand on her shoulder. "Maggie." Her name came out in a husky whisper. "When you broke things off, it killed me. I thought you'd..." The words tangled on his tongue.

"You thought I'd change my mind." Her lips turned down, and she lifted her eyes to his, gaze softening. Moisture pooled near her lower lashes. The longest, blackest lashes he'd ever seen. "And I thought you'd change your plans and come to me."

The desire to hold her overwhelmed him. Not giving into the urge left him feeling as if he were drowning, gasping for air, so he took a step back and schooled his expression. "Let's go eat. I'm getting cranky."

A resigned chuckle bubbled from her throat. "Me, too."

Down the hall to the elevators, they walked in uncomfortable silence. They both reached to press the lobby button, hands colliding.

The touch zapped through Josh like a bolt of electricity. "Sorry." He jerked his arm back.

She did the same. "You can press it."

"Okay." He extended his hand again slowly, carefully. The silliness of it made him laugh.

She gave him a curious glance, which made him laugh again.

"This is crazy." He nudged her with his elbow. "We're not teenagers anymore."

A begrudging smile lifted her lips, the way he remembered. "That's basically what Cammie said when I saw her." Maggie shook her head, causing the mass of curls to brush her shoulders. "We're a mess, aren't we?"

More than he wanted to admit. "I know I am." And his fingers itched to toy with her hair.

Once they'd gone through the food line and settled in a cafeteria booth, Maggie aimed an intense stare at him. "Cammie's paralyzed from the waist down. We don't know if it's permanent."

Nausea swept through him, and Josh pushed his tray aside. One more tragedy in a long line of heartbreaks for this family. The unfairness of it all. Bowing his head, he folded his hands. "Lord, please let the paralysis be temporary. Heal your servant Cammie, in Jesus' name." The lump in his throat kept him from saying more. His eyes burned as he lifted them back to Maggie.

A tear ran down her cheek as she stirred the green beans on the tray with her fork. "Amen."

"Don't worry about J.D. He's my responsibility, and I'll figure something out. I've got two weeks." But he had no idea what he'd do.

"Where is his mother?" Her jaw tightened as she lifted her gaze to meet his.

A loaded question with a tough answer. "She's remarried and living in Nevada with her new husband. A casino executive. Parenting wasn't for her."

"As if that's a choice?" The fire returned to Maggie's eyes. Bitterness uprooted from his past. "Tell that to my dad." The irresponsible jerk had decided being tied down with a family wasn't his thing, left a note, and never looked back. Though Josh's six-year-old heart kept up hope for years afterward. He'd vowed to be a better father than his own, an honorable man like Mr. Marovich. But somehow he'd married a woman who'd repeated the history in spite of his best efforts—desperate efforts at times.

Maggie pressed her lips together, and the blaze receded a bit. "Sorry. I never understood that one either." Her head tilted. "But isn't your mom around?"

"Her company moved overseas, so she took a new job in Atlanta, met someone, and remarried. Right before Trisha left." He picked up his fork and stared at it. "Mom's new husband's a nice enough guy. She took all her vacation days and sick leave to help me out when my marriage first went south. She's taken J.D. up to Atlanta and hired a sitter for some of my two-weeks out." His stomach growled, and he slid his tray closer. "She may retire soon, but that really won't be a permanent fix with her living six hours away. And she's due a bit of happiness with her new husband. I don't want to dump J.D on her every month." He took a bite of meatloaf. Bland, but not bad, considering.

"What about bossy nurse Angie? Isn't her husband a pilot? Who keeps their child?"

"Yeah, Graham's a pilot, but Angie only works part-time. Plus both their parents live here and help them out."

Maggie's fingers massaged her temples as if trying to figure out the mess he was in. "Hmm."

"It's not your problem." He brushed her fingers with his

own. "You've got your family to worry about."

Her gaze traveled to his hand, then found his eyes again. "How'd you end up having Cammie watch J.D. anyway?"

"A fluke. I had to sell the house in the divorce and was searching for someplace to move in a hurry. I was driving around our old stomping grounds to take a look and saw a For Sale sign." He shrugged. "She was outside, saw me. We talked, and she offered to help."

Maggie huffed. "Were either of you going to tell me? I do come here. Occasionally, anyway. Besides, Cammie has enough on her plate already."

Was she kidding? Heat shot to his cheeks. The woman still infuriated him so. "Your first thought is about how the arrangement would affect you? My life was falling apart and my kid had no mother."

"Sorry… It wasn't my first thought…about you, I mean him. He's precious." Maggie's brows did that scrunching thing they always had when she was upset.

A bit of his anger receded. "Cammie said she needed the money."

"She needs money that bad? Why wouldn't she tell me?"

"That's what she said." Guilt knifed him. He shouldn't have lit into Maggie that way. Both he and Cammie had known the arrangement would likely upset Maggie. "The antique business is down, I guess." He snapped his fingers. "Oh, and she wants to send Dahlia to private school."

Maggie seemed to let that sink in and took a few bites of her food.

Josh followed suit. He should eat. This probably tasted better than what he'd find in his freezer at home. If there was anything in there at all.

"I have to get them all out of here before the storm." She

dropped her fork onto the tray. "Permanently, if it's up to me."

"Maggie." He kept his voice low and controlled. "You can't keep running every time there's a storm. Life happens, accidents happen. People have heart attacks, get cancer—"

Her chair pushed back with a scrape. "I've faced plenty of storms. But I'm not looking to run headlong into them."

One look at her expression told him he'd hit a nerve. He'd forgotten about her mother's cancer. What an idiot he was.

She jabbed a finger at him. "You should get your son to safety."

Apparently, the conversation was over. He watched her stomp away. Again.

He knew better than to chase her down and try to talk sense into her stubborn head. Once she got into that mode, reasoning wouldn't be possible. He also knew she had too much on her plate. There was no way she'd be able to take care of the store, her elderly aunt, a ten-year-old niece, and be here at the hospital. Maggie wouldn't want help, but too bad. A crisis changed things, and last time, he'd been too caught up in his own grief to realize that. He'd help until Cammie had a better prognosis. Then he'd likely have to get out of their lives altogether. Again.

Josh picked up both their trays, emptied the half-eaten food, and set them on top of the trash can. On the way to the parking lot, he replayed the conversation with Maggie in his mind. He'd have to learn to think before he spoke if he was going to help Maggie—to avoid stepping on a land mine of emotion. Topics like cancer, piloting, parents...the weather. Were there more?

Why had he bought the house next door? He'd known better. Known that Maggie would be hurt. Known that seeing her would slash both of their hearts open again. But he'd held out hope that the arrangement with Cammie and J.D. could work…and maybe, just maybe, he'd held out hope for him and Maggie.

That had been a mistake.

Josh clicked his key fob and opened the truck door. He might as well face the facts. He'd need to find a new nanny for J.D., and probably sell that house, too. Or find a job with slightly normal hours, like teaching at the maritime school, maybe running harbor tugs or cargo surveying. Another reality that would tear his heart to shreds. Besides being a father, piloting was his life. Without it, who was he?

Chapter 5

Run from storms? So exasperating. Why could that man still splinter her heart after so long? Chin quivering, Maggie fought to keep herself from sprinting away from the cafeteria. Blasted Josh. With his same blue eyes and tanned skin, only now small smile lines crinkled the corners of his temples. The way those eyes adored his son...held such compassion even when he looked at her...

Enough with Josh and the past. She was here for Cammie, and there was a hurricane brewing out there somewhere. Brushing tears from her cheeks, Maggie kept walking until she reached the parking lot and popped the trunk of her car. Her computer lay tucked between her emergency kit and the case of bottled water and other disaster supplies she always kept stocked in the Acura—just in case. After retrieving the laptop and a water, she sneaked back toward the entrance, hopeful she could avoid Josh. He should go home to his son.

Finally in the bright light of the ICU waiting room, Maggie flopped onto the couch and unzipped her computer case. She'd stay until the next visiting hour and then go home to change and check on Dahlia and Aunt Ruth. Until then, she could pull up the latest storm prediction models. She'd look into spinal injuries, too. Oh, and that young Dr. Castro.

If Cammie never walked again, life suddenly just took a radical turn for all of them.

After accessing the Wi-Fi, she opened several meteorology sites and logged into her work email. First the hurricane in the

Gulf. The storm looked to have stalled west of Miami, dumping rain with its outer bands. But it hadn't made landfall, so it still posed the threat of strengthening and veering their way over the next week. Exactly as Katrina had.

They'd need to ready the house soon. Like tomorrow. But she'd also promised to open the store. And someone needed to be here to get updates on Cammie. How in the world could she be in three places at once?

She pulled her phone from her purse and set the alarm for five a.m. It would be a long day. Did Dahlia have school, or had it been cancelled in case the hurricane sped up? Or were they already on Thanksgiving break? Dahlia could be helpful to have around at the store…unless she would spend the hours being sulky. Better to see if school was open.

Onto the next crisis—paralysis. Maggie scanned article after article on spinal injuries, possible treatments, and then did a search on the good doctor. Kyle Castro seemed to be a respected specialist. Board certified and highly recommended. Still, calling a few friends in the medical community wouldn't hurt, just to make sure he was the best choice to continue treating her sister. She couldn't take any chances with such a serious issue.

An hour passed, and families in the waiting room began to stand and edge closer to the ICU entrance. A minute later, a nurse stuck her head into the waiting room. "It's time."

Maggie followed the somber crowd into the quiet hall. Quiet other than the beeps and the whooshing air of ventilators. A few hushed voices came from one area where a doctor and nurse worked on a patient.

Maggie reached the glass room where Cammie lay sleeping. With those raw scrapes and bruises, her sister looked so fragile and weak. The skin near her brow had swollen. With all the equipment attached, it would be too easy to accidentally dislodge the IV or some other important monitor. Worry nagged Maggie. She scooted a chair close to the bed and laid a hand over Cammie's fingers.

Lord, please heal Cammie. And please let us escape the storm this time. All the storms. The hurricane, the store, Josh... Help me stay strong for my family. I need a plan to keep everything under control.

Too quickly, the thirty-minute visiting time ended, and Maggie made the zombie-like walk back to the waiting area with the other anxious families. She checked her phone. Dahlia would be, or rather *should be*, in bed, but she'd better go check in on her niece and Aunt Ruth to make sure they were okay. Today had to have been a horrendous one for them, too.

The drive back to the house passed in a blur. Was there anyone they could hire to run the store so she could stay with Cammie? Was it okay to leave Dahlia with Aunt Ruth for long periods of time? What could she expect from a ten-year-old girl and an eighty-five-year-old woman? Churning thoughts of how to best manage the situation left her drained. Too many variables to predict how to fix things. By the time she reached the driveway, a tension headache clamped around her skull. All the lights still shone at Aunt Ruth's. She glanced next door and blew out a long breath. Lights were on at Josh's house, too. Pain squeezed her heart with renewed force. Why couldn't he at least be five blocks over, or down the street? Anywhere but next door.

Since she couldn't get him to move—yet—she'd try to pretend the home belonged to someone else. Someone old and grumpy who kept to himself at all costs. She opened the car door and stepped out into the breezy night, probably about sixty-eight degrees still. They needed some cooler air to push in and blow the storm away. Leaves and pine straw cluttered the sidewalk. When would she have time to rake on top of everything else? The last thing they needed was for Aunt Ruth to slip in the pine straw and fall. They could hire a yard man for a few months. Would Cammie be well in a few months? Or ever?

Maggie's feet slowed at the front porch steps. How many adjustments would they need to make with Cammie in a wheelchair? Ramps, handrails, bathroom remodeling—and who knew what else—would have to be done regardless of whether Cammie insisted on staying here or agreed to move up to Jackson so she'd have help.

Inside, the television screen flashed with a cartoon of some sort, but the sound had been muted. Maggie blinked twice at the sight on the couch. J.D. was curled under the pink afghan her mother had made for Dahlia. Why was he—?

"I thought I heard you come in." Warm breath pressed against her ear. Low and gentle, Josh's voice washed over her, sending chills scampering down her spine. "Dahlia's still awake if you want to say goodnight."

Why did he have to be so caring? He was no doubt a great father. But she couldn't go there. And he shouldn't be in their house. Maggie steeled herself against the churning wave of emotions and turned to face him. He was way too close. "What are you doing here?"

His fingers touched her elbow, and he nodded toward the hall. "Reading and talking to Dahlia. We were getting ready to pray when I heard your car door."

Pray? Her feet followed him numbly down the hall. How could she say anything negative when he was praying with her niece?

Preteen and little girl converged in Dahlia's room. Maggie scanned the lime green comforter and the turquoise accent wall behind the twin beds. There hadn't been time to really look around earlier. Some sort of white flowery light fixture hung over the bed, and two smaller versions stood as lamps on both night tables. A large green letter D hung alongside a funky-colored bulletin board with pictures of kittens and a pop band Maggie had never heard of.

"Hey, sweetie." Maggie sat on the side of the bed and stroked the hair from Dahlia's face.

"How's Mom?" Puffy circles plumped the skin beneath Dahlia's eyes.

Poor baby. Answering the question vaguely seemed like the best idea. "Nothing has changed."

Josh made his way to the opposite side of the bed and sat. "We were about to pray. Do one of y'all want to start or would you like me to lead?"

The twin mattress shifted with his weight, and Maggie's gaze traveled over him. His shoulders were wider than she remembered from way back. His chest had broadened, too. Her cheeks heated, and she pulled her gaze away. The Josh she'd known was still a teen when he'd left. Now he'd become a man. A father. A good looking man with nice muscles…

"You pray." Dahlia's voice was quiet, but it quickly doused the heat traveling through Maggie.

Dahlia squeezed her eyes closed.

With a hesitant move, Josh clasped Dahlia's hand, then covered Maggie's. His fingers were rough and calloused and strong. So much like what she remembered of her father's. Like a ship pilots would be, of course.

Pilot. That was the problem.

"Is that okay with you, Maggie?"

"What?" Her stunned mind tried to focus on something besides the warmth of his hand on hers.

49

"If I pray? Unless you want to?"

An ache that was bone deep washed over her. "Go ahead."

"Lord, we are thankful for Your daughter Cammie. We love her, and we know You love her even more. We are thankful she is in the care of a skilled doctor. Today was a scary day, but we know You weren't taken by surprise. You are in control, and we ask You to be with us, to calm our fears, to strengthen our hearts, and we ask for complete healing for Cammie. We turn her over to Your loving hands, Lord. Let Your will be done in all our lives. We praise You and bring these requests in Jesus' name." Josh gave Maggie's fingers a gentle squeeze. "Amen."

"Amen." Maggie's single word came out scratchy and broken.

Breathing deep, Josh leaned in and gave Dahlia a hug. "Good night, darling. I should get my little sailor off the couch and into his bed, but you have my number. If you need anything, call me. I'm right next door."

Maggie pressed her eyes closed to keep from rolling them. *Right next door.* Like barely twenty feet away from exterior to exterior. At least tonight his presence would give her some peace when she went back to the hospital.

She stood, then bent to kiss Dahlia's forehead. "I want to go back to the hospital in a while. Are you okay with Aunt Ruth here?" She cleared her throat. "And Josh, you know…" She nodded toward the window. She couldn't bring herself to say next door again.

Dahlia nodded. "I like that you're checking on Mom. Stay all night if you want. I know you'll make sure everything's legit."

"Yep. I'm staying on top of those medical people." She tried to force a smile for her niece. But was she really doing all she could? Was there a way she could insist they let her sit at Cammie's bedside? She'd ask around, maybe even call bossy Angie to find out for sure. Nurses always knew the real story about the hospital's units and about which doctors were any good.

"I'll go now." Josh stood, took one step, and stopped.

Good. Go. Maggie's chest tightened. This room was too small with him in it. She could barely breathe. Or keep from saying something she'd regret.

"See y'all tomorrow." His footsteps fell quietly on the hardwood. Like a man who'd learned to walk softly, so he wouldn't wake a child.

"Bye," she managed to squeak out.

"You can go now, too, Aunt Maggie, if you want to be with Mama." Dahlia grabbed an old phone Cammie had given her and lay back against her pillows. "I'm going to listen to some music and try to sleep."

"Okay." Her niece looked fragile and small as she placed earbuds in her ears and closed her eyes. Should she really leave her with Aunt Ruth? Dahlia had said to go. And as much as she hated it, Josh was close.

Maggie walked from the room but hesitated in the hall. Josh scooped his son against his chest. Cradling the sleeping child, he gave her one last look before exiting quietly. The door creaked as it shut, and he was gone. Carrying another little piece of her heart with him.

She grabbed a diet soda from the refrigerator and went back toward the hall to check on Aunt Ruth. The house was awfully quiet now, but her aunt had always been a bit of a night owl, staying up late to watch TV. Maybe the stress had taken its toll on the elderly woman.

Maggie tiptoed closer to the master bedroom, and the glow

from the screen met her at the entrance. So not much had changed in that regard except the volume. The sound was muted, and after the way they'd had to turn it up at the hospital... Worry pricked the back of her neck as she moved closer to the mound of comforter and pillows. It was hard to make out much under the dark antique canopy bed. She reached out and touched a bump that looked to be a foot. "Aunt Ruth?"

"What in the world!" Her aunt sat straight up, eyes wide. "Lands sake, child. Warn a person. I thought a bat had gotten in the house again."

Maggie fought a laugh. "A bat?"

"We had one trying to live in the chimney, and a couple of months ago, it flew right in the house, that little furry monster with beady eyes. I know they catch mosquitoes, but some of them have rabies. Me and Cammie liked to never get it out of the house. Chasing it around with brooms and a mop." She shook her head. "If it weren't for Josh and his fishing net—" She stopped abruptly like she'd let a secret slip and looked up at Maggie. "Sorry, but it is nice to have a man around sometimes."

"Makes sense, I guess." Another little sliver of hurt needled into Maggie's chest. Yes. It would've been nice to have a man around. Hadn't she thought the same thing over the years? She'd tried dating. Really tried. But no one ever lived up to what she'd been looking for. No one had ever understood her either. No one had ever felt like home the way her best friend Josh had.

"I'm going back to the hospital. Call me if you need anything. Or get Josh." She tried to keep her tone even. Not full of the sarcasm she'd felt saying those words.

"We'll be fine."

All the way to the hospital, Maggie fought to still her emotions. Tears built up and blurred her vision, but she rubbed them away. It wouldn't do any good for her to lose control. Everyone was depending on her. In the parking lot, she squared her shoulders and took a deep breath. "Help me, Lord. I can't fall apart."

A cold wave of fatigue settled over Maggie in the ICU waiting room, as if her arms and legs thrummed a heavy, achy tune. She took a seat, leaned her head back, and let her heavy lids shut. Visions of blue eyes filtered through her thoughts. Sparkling and deep like sky and sea. Josh's eyes, and that adorable little boy's, too.

This accident and the timing. The weather. Josh. The perfect storm to destroy her heart.

All over again.

Darkness crept in.

The dream fired up. Wind, rain, thunder. The turbulent surf burying her father, ripping him away. She held out her arms, but she couldn't grab hold of him. She stretched out her hands, begging for something, anything, to help her reach him.

Then she and Josh were on the sailboat steering out to Deer Island, happy and smiling, the sun bright and warm against her shoulders. Suddenly, the water started to churn with enormous green and brown swells. Gulls circled, mocking them as a wave crashed against the hull and capsized the boat. They held on and fought the currents, but Josh was torn away.

No!

Farther and farther. She tried to catch him but sunk into the depths. The weight of the water crushed her chest. Air. She needed air!

Her eyes popped open, and she gasped. Lungs filling with oxygen and the scent of antiseptic. She glanced around. Where was she?

Bright lights. A lady sleeping across the room on the hard plastic chairs.

A door opened, and a woman in scrubs entered. Maggie blinked. The hospital. What time was it? Her fingers dug around the seat until she felt the cool screen of her phone. Four-fifty.

"Y'all can come in now. It's close enough to visiting hours."

Maggie followed the nurse down the hall. "What time will the doctor be by again? I need to do a few things for my sister at home."

"Probably mid-morning, no way to know. You can write your name and number on the whiteboard for him or any of us to call you."

Cammie's lids lifted when Maggie entered. "Go home and open the store. Keep my phone with you in case vendors call. They pay people to take care of me here." Her scratchy voice held a ring of big-sister authority.

"I will in a minute, but I waited all night to see you." Maggie moved to the side of the bed. "You can at least let me look at you while I can. How are you? Can I get you a Sprite or something? Can you eat?"

"Don't worry so much." She pointed to the rolling tray beside her. "They brought everything I'm allowed to have." A plastic cup with a straw and an empty container of pudding stood there.

"That's not much."

"I'm not exactly running off the calories." Her eyes closed. "Pull up a chair and sit with me if you're going to stay. I'm not much company right now."

Maggie complied. If she were in Cammie's place, she

wouldn't be good company either. But Cammie had always been the patient one. For a Marovich.

Cool air blew from a vent above and sent a shiver across Maggie's shoulders. She crossed her arms and watched her sister sleep. The machines kept up their constant beeps and whooshing. A patient across the way moaned and hollered periodically. The best way to pass the time might be to develop an orderly plan for the day, and listing it on her phone seemed like the best thing to do. The time passed quietly. At last, Maggie rose, stretched, then bent down and pressed a kiss on Cammie's forehead. "I love you, sis."

"I love you," Cammie whispered. "Thank you."

The prospect of working at the store and readying the house for a storm held less appeal than sitting at the hospital, but she'd promised.

~~~

Always nice to wake up in his own bed. Not that he'd slept much in the night. Josh stretched, careful to avoid bumping into J.D.

How did that booger always end up under the covers with him? He watched his son's chest rise and fall, thinking back to that first day he'd brought J.D. home from the hospital. So tiny and helpless cradled in his arms. How he'd vowed to be a good father like Mr. Marovich.

And J.D. owned his heart, that was for sure. Maybe Maggie had been right. Maybe he should travel inland in case the weather turned bad.

There were no evacuation notices yet, though. The storm could stall out and only dump a bunch of rain. Plus Maggie would need his help, like it or not. He pushed away her hurricane nonsense as he pressed to his feet. Not every storm was a Katrina. People here weathered the small storms. Knew what to do. The town didn't run away every time the wind blew.

Like both the women in his life did.

Of course, Maggie had given him the choice to follow, unlike Trisha.

His feet led him down the hall to the coffee pot in the kitchen. His only addiction, but a strong one. He ground the Guatemalan beans and took a deep whiff of the robust aroma before pouring black granules into the filter. Guatemalan was the best coffee in the world, as far as he was concerned. Thankfully, he piloted ships from all over the globe and could get the good stuff from a few Central American friends he'd made.

Outside the kitchen window, swallows filled the limbs on one of the moss-covered live oaks still standing in the backyard. He and Maggie spent many days climbing the old trees' sprawling limbs. They'd fished together. Ridden their bikes round and round the blocks of this neighborhood together. Grown up together. Shared their first kiss together.

The image still struck a blow that left him aching for air. He'd loved the girl as far back as he had memory. Buying the house beside Cammie hadn't been the best idea. He had to have been subconsciously hoping he'd run into Maggie after Trisha left. Maybe not *sub*consciously at all.

The flash of an orange shirt caught his eye, and a wave of almost black curls. Maggie already plodded around the yard next door in red rain boots. What was she doing back from the hospital and outside so early?

She entered the dilapidated shed and threw miscellaneous pieces of wood and old tools out the door to the ground. By her jerky movements, he'd guess she was frustrated about something. Not so unusual.

Steam rose from the brewing coffee. A cup of Guatemala's finest might perk her up. Not that she needed more intensity. He chuckled, filled two mugs, and then headed outside.

"You need help?"

A thud echoed as her elbow banged against the frame of the shed. "Ouch."

That had to hurt. Not a good start.

Her brows screwed into all manner of angry angles. "Don't sneak up on someone at this time of the morning."

"Still like coffee?" He held out his peace offering. "It's the good stuff."

The muscles in her face loosened, and she eyed the mug.

Josh took a swig of his and let out a contented sigh. No way would she refuse. Her coffee addiction blew his out of the water.

She stomped toward him. "Fine. I could use more caffeine to get through today."

"No sleep?"

"Some." Her curls shook back and forth. "Hard to rest in those places though."

His thoughts went to his careless words the night before and to her mother's cancer. "I never got to tell you how sorry I was for your loss. I loved your mother, too."

Her features softened, and she gripped the cup with both hands as if holding onto a lost moment. "My parents loved you. Like the son they never had."

The gates of his heart pried open, allowing memory after memory to parade through his mind. The ones he'd lain awake all night banishing. Her dad teaching them to drive. Her mother always pinning on his boutonniere before the high school dances. The whole family sailing out to Deer Island. His eyes stung—both from the grief and the lack of sleep.

"Cammie said you took good care of your mother when you moved her up to Jackson. Flew her all over the country for second opinions and treatments. Were at her side until the end."

Maggie's lashes lowered, and she gave a slow nod.

A sobering hush fell between them, sucking up all the air. Even the swallows quieted in the solemn moment.

Josh struggled to find words. Why exactly had he come out here? "You like the coffee?"

"It's good."

"Just good?"

Her gaze lifted to meet his, a bit of the sass returning. "Glorious. Thank you." She chugged back another gulp. "Now I'm off to find the storm shutters I bought for this house. All I can find are the old ones. They probably never even unpacked the new ones."

"Tried the attic?"

"It was such a mess up there last I looked." Her head dropped back with a sigh. "And I need to get this finished so I can open the shop at ten. I haven't figured out if I can leave Aunt Ruth at the shop alone when the next visiting hours roll around. I'd like to talk to the doctor again if I can catch him."

Sounded like an invitation if he ever heard one. "No need to beg. I'll be happy to help."

Chapter 6

She hadn't asked for Josh Bergeron's help. Now she had to spend even more heartrending minutes with him. Face searing as annoyance burned across her cheeks to the tips of her ears, Maggie led Josh to the attic pull in the garage. She did need to get to the store, so his intrusion might be marginally helpful.

Once the ladder extended, he took a step up, but stopped. "Oh, can you check on J.D. while I look around up here?" His eyes widened into a pleading gaze. A flirty gaze.

She remembered that look all too well. Like when he'd talked her into skiing in a bayou full of alligators. She'd held on tight to the rope that day and moved into the boat at a speed akin to pelican diving for a fish. Now, her jaw tightened as she tried to come up with an appropriate retort. She sure didn't want to unearth more of the past.

"You know," Josh continued, "J.D. talked about you when I got home last night. How you read to him and colored a puppy with him while you were in the hospital waiting room. He's dying for a puppy, but it's hard enough finding someone to watch…" He blew out a long breath. "Oh, and you gave him spicy candy he thought were called Hot Tomatoes."

That stirred up a chuckle. Hot Tomatoes. "Fine. I'm going over because J.D.'s cute, and his father left him all alone next door."

"Bad me. I didn't want to wake him when I first got up, and I didn't know you'd rope me into all this work."

"Rope you? Really?" She turned toward the open garage

door. "You practically begged to help me, and you know it." She stomped into the squishy wet grass between the two yards.

His rich laughter trailed her.

Of course he'd laugh. He'd gotten his way like always. After climbing the cement porch steps and opening the door, a cautious step brought Maggie inside the house. No surprise, the decor reeked masculine and nautical. A map and an antique ship's wheel hung on one wall. A large marlin mounted on wooden planks hung above the fireplace. Humph. If she were in charge, that thing would be in a back bedroom or the garage, not in the living room. Most of the rest of this tacky decor, too.

She couldn't help but look around and imagine what if. What if she'd stayed? What if they'd made it to the altar? What if they'd had children? Would they be good parents together... a team like her own mother and father? Smiling pictures of the blond boy at different stages hung along the wall in the hall, and she ran her fingers over the glass. Something pinched inside, and she ached for the life she might've lived.

Shake it off. Even if she had stayed here, they probably never would have lasted, the man was so stubborn and single-minded. *One way. His way.* She continued down the hall. The first room held a blue chest of drawers and twin bed made to look like a sailboat, but the covers lay flat. No J.D.

Her stomach did a little flip. Where was he?

She quickened her steps. The next room looked to be an office, and the walls were bare. The perfect place for all the old maritime junk.

In the last room, a small blond head lay on a pillow in the middle of a king-sized bed. The vision caused her insides to pinch harder, and she held her breath. *Lord, he's beautiful. Did I make a mistake?* Would that precious child have been hers? Instead, J.D. had a mother who wasn't interested in her own flesh and blood. How was that even possible?

Moisture fought its way out from her eyes and rolled down her cheeks in big sloppy tears. She sniffled and mashed them away.

The sheets rustled. He must've been waking. She used a corner of her T-shirt to make sure she'd cleared all the evidence of her ridiculous emotions.

J.D.'s eyes blinked open. He looked her way, and then he shot straight up. "Hey, Miss Maggie."

"Good morning, pumpkin."

"I'm not a pumpkin. I'm a boy named J.D. We drew pumpkins at preschool."

A laugh loosened the ache inside. "I know, silly. Pumpkin is a nickname because you're cute and sweet." She sat on the edge of the bed and tweaked his nose.

"But I already have a name."

She couldn't help but run her fingers across a wayward strand of his hair, pushing it down. The strand was soft and feathery under her hand, stirring up more raw emotions. "Right. Your name is J.D."

"No." His nose scrunched up, and he cocked his head. "Like pumpkin, but not."

"Okay." Whatever he said. It was too early for her to make sense of it. "You want breakfast? Your dad's next door helping me get storm shutters from the attic."

"Captain." He scooted to the edge of the bed and slid to the floor. Prints of red sailboats covered his blue pajamas.

Boats everywhere. There was no escaping them. Maggie stood and considered his word. "You want Captain Crunch?"

"What's that?"

"It's a cereal, and you said captain."

"My other name is captain. Sometimes mate, too. Or

sailor." He stared at her like she was pretty dense.

"Oh." It figured. Josh was totally indoctrinating J.D. into the dangerous life of the sea.

They entered the wood-paneled kitchen. So dark. The walls could use a fresh coat of a light paint. Or maybe he should change out the dark paneling for a narrower beadboard. Maggie opened the refrigerator. "What do you eat for breakfast?"

"Daddy cooks eggs. But I want what you said." His arms crossed, and he stared up at her with puppy-dog eyes.

"What I said?" A prick of uneasiness brought her brows together.

"Captain cereal."

Uh, oh. A sinking feeling told her she'd misspoken. "Where do you keep the captain cereal?"

"We don't have any."

Of course they didn't. "How about we have eggs like Daddy makes?"

He shook his head. "You said captain cereal. I'm a captain. I need captain cereal."

"I can make the special Maggie's cheese omelet."

His disappointed face aimed up at her.

"Let's go next door and see what cereal Dahlia has." Or go let Josh take the flak for her mistake. She held out her arms, and he willingly came to her and snuggled close.

Though she hated to admit it, she could get used to this warm toasty feeling. But she obviously had a lot to learn about kids.

~~~

Maggie had been right about one thing. Josh wished it hadn't been *this thing* as he bent over and cut open another box. Cammie and Ruth had never opened the new storm shutters.

This project would take a while, and he still hadn't found the socket set he'd need. Probably in storage. Either that or Trisha had made off with it. Like she had with most of his money and belongings. Why, he couldn't figure, since she'd left him for a casino mogul.

Anyway, he'd have to run to the hardware store.

"You're not making much progress, from the looks of it." Maggie's voice snuck up from behind and coiled around his heart.

Josh turned to find her standing in the garage looking at the panels on the ground. J.D. was settled happily on her hip still in his pajamas. Didn't she know to dress him before bringing him out? "Morning, captain." It wasn't until he pressed his lips to the little boy's cheek that Maggie's sweet floral scent drifted to him. She was so close. A current jolted through him. Heated his chest. And for one moment, the world seemed right.

But no. That scenario would never be. She'd never come back here. Or to him. He glanced at her face but she cut her eyes away. Had she felt it, too?

"I want captain cereal for breakfast." J.D.'s voice brought Josh crashing down to earth.

"What?" The sentence hadn't fully reached his brain.

"Miss Maggie told me about captain cereal. I want some." J.D. played with one of Maggie's curls as he talked. The picture pecked hard at Josh's heart.

Oh, man. This was messed up. "She did, huh? We usually have eggs."

Finally, she looked Josh's way, her dark eyes narrowing. "A misunderstanding, okay? Is it acceptable if I check to see if Dahlia has any, just for today?"

"Please, Daddy?"

63

They had him at *captain cereal*. "Just for today, sailor?"

"Yes, sir." J.D.'s head nodded.

"Carry on then, sir. And ma'am." Josh saluted them both and held back a smile. The two looked so perfect together. "Can I have some, too? I have to go to the hardware store before I can finish this job anyway."

Something like a growl vibrated in Maggie's throat. "Seriously?"

"I'm not one of those fly-by-night installers who throws on shutters without the proper tools, ma'am."

Trudging forward, Maggie sighed. "I've got to figure out if Dahlia has school and open the store."

He followed them through the garage and into the kitchen. "You don't have to be here for me to do the job. You can trust me."

"Humph. We'll see. Not that I have much choice." Maggie set to work, searching out a box of captain cereal, which could've been any of them as far as J.D. knew. She found the real deal. The blue-and-white bowls clinked as she set them on the counter and threw a spoon in each. She turned Josh's way with raised eyebrows. "You just gonna watch?" The dark eyes drilled into him.

"Huh?" Boy, she had him mesmerized.

"You could get the milk if you wanted to be useful. Can I trust you with that?" A slight tease filtered through her harsh words.

"Oh. Yeah." He'd been caught staring, enjoying the view of her piddling around the kitchen with J.D. on her hip. He grabbed the carton from the refrigerator and waited until she filled two bowls with cereal. "Aren't you eating?"

"I need to wake Dahlia first. The school is still open last I heard."

He poured milk over one bowl and took it to the table. "I'll let the captain get started, and I'll wait to have mine, too."

"Why?"

What she didn't know about kids could be hazardous to all their health. Mental and otherwise. "You might need all hands on deck to get that one out of bed."

~~~

The smirk on Josh's face poked at Maggie's nerves. Again. She'd not asked for his help, but of course, he was on her heels like he owned the place. He wasn't the captain of this ship. She trudged to Dahlia's room and flicked on the light. "Good morning, sunshine."

"Turn that off." A pillow covered Dahlia's head. "What are you doing?" A grumpy snarl arose from under the lime green lump.

"You need to get ready for school. Do you ride the bus, or does your mom drive you?" Keeping one's voice perky took a lot of patience. Maggie pinned up her lips in a grin.

Hands reached out and punched the pillow tighter over the bulge that was Dahlia's head. No answer.

"Dahlia, let's rise and shine and give God the glory." That's what her mom had always said. Maggie sat on the edge of the bed and rubbed what looked to be the girl's shoulder. "Come on. We're serving up Captain Crunch in the mess hall." Did she really use the term *mess hall*? Just like her dad. What this place did to her in a day…

"I'm not going to school."

"What? You don't have school today?" Probably a fib. "I better check the website again to be sure."

"We have school." The pillow spoke again. "I'm not going."

Josh stepped closer to the bed. "Um, Maggie—"

65

"Why aren't you going?" Maggie shot her toughest back-off look at Josh.

"You might need help at the store."

"I'll manage, sweetie. You don't have to worry. I'm here to take care of things."

An elbow nudged her. Apparently Josh thought he should interrupt. He mouthed words, but she waved him off.

"Aunt Maggie, we're not doing anything except making Thanksgiving crafts, and my mother was *practically killed* in a tragic accident, and I am *not* going to school."

Emotion punctuated Dahlia's words and quivered in Dahlia's voice.

The sentiment wrestled against Maggie's resolve. She hadn't considered how deeply the accident had affected her niece. Seeing one's mother injured and then taken away in an ambulance must have been traumatic. How awful for a child to endure.

Yet Dahlia had carried Josh's son home, made the call for help, and cared for J.D. until she arrived. Dahlia was strong, but still a little girl. Maggie cut her gaze toward Josh, who wore a look that spoke *duh*. So that's what he was trying to tell her. He might know a bit more about children than she did. He was probably a good father.

"Sweetie, your mom's going to get better. I was with her before I came home." Of course, Cammie had looked about the same as she had the night before. Groggy and beat up.

The sheets rustled as Dahlia turned over and finally poked out her head. "Like my grandma? She never got better. Or Grandpa? I never even got to meet him." Worry carved a line between her brows.

The words knifed Maggie's chest. "It's nothing like what happened to my mother or my father. Your mom will be home before you know it." *Please, Lord, let that be true. And let her be walking.*

"I wish I'd known Grandpa. It would've been cool to have a dad like him." Dahlia eyed Josh.

Bending to one knee beside the bed, Josh offered a tender smile. "Your grandpa was like a father to me when I needed one. I could return the favor. Teach you to fish and take you sailing—"

Wait…what was he offering? To be her niece's father? And sailing? "No. Not sailing." Maggie's voice came out too harsh.

Both heads twisted toward her.

"I mean, let's talk about this later. You don't have to go to school. You can come to the store with me."

"Well, if I'm staying home, can I sleep in? You can come get me at lunch. Or I'll walk over when I wake up. It's only two blocks."

The girl was good. She had to give her that. "Okay, mini-me, that wasn't the deal."

J.D. took that moment to appear and jump onto the bed. "I'll go to the store with you, Miss Maggie." Milk circled his mouth as he smiled.

If that wasn't the most precious thing she'd ever seen… "You sure ate quickly. Did you finish all your cereal?"

"Yes, ma'am. I like the Captain. Can we buy some more?"

Josh leaned across the bed and scooped his son up in one fell swoop. "We'll see. And you can stay home and be Daddy's helper today."

"But I want to go with Miss Maggie." J.D.'s brows met above his nose.

His expression caught hold of Maggie's heart. Kids usually didn't give her this much attention. Of course, she hadn't been around many besides Jane's kids and Dahlia. She hated to disappoint him. "I guess I could take him. Do you have some kind of sling I can carry him around in?"

That drew a laugh from both Josh and Dahlia.

At last, her niece sat up. "He's not a baby, Aunt Maggie."

"What about a backpack? I've seen bigger kids in those."

"There's not room to walk around with a backpack in an antique store." Dahlia rolled her eyes. "Next stupid idea."

"Stupid idea? I'll give you a—"

"Hey." Josh stood and pressed his forehead against J.D.'s. "I need my first mate and Dahlia to stay with me this morning. It'll take all hands on deck to get the shutters up, and then we'll pick up lunch for everyone and go hang out with Maggie at the store."

"That could work." The man did have a smidgen of sense. Maybe. Sometimes. But what did he mean by hang out? Not him, too, surely. He had to know she didn't want him distracting her.

Like he was already.

She had a headache as it was.

"I'll see if Aunt Ruth is up." She'd have to have someone familiar with how to run the business. Maggie smiled at the children and then made her way down the dark hall to Aunt Ruth's room. A faint glow came from under her great aunt's door. And the scent of Chanel perfume, a fragrance both Aunt Ruth and Mama loved.

Memories surrounded her, almost swallowing her...

Mama and Cammie moving in with Aunt Ruth after Katrina once new sheetrock had been put in.

Mama hoping against hope Daddy would be found and they'd rebuild on the old foundation a few blocks over.

Then reality had struck.

More like reality had slapped them silly. Daddy was never

coming back. The insurance company wasn't going to cover what they deemed *flood damage*. Cammie was pregnant and would have to quit her classes at Tulane and come home to take care of a baby while Mama went back to work. All three women had insisted that Maggie go back to Mississippi State and get on with her life. As if...

The door creaked open, and Aunt Ruth appeared. "Oh! What are you doing, Maggie? You scared the life out of me, like seeing a ghost standing there."

"Sorry." She knew the feeling. "I was just about to knock." Aunt Ruth was dressed to the nines, short hair poufy but sprayed in place, face powdered, and red lipstick circling her lips. "You look ready for a day of selling antiques."

A big smile accompanied a slight giggle. "Born ready for that, sweetie."

"Great."

Aunt Ruth took small, shuffling steps beside Maggie down the hall. She seemed to favor one foot, causing a small limp.

If her aunt fell or something... "Have you hurt your foot?"

"My rheumatism. The weather and all."

Yeah, the weather. Maggie breathed a shaky sigh. She hoped it was only the weather causing Aunt Ruth's pain. The house was being prepared for the storm, but someone needed to be at the hospital when the next visiting hour came around. Could Aunt Ruth be left alone at the store if something happened with Cammie?

Chapter 7

After pulling up to the old storefront on Washington Avenue, Maggie checked her phone. Nothing from the hospital so far. Should she call?

Aunt Ruth patted her hand. "God's in control. We just have to do our part."

The statement grated against Maggie's already frazzled patience. "But what's my part? What's most important? The store? Holding Cammie's hand? Taking care of Dahlia? Watching the weather?" *Which one, God?*

"One moment at a time, Magnolia. That's all we can manage—the moment we're in."

So the store, since that's where they were. She might as well get out and attack that challenge. Maggie pushed open her door and stepped out onto the cracked pavement. The turquoise awning above the entrance looked new. A shame since if a hurricane made landfall, the storm winds would likely slice it to shreds. The cute wrought iron benches and planters filled with pansies would need to be carried inside, too. She nudged one of the pots as she passed. The things were heavy, but surely Cammie had a dolly somewhere.

Aunt Ruth slowly made her way toward the door with the keys. Maggie hurried to offer an arm. "Can I help?"

"I'm fine." She shooed her away. "I'm not as fast as I once was, but I've been walking for a while now."

Still stubborn, like all the women in this family...

With each step her aunt took, Maggie flinched, hoping the

elderly woman wouldn't trip. Each crack and dip in the sidewalk looked like an accident waiting to happen. The coastal soil didn't allow concrete pathways to stay level for long.

Finally inside, Maggie set her purse under the sales counter. A coffee pot, a gallon jug of bottled water, and a can of New Orleans' finest grounds—from Café Du Monde, of course—sat on a shelf nearby. *Thank you, Cammie, for the easy caffeine access.* Apparently, Cammie loved the stuff as much as she did. Maggie wasted no time filling the carafe and adding the dark roast. She pressed the *on* button, and the aromatic chicory joined the scent of whatever floral fragrance Cammie was using to make the store smell fresh. Her sister had always been obsessed with air freshening techniques for ambiance around the antiques. But really, Cammie had always been obsessed with all things perfume and fragrance. A bit of a smell snob. Maggie chuckled at the memories of Cammie claiming the perfumes Maggie wore gave her a headache and insisting the whole family needed to shower after a walk around the block.

The silly memory was a good one now, and it excavated others with it. A memory of Sunday afternoon strolls with Mama and Daddy, another of shopping with friends in high school, Cammie styling their hair for homecoming...

Maggie shook her head. There was no time for strolling down memory lane. She needed to get down to business.

Aunt Ruth puttered around, rearranging items on the shelves and dusting. Not that the store needed cleaning. The place was immaculate. Clean. Orderly. Even the baseboards looked freshly scrubbed. Cammie ran a tight ship.

Maggie strode to the stockroom. Spotless. Only one large shipping box needed to be unwrapped. After she figured out how to get the cash register going, she'd open it up and see what it held.

Maggie returned to the showroom. "Aunt Ruth, do you know how to get this machine started?"

No answer. Maggie wound around the aisles until she reached her aunt and tapped her shoulder.

"Oh!" Aunt Ruth clutched her heart. "You scared the life out of me, child, sneaking up on me like that again. You always were a tricky one."

"I'm sorry, I didn't…" Add hearing-aid to the to-do list. "Do you know how to operate the cash register?"

"Oh, she got a new one not long ago. Once we get it going, I might be able to help, but the thing's high-technical. Dahlia knows. Josh probably knows, too."

"Josh? Why would he know?"

"He helps out now and then. More lately, if Cammie needs to be off when he's home. It's a nice tradeoff for them. They help each other, being single parents and all."

A vise locked around Maggie's chest. Was there more to the new arrangement than single parents helping each other? "How nice for them."

Her aunt shook a finger at her. "Now, Magnolia, don't get your unmentionables twisted, as they say. It's not a romantic thing. It's the practicality of surviving their difficult situations."

No one used the word unmentionables anymore, much less twisted unmentionables. And what was with Aunt Ruth calling her Magnolia? Maggie held in the smart replies popping up in her brain and sighed. Two single parents helping each other out made sense. And she'd love Cammie to find a nice guy. If it were *any other* nice guy in the world.

Maggie walked back to the cash register. Wading through a ton of sand might be more fun than the prospect of calling Dahlia or Josh for help. There had to be an instruction manual around. She was pretty good with computers. Her job in meteorology kept her on the crazy technology twenty-four seven. Good thing she'd come in early.

Thirty minutes later, Maggie threw the thin manual against the wall and groaned. The store was supposed to open now. Calling Dahlia seemed to be the only option, because she wasn't asking Josh. She dialed the house phone. It rang until the machine picked up. Which meant she'd be left calling Josh either way. Or she could skip entering purchases and write them on paper. Not a real option, though. She'd promised to do this, and if she was going to do it, she was going to do it right.

Josh's number was taped behind the counter. Maybe for Dahlia and Aunt Ruth, because Cammie had it in her phone. Reluctantly, Maggie retrieved her cell from her purse and forced her fingers to press the numbers.

"Hello." His low voice haunted her like a ghost from her past…which he was.

Maggie blew out an extended sigh combined with a groan. "I need to ask Dahlia how to operate the stupid cash register."

Laughter rumbled through the line. "I might be able—"

"Just put her on." Of course he found humor in her weakness.

"Aye, aye, sir." More chuckling.

She'd pinch him if he were here. No. He'd probably enjoy it. And start tickling her like he always had when they were kids. Okay, and when they were teens, which usually led to kissing. More memories flooded her mind. They hung heavy around her heart, squeezing…crushing.

"Aunt Maggie? Hello?"

"Yeah." She snapped herself back to the present. "How do I work this crazy machine?"

Dahlia started spouting instructions. Maggie blinked hard.

She should really pay attention and squash thoughts of Josh, once and for all. Like she'd been trying to do for more than ten years. The other reason, besides hurricanes, that kept her from visiting her family on the Coast as often as she should. She couldn't stand the thought of running into him, or worse yet, hearing something terrible had happened to him. Like what happened to her father.

"Got it, Aunt Maggie?"

"Run through the instructions one more time."

Once Dahlia growled and explained again, Maggie had it. Aunt Ruth turned the *Closed* sign in the window to *Open*, and they waited for the first customer.

Aunt Ruth neared and wiped the clean counter. "I hope the ads Cammie placed in the paper bring in some business. The economy is down, and people don't buy real antiques so much. They love painting those flea markets finds."

So Aunt Ruth knew about the slump. "How bad is it?"

"What?" She leaned her head closer.

"How bad is it?" Maggie spoke so loud, she felt she was shouting.

"We break even, but don't make much after paying our small salaries."

"You could retire and close the store. Cammie could find another job." She added volume to her tone by pushing the words up from her diaphragm.

"Cammie loves the store because Dahlia can be here after school and during the summer. She doesn't want her home alone. There's all kinds of trouble out there for children these days."

"Is that why she wants to send her to private school?"

"Some kids have been ugly to Dahlia. I think it's hurting her feelings, and she comes home and takes it out on Cammie."

That explained the smart mouth. Poor Dahlia. There had to be a solution. At least now she better understood why Cammie had taken on babysitting J.D. Plus, the boy was pretty cute. Both kids were.

"We'll figure out how she can make the new school happen. We can try for after Christmas, if there's a spot." She'd pull every string she could, and she'd make Josh Bergeron do the same. He had to know someone with influence around the area. "What about selling furniture on consignment? Then you wouldn't have to purchase inventory. We could refinish some of our own flea market finds that don't look so hot with paint in those trendy colors. We could sell the decorator paint, too. And add candles and local pottery. People love scented candles. Of course, they'd have to go through the Cammie scent approval."

A smile lifted Aunt Ruth's lined cheeks. "Aren't you like a dog with a bone? But talk to Cammie before you make any big changes. I signed the store over to her five years ago. The house, too. She's taken such good care of me all this time. She's the child I never had." Her eyes widened, and her hand went to her cheek. "Not that you aren't—"

"I understand. Don't worry." Maggie smiled. "You've helped Cammie, and she's helped you. I'm glad you had each other."

"You don't have to be alone, you know? We can all be together."

Not that again. She wasn't moving back here. The glass entry door chimed. "I think we have a customer." Saved by the bell.

Chapter 8

"Up to the mast with you. Keep an eye out for pirates." Josh hoisted J.D. onto his shoulders in the crowded parking lot of the hardware store.

"Aye, aye, sir." J.D. slipped into place and patted his hands on Josh's forehead.

The sky alternated cloud cover and spills of sunlight. One minute a wind whipped up and the next, all became still. The weather was about as confusing as the emotions churning through his mind.

Giggling, Dahlia walked beside Josh. "He's so cute."

"I agree." Josh smiled down at her. "You're not too shabby yourself. Pretty like your mama and…" Why'd he start that?

One side of her mouth quirked. "Aunt Maggie?"

Harpooned by a ten-year-old girl. "Yeah. Her, too."

"Everyone says I look like Aunt Maggie." She shrugged. "So y'all were a thing?"

"What, us? A thing?" Could he play dumb? "What's a thing?"

Dahlia's fists went to her hips and she gave him a hard stare. "Don't go to Broadway. You won't get the part."

Way too much like her aunt. "We grew up together. Spent all our time together. Dated." He hoped that answer would be enough to quench her curiosity. Meanwhile J.D. made boat motor noises above and seemed to be using his dad's ears as steering levers.

"I heard Mom tell Aunt Ruth that Aunt Maggie never got

over you. That's why she's not married."

The words both anguished him and gave him hope. If only Maggie weren't so stubborn. Or was he the stubborn one?

"But you must've gotten over her because you married J.D.'s mom." Another hard blow. It seemed Dahlia wasn't giving up any time soon.

And had that been a question or a statement? Kids could be so blunt. "I guess I gave up on Maggie ever coming back, and I met Trisha."

"So you loved both?"

Good grief. The girl was worse than a shrink. Even if he knew the answers to all her questions, which he didn't, he'd rather not poke around those tender wounds. He'd thought he'd loved Trisha once. Except he'd obviously never really known the woman. Not deep down. Josh lowered J.D. to his hip before they entered the glass doors of the hardware store. The last thing the boy needed was to bump his noggin. They'd learned that one the hard way.

"Daddy, look. Candy!" J.D. struggled to slip to the floor and escape.

Thank the Lord. If Dahlia liked junk food, too, she might lose interest in her inquisition. Josh set J.D. on his feet but held onto his hand. "Not yet. If you're a good boy, I'll buy you and Dahlia a treat when we finish shopping." Between the sugary cereal and this candy, he'd need to make sure lunch was healthy, at least.

Tools stood in waist-high carts and displays, shiny and new. Saws and drills hung neatly on an endcap. Grills of various sizes and price ranges lined the wall near the cash register. He eyed one that held a side table fryer. That would be nice to cook seafood in. He inhaled deeply. Dusty and metallic. Man, he loved the hardware store. Was this how women felt when they went shopping?

"You didn't answer my question."

He looked down to find Dahlia's brown eyes staring up at him. The women in this family were tenacious.

"Okay, but first, I'd like to ask you a question. Why do you want to know this information?" Let her chew on that for a half minute while he looked for the right aisle. Usually five sales clerks tried to help him, but they were all leading customers around today. Others prepping in case of a storm, no doubt.

"Because I don't understand adults." Dahlia paused, biting her lip. "Like my dad. I've never even met him."

Josh's stomach lurched. So Dahlia had reached an age where she'd started to wonder about her parents' relationship. Someday J.D. would do the same. He'd ask questions about why his mother left him. The realization pitched Josh's stomach into a deep current. The hurt of parents who didn't care enough to be a part of their child's life was all too familiar—his own father'd dumped him and his mom like a load of rotten fish. How a parent could cut and run on a child, Josh would never understand.

He met Dahlia's gaze and forced a smile. "Adults do stupid things, make big mistakes, and it hurts. I told you my dad left me and my mom, so I know how hard it is, but you do the best you can and lean on God. He can become a Father to you." He tweaked her chin with his free hand. "And you're lucky. Your mom loves you something fierce. Plus Ruth and Maggie."

"Aunt Ruth's in her eighties. What if something happens to Mom? What if she doesn't get well?"

God forbid. "She will, but you have your aunt Maggie." Dahlia's watery gaze plucked at his heart. "I told you I'll hang around, too."

Her lips pinched together, and she looked away. The child

was really taking the accident hard. He gave her shoulder a squeeze and prayed she'd find peace in all this. "Let's finish up, and I'll get y'all a treat."

He located the aisle of sockets. With the right tools, the windows wouldn't take him too long. Despite the fact that he should probably be searching for new childcare options, he would stay close to the Marovich women. Dahlia needed him now.

Maggie, too, whether she'd admit it or not.

~~~

Had the school let out early or had the three lanky teens entering the store skipped? Maggie pretended to rearrange a nearby shelf of antique paperweights to keep an eye on them. Every time they touched something, she cringed. They'd come in laughing and talking loudly. Not really the antique store type, but a parent could've given them money to Christmas shop. Possibly. Okay, she was probably deluding herself.

Near a shelf of crystal bowls, one boy grabbed another's hat and made a joke about his hair. She took quick steps to them, right as a shoving match started. "Hey! Stop that, and get outside before you break something. Now." Her voice roared in her own ears as she gave them her best crazy face.

In unison, the boys' heads jerked her way.

"You heard me." She stomped closer. "What are you waiting on?"

"She's nuts, man." The tallest of them shook his head and turned toward the door. The other two followed.

"That's right. I'm nuts. Warn all your friends."

Aunt Ruth came out from the back as they left. "Maggie, did you call me? I thought I heard you."

Yep. She'd been that loud. "No. I was talking to some kids."

"Oh. Could they go buy us some lunch? I'm ravenous all of a sudden."

"I don't think so." Maggie couldn't help but chuckle. "Josh is bringing lunch soon."

"Could you call and ask him to hurry? I don't know if my blood sugar can wait."

Her blood sugar? "Are you diabetic now?"

"Sometimes hunger hits me like this. Always has. Makes me cranky. Lightheaded."

Must run in the family. "Is there some juice or cookies around? That usually helps me. I don't want you fainting."

"Call Josh. I bet he'll come on over."

Not again with calling Josh. It was barely eleven o'clock. They could have lunch delivered, but then she'd need to at least send Josh a text so he wouldn't bring more food. A no-win situation. "Okay."

She texted him instead of calling.

Aunt Ruth says her blood sugar needs lunch ASAP.

A second later, her phone vibrated.

Not a problem. Sounds familiar. Any special requests?

Having an extended conversation wasn't her plan.

No.

Be there soon. I know a great place, and it's a buffet so it won't take long at all to fill up some to-go boxes.

Good for him. She'd head to the back and open that big delivery box. If she timed it right, she might miss Josh's visit all together. But what if those boys came back? Did Cammie have a problem with crime? Her aunt might not even hear someone come in. There was no way she could be left at the store alone for an extended period.

Maggie chewed her bottom lip. She could go in the back and open the box, but come check on things every few minutes.

"Aunt Ruth?" Maggie tapped her arm. "Can you stay behind the counter while I go to the storage area?"

"Of course I can, sugar."

Maggie took her leave and began a search for the box cutter. Most of the extra small-size inventory were in labeled clear plastic tubs. A vintage post office sorting cabinet held ribbons, tissue paper, tape, bows, and jars, but nothing to cut with. Another set of shelves were affixed above a counter. Good grief, so much bubble wrap. Cammie had miles of it stored back here. Finally Maggie spotted the handle jutting out from the highest shelf with all the cleaning supplies. She stretched on her tiptoes to reach it. Why did Cammie keep everything so high? Rearranging the shelves might be helpful. She could put the things they used every day within reach.

The huge package stood just inside the loading area. It loomed tall over Maggie as she neared. Where should she start? She didn't want to cut in too far and scar an expensive china cabinet or something. Settling on a side corner, Maggie slit the cardboard. Bubble wrap surrounded whatever was inside, so she continued. Once she unwrapped each side, she stripped away the insulation.

Her jaw dropped.

The intricately-carved French armoire standing before her looked so close to the one that had been destroyed in their house during Katrina. It had been in her bedroom. She laid the box cutter on the counter and ran her fingers across the white-finished wood, recalling the happy years with her family. Before the storm. How many times had they hidden in that armoire during a game of hide-and-seek? Or pretended they'd found the wardrobe to Narnia and filled the thing with *talking* stuffed animals?

Had Cammie intended to sell this piece or had her sister ordered it with other intentions? Maybe to keep herself? The piece had always been special to them.

Now that she thought of Cammie, she really needed to call the nurse's station to check on her. In fact, she should be at the hospital, but here she stood wading through too many memories. Her father playing Frisbee with her, Josh, and Cammie in the front yard. The smile that lit up Daddy's face and the encouraging words, whether she made the catch or missed. Her mother cooking up enormous, mouthwatering pots of gumbo or red beans for them all. Sitting around the table with family.

Her stomach gurgled. An early lunch might be a good idea, but every time she saw Josh, the hurt cut so deep, she wanted to pluck her eyes out. When she'd left him years ago, she'd blown up, said things she shouldn't have. And there were some words a person couldn't take back.

"Miss Maggie?" A small voice jerked her head around.

J.D. stood by the counter, staring at the box cutter, his hand hovering over it. "Daddy said to tell you we brought lunch."

Maggie forced the residue of memories aside and plucked up the box cutter. She strained to place it back on the top shelf. No wonder everything was out of reach. "Thank you, pumpkin—I mean captain."

"You can call me pumpkin, I guess. Since you're not a sailor."

Thank goodness. He was such a doll, her arms ached to hold him, an unfamiliar sensation for her. "Can I pick you up and give you a hug as thanks for bringing lunch?"

His chin tilted as his blue eyes studied her. "Okay."

She lifted him up and nestled him close, letting her chin

rub against his fine hair. "You're such a good boy, aren't you?" Like his daddy used to be.

Stop that, brain. Her feet carried her back to the front of the store, despite the fact that she'd been hiding from Josh. She was a little hungry.

"Cammie says I'm a good boy, too. Is she better yet?"

"I don't know. I'm hoping to check on her soon."

Dahlia sat on a stool behind the checkout counter eating from a white Styrofoam container and looking like she was ready to take over. Aunt Ruth had settled next to her with her own box.

A hand skimmed the small of Maggie's back. "I think you'll like the food from this restaurant." Josh's proximity sent flutters through her midsection. "Sit, eat your lunch, and then go see about Cammie. I'll stay."

Her eyes met Josh's unnerving blue gaze. "I couldn't ask you—"

"Yes. You could." He grinned, bringing those blasted smile lines to life. "Besides." He nodded toward Dahlia. "I'll have someone here who actually knows how to run the place and work the cash register."

"You always were a smart aleck." Maggie couldn't stop a smirk. Josh had noticed the same air of ownership in her niece. Dahlia obviously knew what she was doing, and someone did need to see about Cammie. "Fine. I'll let you." An aroma of spices hit Maggie's nose and sent a rumble through her stomach.

"Someone really needs her lunch." More grinning from Josh. "How about we sit on the bench out front and eat?" He held up a white bag, and the steamy scents escalated. "Come on. Get some vitamin D before you go. The sun's peeking out now and then."

The food did smell good. It had been a long day already, and she needed to eat. "Okay. I have a few minutes before I'd need to leave if I'm going to make the next visiting hour." She followed him to the door, still snuggling J.D. close.

She could eat lunch with the man and his boy, right? That didn't mean anything. It sure didn't mean she was going to let Josh be a part of her life.

Not unless he made a different career choice. She couldn't live with the chance of losing him to the Gulf like she'd lost her father. After that crushing blow, it had taken everything within her not to lose her faith. And not without a number of hard questions sent up in prayer. She'd gone from a happy eighteen-year-old with a happy family in a nice home to a devastated young adult who'd had almost everything swept away in a single day. She struggled to understand why God had allowed the disaster.

"Miss Maggie?" J.D. patted her face. "Can you let me down so I can eat? You can hold me again after I finish."

Poor child. How long had she been staring at the swaying canopy formed by the moss-covered branches of the live oaks across the street? "Sure, pumpkin." She set him on the bench and took a step back.

Josh placed a container next to J.D., stretched open a napkin, and tucked it in his son's collar.

J.D.'s nose scrunched as he stared up at his father. "I'm not a baby."

"Oh now, I'm going to use a napkin, too. Remember, we have to look nice to work at the fancy antique store." He unfolded another paper and pushed it under his own collar.

Maggie took in the whole sight of them. Until that moment, she hadn't noticed their attire. She never got far beyond those blue eyes. Both wore khakis and dark blue button down shirts tucked in with brown leather belts. J.D.'s little brown Dockers looked exactly like Josh's. An adorable picture if there ever was one.

"Here's yours." Josh held out another box. "Have a seat."

Taking it, she moved to the other side of J.D. No way she was sitting so close to Josh. She opened her lunch to find fried catfish, turnip greens, and black-eyed peas. The man knew her favorites. Though her hips didn't need the fried food. Gone were the days of eating like a teenager. Oh, well, as long as it was here… She took a large bite of the crispy filet. So perfectly fried, salty, and delicious.

A cool breeze whipped up and ran across her face. Not too cold, though. And the bench was warm enough, but the metal a tad hard, which reminded her she needed to move it inside in case the winds reached hurricane force. As long as Josh insisted on helping, she might as well ask. "Can you take these seats and the planters inside before the storm?"

"I don't know if I'm strong enough for that." He'd sat on the other side of J.D and opened his food, but stopped and flexed one bicep. "I mean I've still got it, but these benches are bolted to the cement to keep people from taking off with them." Josh held his arm closer and raised his brows. "You can test it out if you want, since you can't see it well under the sleeve."

Maggie shook her head. "Put your gun away. You're as bad as Steve at my office." She twisted to look over the back of the bench. "Bolted down?"

"Steve, huh? What's he like? Muscular?"

"Full of Steve." She leaned forward, studied the bolts that held the bench in place. She hadn't noticed that before. A little rusty, but maybe they'd hold. Nothing much she could do about it.

"I've got a muscle." J.D. jerked up his arm, still holding a forkful of mashed potatoes. The white blob sailed off and splatted on Josh's cheek.

"Aw, mate, watch out. I've got my own food to eat." Josh wiped his face with his napkin, smearing the creamy mess further.

Laughter made its way up Maggie's midsection and spilled out. She snorted in her attempt to hold it in. Her amusement was joined by a chorus of the sweetest childish giggles she'd ever heard. J.D.'s chest shook as he chortled harder and louder, followed by a little cough.

"Not funny." After flipping his napkin, Josh rubbed his face again. "And y'all sound like a pair of snorting hyenas."

They both laughed harder. Josh rolled his eyes, but a smile seeped out.

A bell chimed, and an elderly couple exited the art-framing shop next door.

The woman smiled and waved. "We were watching you through the window. Y'all are the cutest little family. Absolutely adorable."

The warbled voice was warm, but reality slapped Maggie like a cold wave.

What did she say to that?

"Thanks." Josh gave a quick smile at the woman and waved, but grief churned in Maggie's stomach.

She closed her lunch and rose. "I have to go. I'll eat this at the hospital."

"Maggie, wait. Don't—"

"No." She pressed one hand out in front of her. "I can't." If she didn't get out of here now, she'd lose it.

Chapter 9

A truck in front of her came to a sudden stop, and Maggie slammed the brakes of her Acura. The box of food Josh had bought her slipped from the edge of the front seat to spill onto the floorboard. Black-eyed peas tumbled everywhere. Turnip greens slathered over the beige carpet. That smell would linger for months, maybe forever. Seemed about right. A big mess all over the place. Like every hurt she'd locked inside for years was spilling out again.

Her eyes burned. She wouldn't cry. She'd shed way too many tears already when Josh had chosen piloting over her. But that woman's comment about them being a family had lifted a gravestone and raised up the buried loss inside. And that little boy. And sitting there with Josh, laughing like they'd always laughed. And pretending it hadn't been more than a decade since they'd spoken.

"Lord, help me with this pain. No matter how hard I try, I can't seem to keep my emotions under control around here."

Her grip on the steering wheel tightened, and she focused. Another car pulled out in front of her. She needed to keep her mind on the road. Her family couldn't deal with any other disasters. At least she didn't have much farther.

Once she reached the hospital lot, Maggie checked her eyes in the rearview for any sign of smeared makeup. Not that she'd worn much, but no sense upsetting Cammie. The splatter of greens and peas on the floor continued to heckle her.

"Oh hush. So help me, I'll scrub this car after my visit, and it'll be like you were never even here. You hear me?" Now she was threatening vegetables. Her sanity might be in danger. If only she could scour Josh from her mind as well.

Inside the hospital, she arrived as the last visitors and a nurse entered the ICU. "Wait. I'm coming."

The nurse turned and held the door. "You made it. Take a deep breath."

Did she look as frazzled as she felt? "I lost track of time."

"You're here now."

Maggie neared Cammie's room. A man's voice and then a small laugh came through. Cammie's laugh. That had to be a good sign. Maggie poked her head in to see Dr. Castro sitting in a chair pulled close to Cammie's head. From his profile, he wore a grin way too large for the doctor of a patient who'd recently been paralyzed.

Maggie cleared her throat. Twice. Loudly.

The doctor pushed back and stood, still grinning. "Miss Marovich, good to see you. We have great news."

Her heart skipped a beat. "She can walk?"

His forehead crinkled as the smile lessened. "No, but she has pins-and-needles sensations."

That caused all the smiling? Maggie stared at the man.

"It means she's healing. I know it's a small step, but it's a start."

It wasn't a step at all. The man should learn to word things better. She pressed on a smile and moved closer to Cammie. "Great."

"Why are you here?" Cammie's brows drew together. "Who's at the store? It's not closed, is it?" She must've been getting a little better. All the woman ever worried about was that store. Of course, the business was the sole income source to support three people, so it made sense Cammie would be concerned.

"Settle down." Maggie forced a pleasant expression. "I figured out how to use the cash register, and Josh is there with everyone, so it's fine."

"Okay." Cammie's brow relaxed. "Josh knows what to do."

"Apparently." Maggie beat back the urge to roll her eyes. "And Dahlia?"

The anguished press of Cammie's lips squashed all the ridiculous self-pity from Maggie's mind. "She's worried about you." She turned her attention back to Dr. Castro. "When can her daughter visit? It's Thanksgiving soon and all."

"Give it another day or so. There are a lot of flu bugs going around the schools right now. The last thing we need is for Cammie to catch a virus and have it to turn into pneumonia."

The image of Cammie getting ill whipped up the terror wanting to break out of the mental vault Maggie had locked it in. Her heart thrashed in her chest. If her sister caught pneumonia, would that stunt the healing in her back? Or worse?

Being strong required her to keep that fear tamped down, not become paralyzed by worry and panic.

"You know," Dr. Castro continued, "I'm on call over Thanksgiving, and the hospital is offering a catered lunch. Why don't you all come, and you can take turns visiting then. My daughter will be around, as well as other families. Dahlia won't be the only youngster here."

Maggie let the offer sink in. It would save her from having to cook a Thanksgiving meal, along with everything else. Doubtful she'd have much time to go to the grocery store. "We can chip in or something."

"There will be plenty, but come as my guests."

Dr. Castro sure was being friendly. Maggie checked out his ring finger. Empty. He'd better not be a creep. "Doesn't your wife hate when you have to work on the holidays?"

The smile on his face faded quicker than daylilies in the dark. His Adam's apple bobbed as he swallowed. "I lost her to breast cancer two years ago now."

Memories of her mother struck like a winter wave slapping bare skin. Remnants of those gray days of IVs inserted in PICC lines, catheters, managing pain meds, her mother's endless nausea… The way her mother's body had shriveled away there at the end. She ached for anyone who'd suffered through the horrendous disease. Her mother's encouraging spirit had been the last to go, and she could still hear Mama speak her final words.

Don't lose hope, Magnolia. Take heart, God loves you.

If only she knew how God wanted her to *take heart*. What did that even mean?

"I'm sorry." But she knew how little those words actually helped. There was nothing that could help that kind of pain.

His nonchalant shrug couldn't hide the grief tightening the lines around his mouth. "You didn't know."

"You said you had a daughter, right? How old is she? Who keeps her?" Maybe he knew of good childcare for Josh.

"Anna's ten." He fidgeted with a pen in the breast pocket of his lab coat as if embarrassed by what he was going to say next. "My mother lives with us. She's a widow of many years, so when I lost Leah, she moved in to help."

Sweet, but not useful for their childcare issues. "Makes perfect sense. Our great aunt Ruth and Cammie live together and support each other."

Cammie's brows shot up, and she aimed a barbed stare Maggie's way. "You've seen that I'm okay, so you can go back to the store."

What in the world was with that look? "But Josh is... Never mind." Her sister, the slave driver, even from ICU. "I'll check back tonight, and I'll bring Aunt Ruth and Dahlia later in the week." Unless the hurricane decided to move in. Her empty stomach tossed at the thought.

"Bring Josh and J.D., too, for Thanksgiving. They won't have anyone either."

What was this? The lonely hearts club Thanksgiving meal? Though the idea seemed as smart as bathing a jellyfish, Maggie schooled her face and nodded. "I love you, sis." She clasped Cammie's fingers and gave a little squeeze.

"No sleeping in the waiting room." Cammie closed her hand around Maggie's. "You don't have to come tonight."

Her sister might not be able to walk, but she was sure able to boss. Maggie let out a long sigh. Would Josh have plans to visit his mother in Atlanta for Thanksgiving? She hoped so.

Before she left, she'd find out where Angie worked and see if they could have a chat about the doctor. Maybe even childcare options. Maggie exited the ICU and stopped at the information desk in the waiting room. A woman sat playing Solitaire on her phone.

"Excuse me. How can I find a friend of mine who is an employee of the hospital? I needed...wanted to catch up with her for a second if she's here."

The sixtyish woman looked at Maggie over her reading glasses. "I'm new part-time help, and I'm not sure of the policies for employees." The angle of her body shifted closer toward her computer screen. "I suppose I could tell you what floor she works on. What's her name?"

"Angie—" Wait. What was Angie's married name? Maggie strained to pull up the information from her tired brain.

Braden? Burton?

The woman's forehead crinkled with wary expectation now.

"Bernard. I think. I mean I knew her maiden name, but it's been a while."

Slow fingers pecked on the keyboard. "Let's see if this is the right place to punch it in. Angie B-e-r-n-a-r-d?"

"Right." Weren't the older generation supposed to be better at typing? They'd had to learn on old-fashioned typewriters.

Once the clerk figured out how to find the information, Maggie made her way down one floor. She probably could've walked around asking and figured it out quicker. At the nurses' desk, Maggie waited for one of the staff members to catch her eye. They all had conversations going, either on a phone or with other medical personnel.

Finally, a short man in blue scrubs looked up. "Can I help you?"

"Is Angie Bernard here?"

"She's off today. Can someone else help?"

"I'm a friend. My sister's upstairs. No worries." Well. She wished there were no worries.

~~~

Josh rang up another customer while Dahlia and J.D. played a game of Connect Four in the corner. Cammie stocked quite the collection of games and educational toys to entertain the children. Though only smaller items had sold since he'd been the one minding the store, business had been brisk, which should help Cammie's finances. The door chimed, and Maggie marched through, sweeping his breath away.

Every. Single. Time.

"How's Cammie?" He kept his voice low to avoid drawing

Dahlia over.

"Pins-and-needles sensations. Supposedly a good sign." Maggie blew a strand of hair from her face.

Man, he'd love to tuck it back for her. Instead, he jammed his hands in his pockets. "Sounds promising." He hoped.

"I guess. The doctor said Dahlia could come up for Thanksgiving lunch and a visit with Cammie. Are y'all traveling to Atlanta?"

Was she trying to get rid of him already? Or offer an invitation? "Mom's in California with her husband's kids. They'll be with us for Christmas."

"Miss Maggie's back." J.D.'s voice sang as he ran at her and grabbed her legs.

For a second, Maggie's eyes widened. Then she recovered, lifting him up for a hug. "I was only gone a little while, pumpkin."

"Do you want to play with me?"

"Uh, okay." More bewilderment roamed her face.

Josh took a step closer and held out his arms. "Let's go for a quick walk while Maggie gets settled in."

"No." His son's brows scrunched together.

"Now, J.D., that's not how we talk." Josh tried to give him a stern look, but it was such an adorable picture.

"No, sir." The small lips formed a pout.

"I have an idea." Maggie tipped J.D.'s chin. "I'll show you something I always loved when I was little. Then you can take it home and play with it more, if it's okay with your dad."

"What is it?" Puppy-dog eyes stared up at Maggie. The boy was a charmer already.

A vision of Trisha materialized. Dressed to the max, nails perfect, eyes flashing. The woman had been smooth. Josh pushed away the image. His son would not turn out like her.

"There's a huge box in the back." Maggie gave his son a tender smile. "I'll show you."

"A box? That's not a toy."

"Oh yes, it is." Maggie's lips lifted, a smile brightening her eyes and the soft angles of her face. "With an imagination, anything can be fun."

Josh held in a sigh that really wanted to escape. Right now, his imagination was breaking his heart. Maggie would be a great mother.

After a few steps, she turned toward him. "You've got the front."

"Question or command?"

"Ha. Ha. Very funny."

Command it was, but he'd love to see her introducing J.D. to playing with a box. Well, he'd love seeing her do anything.

He should leave town before J.D. got too attached. Okay, before he got attached, too.

~~~

In the back room, Maggie located a pack of washable markers and used duct tape to reassemble the box she'd flattened. Once she had it squared off again, she stood beside J.D. and motioned toward the enormous brown rectangle.

"What do you see? A castle? A Jeep? I'll make some slices with the box cutter when you decide, and you can use markers to decorate our imagination-creation."

His face screwed together, and he scratched behind his right ear. Like Josh always did when he was concentrating. "Pilot boat."

A small sigh seeped from her lips. "Are you sure it's not a fort?"

"Nope. Pilot boat."

"Okay." Might as well keep stirring up all the painful debris from her past. She mashed her lips together and tried to look pleasant. "I'll lay it sideways and cut a circle at the top and on the side for a gangway, so you can ride in it. You can color while I work."

"Aye, aye, sir." J.D. saluted, his eyes bright with excitement.

After thirty minutes of cutting and snipping, the boat began to come to life. Her fingers throbbed as she worked the scissors to complete the sides. This had looked easier when her dad had done it. Finally, she finished. She glanced at J.D. from her spot on the concrete floor.

"Okay, sailor. All aboard."

He took it all in. "Wow. Thank you, Miss Maggie." His arms wrapped around her neck and squeezed, undoing every single scrap of her heart.

"That is really sweet, Maggie."

She turned to find Josh standing in the doorway, jaw working, smile tentative.

"Brings back memories." His gaze moved from the box-ship to the armoire. "Didn't you have a piece of furniture like that at your house?"

"Yeah." She untangled herself from J.D. and pushed to her feet. "Gone with the deluge."

"I remember how you loved it. You should buy this one."

"It's not the one I had and never will be."

"This piece might be better—sturdier. It will last longer. You should give it a chance."

Why was she arguing with him? "Anyway, now you and J.D. can figure out how to fit the pilot boat in your truck, so y'all can play with it at home."

"We can stay. Help out."

"No. We're fine. I'm fine." With the tightening in her

throat, she felt as though she'd swallowed a life raft. And between the two sets of blue eyes gazing her way, her emotions were about to spill over.

Chapter 10

With Josh and J.D. gone and a lull in the shoppers, Maggie flipped open her computer. She needed to check the latest forecast tracks. A few clicks, and she found the information she'd feared. Though weakened and having drenched the tip of Florida, the storm seemed to be taking aim at Mississippi. Maggie's insides tightened as if iron chains wrapped around each organ and each muscle, paralyzing her. At the same time, a desperate urge crashed over her. The urge to run from the store, hit Highway 49, and not stop until she reached Jackson.

Where were her keys?

"Aunt Maggie? Are you all right?" Dahlia nudged her. "What are you looking at?" Her niece eyed the screen and pointed at the swirling symbol. "Is that the storm?"

Pressing her right thumb into her left palm, Maggie squeezed her hand and massaged. The habit seemed to zap her back from her land of nightmares. She swallowed and picked her brain for words.

"That's the hurricane. They've issued a watch along the Mississippi and Alabama coasts."

Her niece's eyes became twice their usual size. "Are we going to die like Grandpa?"

As scared as she was, Maggie knew better than to terrify a child. "No, sweetie. A watch means it might make landfall within a few days. There's still a high cone of uncertainty. It's not certain. Not like a warning." They should still leave, though. Just in case.

"What category is it?"

"How do you know about categories?"

The smirky expression took over Dahlia's face. "We studied weather at school. I'm in the fifth grade, you know."

"Right." Note to self. Preteens think they're grown-ups. "It's weakened to a category one."

"We shouldn't have to leave if it's only a one, right?"

They would leave now and never come back if it were up to her. "We'll see. They may order an evacuation because winds can still be up to ninety-five miles per hour. Plus there could be a storm surge." The swells that destroyed everything last time.

"It's sunny."

"When the storm is still several days out, the conditions on land can be fair. If we were to go down to the beach, which we aren't, we might see a swell in the water and higher waves. As the storm moves closer, the pressure begins to fall, and the outer bands of clouds start rolling in."

"Oh my goodness. What about Mama?" Terror carved across Dahlia's face, and moisture filled her eyes.

Like looking in a mirror.

Another note to self. Ten was not *really* grown up. Limit scary information. "It'll probably weaken to a tropical storm, sweetie. Most of them do." A fact Cammie had been reminding her of for years. "And if it doesn't, we'll take your mama north with us." Maggie held out one arm to Dahlia. "Come here."

Reluctantly, Dahlia folded into the crook of Maggie's shoulder.

"It'll be all right. We'll pray for your mom to get well and for the storm to dissipate."

Glassy brown eyes stared up at her. "Do you believe prayer will work? Do you believe in miracles?"

"I do believe God can perform miracles." Though many times He chose to answer prayers another way. Why, she still couldn't understand.

The door chimed, alerting them of a new customer. Maggie closed the computer and pushed it under the counter to greet the lady dressed in a trendy pair of riding boots. "Hi. Need help, or just looking around today?"

"Maggie Marovich. How are you?" The woman, probably in her late fifties, looked familiar.

"Okay, I guess." Maggie smiled, trying to wipe the confusion from her face. "How about you?"

"You don't remember me, do you?" The woman stepped closer. "It's okay. It's been a while. I'm Sylvie Daigle, one of your mother's friends. She and I taught at the school together."

"Oh, right." Now it was coming back. "I remember. You had that cool tire swing in your yard." Funny, the things one remembered from childhood.

"The one and only." Her features softened.

Maggie steeled herself. *Here comes the sympathy.*

"I loved your mother. She was a sweetie." Her lips tightened. "Both your parents…amazing people."

"They were." Maggie nodded and tried to pretend she was totally comfortable with the conversation. Mrs. Daigle meant well. "Good people." Would the woman go shop now, or was there more?

"I'm surprised to see you here. Where's Cammie?"

Nope. Not shopping yet. "In the hospital." Might as well spit it all out. "A delivery truck backed into her. Injured her spine."

"Oh, no. You're kidding."

Why would anyone joke about something like that? Maggie tried not to scowl.

Sylvie rushed closer and pulled Maggie into a tight hug. "You girls have had a time of it. I bet you need to be at the hospital but you're having to cover her store. Maybe I can help out."

With those words, Maggie allowed herself to sink into the embrace. "You'd do that?"

"It'd have to be after Thanksgiving because of family and volunteer obligations, but sure. I'm retired now, and I've helped before when Dahlia had a program or was sick. In fact, I'd love to have a store like this myself."

She could buy this exact store if only Cammie would go for it.

"If you're worried, ask Cammie about me if she's able to…" Sylvie seemed at a loss for how to finish.

Maggie released her and nodded. "She's able. I'll talk to her about after the holidays then. Can I get a number to reach you?"

"Sure." Leaning over the counter, she grabbed a pen and paper and jotted it down. "I'll look forward to your call."

Sylvie seemed sincere. Cammie might have an opinion about the idea of paying extra help for an extended period. Not *might*. Her sister always had an opinion. But this could be their ticket out of here, possibly permanently. They only had to make it through the next few days. And the storm.

~~~

The box had to be bent to fit in Josh's truck, but he'd gotten the creation back to its original state. He and J.D. played ships for well over an hour, which got him wondering why he ever spent good money on toys. He should just collect different sizes of boxes and make things with his son.

Josh glanced out the front door. The sunlight was starting to dwindle. It got dark so early without daylight savings time.

"How about we go out for dinner?"

"No, sir." J.D. shook his head.

A polite answer, since he'd phrased it as a question. Which he shouldn't have.

"We could take Maggie with us to thank her for making your box. I mean boat." Did he really offer to take Maggie out when his goal was to spend less time with her?

But the idea seemed to capture his son's attention. And his own.

J.D. stepped out of the boat. "Okay. And Dahlia and Aunt Ruth?"

"Yes, sir." At least his son was being thoughtful.

"How about we make them captain cereal for dinner?"

Oh, how he'd get Maggie back for that one. The sweetened corn cereal sure was delicious, but it was hard enough getting healthy nutrients in J.D.'s mouth. "That's a special breakfast. We need meat, vegetables, fruit. Good stuff."

"But captain cereal could be a special supper."

"Not gonna happen, kiddo. Think of something else."

"Pizza. It can have meat and pineapple. That's healthy."

A chuckle rumbled through Josh's chest. "Can't argue with that logic. I know a great place. Let's go get them before they make other plans."

Running full speed, J.D. aimed at Josh. "Aye, aye, sir! I'm ready!"

Josh caught his son and swung him around. Whether for the pizza or seeing Maggie, he could relate to the excitement. His heart thrummed as he grabbed his keys and headed out the door.

He should've been more careful, though. Maggie might blow the whole idea out of the water.

Darkness already shrouded the parking lot in front of the

store. A group of teen boys lingered outside. An uneasy twitch settled over Josh. He stepped out and pointed a one-fingered salute. "What's up? I think they're about to close."

The tallest boy's head pivoted, caught by surprise. "We're just passing by." He turned to the other two. "Let's go."

Josh leveled his gaze on them. "If you want something at this store, ask for Josh. I'm here most of the time. I'll take care of you." His tone was sharper than his words. He hoped they got the message to stay away from his Marovich girls. Once the boys disappeared around the corner, Josh opened J.D.'s door.

"Daddy, what took you so long?"

"Sorry, mate." He pressed a kiss on the top of J.D.'s head before unbuckling and lifting him out. "Taking care of a little business."

"Miss Maggie's business?"

"Yep." He owed her that much. And more, really. She'd needed him years ago. Needed him to help her pick up the pieces of her life. Needed him to help her get through her hopelessness and grief. Instead he'd followed his dream. He should've at least waited another year…gone to college with her, helped her and her family get settled.

Instead, he'd followed the academy's rules about only leaving for a death in the immediate family.

The door chimed as he entered. Maggie stood inches away, hugging her purse. "What?" Her brows danced and scrunched. "What are you doing here? Again?"

Oh boy. What was he doing here? "Tell her, J.D." Throwing it off on a kid. How pathetic.

"Miss Maggie, we are thanking you with pizza." J.D. nailed his part.

"Thanking me?" Blinking joined the brow movement.

Maybe not quite clear enough, though. Josh nodded. "For

the box-boat. We're taking you all to the pizza place down the street."

Maggie's brown eyes stared at him. Somewhere between simmering suspicion and gratitude, if that were possible.

"Unless, you've already planned out your dinner?" He doubted she had, but she'd probably rather he didn't assume anything.

Still no answer.

Ruth and Dahlia strolled out of the back, flipping off lights as they came.

"Hey, Josh. Hey, J.D." Saved by Dahlia, perhaps. The girl grinned at J.D. "What are y'all doing here?"

J.D. struggled to slip down from Josh's arms. "We're all going to eat pizza." Once his feet hit the floor, he held his arms up for Maggie to hold him. "Right, Miss Maggie?"

Lifting him to her chest, she rolled a glance at Josh. "Seems that way, pumpkin."

Chapter 11

Maggie wrapped her arms around herself as they entered the rustic pizzeria. As much as she hated to admit it, having Josh show up had settled her nerves. Before he'd arrived, she'd been watching those same three boys who'd come in earlier. They'd been milling around outside as dark shadows covered the sidewalk. It was probably nothing, though. Ocean Springs had been safe when she'd lived here.

Maggie held in a groan as they piled into a booth. Historic photos of the Mississippi Coast hung from what looked like salvaged brick, along with more nautical décor. No wonder Josh liked the place. Why would they have a nautical theme in a pizza place?

J.D. snuggled close beside her while they waited for the waitress to deliver his booster seat. Dahlia squeezed in on her other side. Thank goodness. She didn't want to sit that close to Josh. Although, the view was almost as hard with him and Aunt Ruth across the table. Would people think they were a family again? Like her own family growing up. The elusive life she'd always wanted, the life that had always stayed just out of reach. Sometimes she felt like she was rowing against breakers and trying to reach an island shore. No matter how close it seemed, the waves always pushed her away.

A band warmed up as they looked at the menus. Maggie glanced up to check out the musicians. Three graying men must've been following a dream after a recent retirement. They began a seventies tune, confirming her guess. The aromas of yeast and garlic and craft brews circulated, bringing her attention back to the menu. She scanned the variety of pizzas. Way too many options for her tired brain. "What do y'all want, Dahlia, Aunt Ruth?"

"I only want pepperoni and cheese," Dahlia chimed right in. "None of that weird stuff."

Easy enough. "Okay, Aunt Ruth?"

No answer. Her aunt stared at the band.

Maggie reached out and tapped Aunt Ruth's hand. "Do you want to share something?"

"I can't hear you." She pointed at the stage. "The music."

Smiling, Josh leaned near to Aunt Ruth's ear and asked in his deep baritone, "What can we order you?"

"Oh, that tickles, Josh. You don't have to get that close." She rubbed her ear and cheek as if shooing away an insect.

Josh's eyes saucered, along with his mouth.

A chuckle fought its way out of Maggie's lips, despite her best attempts not to even glance Josh's direction.

"I'll share whatever everyone else wants." Aunt Ruth still rubbed her ear.

"I'll share with you, too, Miss Maggie." Blinking inno-cently, J.D. tugged on Maggie's sleeve. And her heart. "I have to eat healthy, though. Pineapple and meat pizza."

How sweet. And heart-melting. "Then we'll get a large pepperoni and a large ham and pineapple."

Josh motioned to the waitress, who neared. "We're ready. All on one ticket."

"You don't need to buy." Maggie waved him off. "You helped me, too, today." As much as she hated to say it, she needed Josh's help now.

She'd needed it after her father died, but he hadn't been there for her.

"This here dinner is from J.D." Josh's nose crinkled up like a little kid's. "He insists." He placed the order for them all.

Always being cute and funny. She really needed to put her guard up because Josh seemed to be laying on the charm.

The band played louder, pounding out a strange version of *Hotel California* with... Were those wind chimes and a cowbell? She'd noticed the wind chimes in the last song, but the sound had sort of fit that tune. Sort of. Shifting her attention to the stage, Maggie took in the performers. The guy on percussion had an array of strange instruments. Maracas, a gong, bongos, and was that a gourd? The day kept getting weirder.

The long song took more unexpected turns and twists, an Eagles medley of sorts, but finally ended by the time they'd finished their pizza. Another peppier tune she didn't recognize began, probably even more ancient, with even more cowbell, if that were possible.

"You and Josh should dance." Dahlia giggled. "This old-school music is from back when you were young, right?"

Hardly. "I'm not *that* old." Maggie let her gaze slip to Josh. The stinker's mouth quirked up into a grin, showing more teeth than a horse begging for a carrot. "I'm not in the mood to dance."

"I'll dance." Her aunt scooted out of the bench. "I can still kick up my heels."

For all that was right in the world, couldn't they pay the bill and go home? "Please keep your heels on the ground. I don't want anyone else getting hurt."

"You worry too much, Magnolia." Aunt Ruth gestured broadly. "We have to live life while we have it. You should've seen me and Wilbourn dance the night away at the Fais-Do-Do way back when."

"What's the Fais-Do-Do?" J.D. scratched the back of his

neck.

"Oh, it's a fun Cajun festival. Your daddy can take you to one the weekend of the Blessing of the Fleet. They hold it at Point Cadet." Aunt Ruth held a wrinkled hand toward Josh. "How about a dance?"

"Of course." If his eyes and mouth were saucers last time, now they were platters. "Let's go."

Josh and Aunt Ruth danced the entire song. Her aunt had always loved to cut a rug, but who knew the elderly woman still had that much energy? Too bad Aunt Ruth and Uncle Wilbourn had never had children. She would've been a fun mom. The thought swamped Maggie's spirits. Would she be childless, too? At the rate she was going, chances were good she'd never marry or have kids. Would Dahlia care for her when she was elderly like Cammie had Aunt Ruth?

Arm in arm, Josh and Aunt Ruth returned to the table as a Jimmy Buffet tune began.

"Your dad loved some Jimmy Buffet," Josh yelled over the growing volume. "Do you still have any of his old albums?"

Didn't Josh know everything they'd owned had been destroyed in the storm? A pulsing current of adrenaline and anger rushed through Maggie's veins. How could he forget? "No." She pressed the answer through clenched teeth.

"I wasn't thinking..." His features softened. "I've been collecting the records your father liked for years. I'd love for you to have them."

A bit of steam receded. She could've done that herself if she'd wanted to. The memories were still too painful. But it was sort of nice that Josh had offered. Shaking her head, she shrugged. "You keep them."

"Remember when we used to sing karaoke to *Cheeseburger in Paradise*?" His lips formed a lopsided grin.

"We were terrible." Although, every time the stupid song played, she relived the fun memories.

"Oh!" Dahlia elbowed Maggie. "Do it. I want to hear y'all. I'm sure the band will know it. They're playing other Jimmy Buffet tunes."

Rubbing the place where her niece's sharp elbow had dug in, Maggie turned to stare at the girl. "You know his songs? Aren't they too ancient for you?"

"Me and Mama play them in the car and sing. They're fun. She has them on her phone." Dahlia's lips twitched at the mention of Cammie. "Please? You and Josh sing."

"Hey, I'm on board." Josh slipped out of the bench again. "Unless you're scared, Magnolia?"

Her real name, the way he'd always dared her, and wasn't he always on board? That was the problem. Of course she was scared, but she wouldn't show him that. Her emotions hadn't ever changed a thing about what the man did, once his mind was set. "Fine, but I'm warning you. It's not gonna be pretty." And it would likely further her undoing.

~~~

What was he doing, about to parade toward the stage to ask the band to play this song? Josh gave Maggie a wide berth as she climbed out of the bench. His heart had lurched when he'd made the faux pas asking about her father's albums. What an idiot he was. Now he'd acted like reliving this memory wouldn't gut the both of them. He kept veering off course in his attempts to help the Marovich women.

"Shake a leg, if we're doing this. Don't stand there staring at me." Brows raised, Maggie waited beside him. "I'm not doing the asking, you are."

Josh took quick steps toward the stage. Had he been staring? Again? Her dark curls were to blame. Or maybe her eyes, unfathomable pools, dark as a cloudy night on the sea. Or the memories he'd stowed away deep in every part of his very being. Why hadn't he done what she'd asked way back when? Maybe neither of them would be in such a squall.

The lead singer paused to take a sip of water between songs, the perfect timing to ask. He nodded at Josh. "Hey, man. You got a request?"

"An odd one. Can we sing *Cheeseburger in Paradise* with y'all?"

Lines crinkled the corners of the musician's temples. "Not that odd. You'd be surprised the requests we get." He waved them toward the microphone and gave instructions to the rest of the band. "Rock on."

The cowbell clanked a beat, and the keyboard player banged out the tune. Josh stifled a laugh, raised his brows at Maggie, and started singing.

Her mouth quivered in an awkward attempt not to smile. This might be fun after all.

She joined in quietly, but as they moved into the chorus, her voice grew strong. Dahlia and J.D. ran to the dance floor. They jumped around, swinging their arms and singing at the top of their lungs right along with them.

A loud laugh erupted from Maggie. She doubled over, holding her stomach. Man, that laugh sounded as good as the whoosh of the wake running behind his boat on smooth seas. Maybe the locked-away memories should be aired out in the sun now and then.

The last chord of the song ended, and people at tables clapped and cheered. Well, most were laughing.

The lead guitarist nodded. "You wanna sing another, or do y'all have a dance request?"

Before he could stop himself, Josh blurted out, "*Down

Around Biloxi," and he held out his hand to Maggie.

Her smile faltered. She stared at his hand as if it were a circling barracuda. Her fingers finally lifted to his, and they stepped down to the dance floor.

J.D. and Dahlia cheered, but Maggie's face crumpled.

What could he do to help her? With her hand still in his, he twirled her then dipped her back. Low.

J.D. giggled. "Do it again, Daddy."

With Maggie gazing up at him, Josh fought to get his bearings. An almost smile lifted her full lips. Good grief, the urge to kiss her seized him like an undertow, sweeping away the last of his good sense. He pulled her up close to his chest. She still fit nicely there, like she always had. Warmth spread through him, familiar as home and the sea and the tides, yet tantalizing and terrifying as a waterspout traveling straight toward him. Before he realized it, the song ended.

Maggie pushed away, curls hanging across one cheek. Her chin dipped. "Can you take everyone home, say prayers with Dahlia? I need… I want to go see Cammie now."

"Of course. I got this."

"I'll go tell them goodbye."

And as quickly as an anchor dropping in deep water, she disappeared.

Chapter 12

Shadows stretched across the hospital parking lot between the hazy glow of streetlights. Maggie parked and let her head drop against the cool steering wheel.

Oh, Josh. Why do you have to be so stinking wonderful?

The way his arms had laced around her, strong yet gentle. The way he made her laugh. The way she fit right into the crook of his shoulder. The few moments tucked there set her heart adrift aimlessly into that hollow sea of the past.

Tonight had been yet another glimmer of the life she might've had. Was it the knowing or the not knowing that dealt the harshest blow? She'd need a mountain escape once their lives got settled. If they did get settled. Maybe someplace in the Smoky Mountains away from the oceans and tides. Like Gatlinburg. She hadn't been there in a while. Or North Carolina. Someplace with a lawn chair on the porch of a remote cabin, someplace she could stare out into the cool mist of a fog-laden valley.

Last time she'd taken Cammie and Dahlia, the cabin she'd rented had a hummingbird feeder. The tiny colorful creatures had entertained them for hours. That and the hot tub. She could do that again, add a little hiking, and the plan sounded perfect for forgetting this whole mess. And Josh.

Of course…Cammie might not ever hike again. The realization rolled over Maggie like a swollen mountain river. No. She couldn't think like that. They had to get Cammie well. God needed to heal Cammie. He owed their family that much.

111

She'd already lost her parents, her home, and the love of her life.

Not Cammie, too, Lord. I'm begging you. I need her to heal. I need her to make it.

Headlights flashed across the lot, and Maggie lifted her head. She should pick up the pieces and go inside, not sit in the parking lot like a weirdo. Sucking in a breath which raised a bit of the residual turnip green aroma, she exited the car and retrieved her computer from the trunk. A Gulf breeze kicked up and caressed her cheeks, almost soothing the war raging inside her. Funny how deceptive the wind and water could be. One day a gift, another day, they blasted until you were bent and broken and empty.

She made the familiar journey to the ICU waiting room and plopped into a seat. She had thirty minutes to wait until they let the families back. That would give her time to decompress and check the forecasts at the National Hurricane Center, as if those two things were possible simultaneously.

"Hey. I heard you were looking for me." Angie appeared from seemingly nowhere and sank into a chair beside Maggie. Instead of scrubs, the nurse wore jeans and a T-shirt. "I thought I might catch you here. We should exchange cell numbers."

"They said you were off today. I hope you didn't make a special trip." She hadn't left a message for her. Maggie swept a glance over Cammie's high school friend. No makeup and her red hair in a ponytail.

"My son has a stuffy nose, and I needed to run out to pick up a decongestant. It wasn't out of the way. Can I help you somehow?"

Stuffy nose? Maggie's stomach lurched, and she scooted away to allow a few more inches between them. If Cammie caught something, it could be dangerous. "Is it contagious? The kids played together."

"No fever, so I doubt it."

She doubted it? Where was the hand sanitizer? They better get this conversation over quickly, so Angie could leave with her germs. "I wanted to ask you about Dr. Castro. Nurses usually hear things, right? Is he a good doctor? A nice guy?"

"The best. I'd want him for my doctor. He's a very nice man, too. Well respected in the community."

Whew. "Great. That's all. You can go back to your little boy." Maggie gave a little wave. "Thank you." *See you later. Don't go near Cammie.*

"You're welcome." Angie inched forward but didn't stand. "You know, Graham says Josh is the best pilot he's ever worked with. It's like Josh has a special sense about the sea. He's meticulous. In tune with the river. If there's a rescue, they want Josh leading the way."

And why did Angie feel the need to share this? "That's all he ever wanted. To be a pilot like my father." More than he wanted anything else.

"But you want him to give it up?"

Really? This was none of her business. They weren't that good of friends. Angie had always been close to Cammie. Maggie checked the time on her phone. Still twenty minutes before she could escape to visit her sister.

Angie hadn't moved. She sat there waiting.

"The Gulf stole my father." Bitterness surged through Maggie's veins like toxic waste burning and poisoning her attitude. "My boyfriend, who was also my best friend, left the family he claimed to love when we needed him most. To become a pilot."

"Hadn't he already left for the Merchant Marine Academy

before Katrina hit?" Angie's cross-examination was becoming more and more maddening. Each question dredged up additional wreckage from Maggie's past, laying open the festering wound she'd covered for so long.

"He'd barely gotten started at Kings Point when the hurricane made landfall." A lump formed in Maggie's throat. "My family had always been there for Josh growing up. My dad was like a father to him. All those years. Then when we needed... I needed him..."

"Oh." Chewing her lip, Angie gave a slow nod. "We lost our house, too, but no one from our family. I'm sure it was a tough time."

The understatement of the decade. "It was."

"Maybe staying the course was his way of honoring your father."

"Maybe." Maggie checked the time again. Since when did the clock move so slowly? "What does it matter now?"

"I remember how close y'all were. Josh is a good man, and that J.D. is a doll. Circumstances have thrown you together again. The way he looked at you the other night... You two might have another chance if you could let go of the past. Move beyond the anger and the fear. The resentment and bitterness have to be getting old."

"Resentment and bitterness?" What had Cammie been telling people? Or was it Josh?

"It's obvious you're still holding onto that anger. Forgiving him for not being there for you could free you from all that baggage. It could free you to move forward. Maybe even forward with him. Together."

So now she looked like a bitter bag lady. A twinge of guilt warred against her defensiveness. She hadn't really wanted to forgive Josh even after all this time. Blaming him for her hurt kept her from turning her anger to more dangerous places. Possibly unholy places.

And if she forgave Josh, it opened her up to deeper digging into that place where blame and hurt had hollowed her out... Her throat tightened. If she forgave Josh, she'd have to allow the questions to come again. Questions like why God had allowed such death and destruction to be unleashed. Why weren't her prayers answered? She'd cried out for God to weaken the hurricane. She'd begged for it to dissipate, to miss her hometown, her house. She'd pleaded for her father to make it home.

And His answer had hurt. Still did. It had wounded her faith. Hadn't her family been devoted servants? They'd tried to follow Him. Follow His Word. Didn't He love them? Didn't He hear their cries?

"I can't do this right now." Maggie covered her face with her palms, tears stinging her eyelids. "I have to be strong for my family."

"Sometimes, you can let other people be strong, hold you up. You don't have to do everything yourself. I go to the same church as Cammie. I can set up meals for y'all, some help with Dahlia, Ruth, the store even. And you can let Josh help while he's here. Let that wall down you've got built up about him... about coming home."

Good grief. Why was the woman stuck on Josh? Maggie's jaw clamped shut. She didn't need Angie's psychoanalysis, and there were plenty of restaurants in downtown Ocean Springs where they could buy dinner. And the store? How would they know if they could trust someone in the store? Cammie wouldn't allow that.

"Come on, Maggie." Angie's tone softened. "At least let me set up the meals a few times a week for Dahlia and Ruth."

Dahlia and Aunt Ruth needed decent food. "We can exchange numbers if you want. I'm sure a lot of people are traveling for the holidays, though, so if you need to wait on starting the dinners, I understand."

"Let me worry about that." Angie touched a few buttons on the screen of her phone and held it out. "Type your information here. I'll get something going."

Maggie complied, and Angie left promising to set up a couple of dinners the following week, if possible. If not, then after Thanksgiving.

How long would Cammie need her to be at the Coast? The doctor had said several days in ICU, then a room, then rehab. Maggie did a quick calculation. She'd need to take a leave of absence from work. Again. How often did they allow family leave? She'd worked hard to move up in the ranks since her mother's passing, and the Weather Service would hold a job for her, but maybe not the *same* position.

The door opened to the ICU, and Maggie stood. It didn't matter what job she held. Cammie's health was most important. Family was what mattered. And the idea of letting God's people help out lifted a bit of the weight from her shoulders.

She followed the too-familiar faces of the other families down the hall until she reached Cammie's room. Dr. Castro sat in a chair beside the bed, smiling like they hadn't a care in the world. The man sure did visit his patients an awful lot.

And the blush on Cammie's bruised cheeks indicated she was enjoying the visit. A lot. Their gazes seemed to be locked on each other.

"Knock, knock." Maggie spoke quietly but felt the need to announce her presence since neither Cammie nor Dr. Castro had glanced her way.

"Oh, hey." The doctor stood and swept his hand toward the chair he'd vacated. "Take my seat. I should finish my rounds anyway." He smiled once more at Cammie. "See you in the morning. Keep up the good work."

"Wait. What's the news? What work?" Someone needed to give her some specifics. This affected too many lives not to know.

"Your sister has been compliant and still, which has allowed the swelling to go down. Then she allowed me to stick her with a needle." His grin broadened. "And she felt it."

Her sister's tired eyes twinkled. "I moved my toes a little bit, too."

Hope surged inside Maggie's chest. "Now that does sound like good news." Maybe God was answering their prayers this time.

"It's great news. See you tomorrow." The doctor left them alone to the sound of beeps and whirs of machines.

Maggie took his place in the chair. "So he's *really* friendly."

"He's wonderful. If I have to go through this junk, at least the staff is nice."

"Angie came by a minute ago. She's setting up dinners for us, starting soon."

"Perfect." She took a small gasp of air. "That'll help. How's the store?"

"It's fine. Should I board up the windows soon? Josh helped with the ones at the house, although he still hadn't covered his own the last time I looked."

"No. Do *not* board the store."

"Why?"

"Not unless you see the bakery down the street close. They're always the last one." She sucked in a shaky breath. "Need the business open."

117

"Whatever you say." And if the store got wind damage, maybe insurance would pay it off, and they'd finally move up to Jackson. "Can I bring you something from home? Or the gift shop? It's still open."

"Brush my hair? They put toiletries in the nightstand."

"Sorry. I should've thought of that." Maggie opened the drawer and grabbed the small brush. It wasn't like she hadn't cared for a hospital patient. "You look pretty, as always." She fought the tremble in her hand as she ran the brush gently across the silky honey-colored strands, the color their mother's had been before it grayed, then was lost due to the chemo. There was an intimacy in caregiving. A bittersweet closeness that bore into a person, forming a sad but indescribable bond. "I can wash your face, put lotion on your hands and feet, if it's okay with the nurses."

"They gave me a sponge bath. No need to worry about the rest for now." Her eyes widened. "Unless I smell bad or something."

"You're fine." She laid her palm against Cammie's cheek. "Always beautiful." She smiled and tweaked Cammie's nose. "And smelling fresh as a flower." Her father's favorite saying popped right out.

"You're a good baby sister, you know?"

"Best one you've got."

"Josh is helping you?"

That came out of nowhere. "Yeah."

"He's a good guy. Always has been."

"Okay." Where was this going?

"Go on back home now. Give Dahlia a kiss from me." Her sister's lips quirked. "Maybe give Josh one from you."

"Stop. Not happening. The Josh part anyway."

"You can at least be friends now, right?"

"That I'm taking care of business is all the business you need to know." She pressed a kiss on Cammie's forehead. "I love you, and I'll see you tomorrow. Call me if you need anything."

The halls seemed quieter as she retraced her path to the front door. Melancholy stole over her despite the good news about Cammie. She'd hoped before, prayed before, trusted before. The fall from the heights of hope hurt something fierce. Better to keep expectations low. She pushed that small parcel of emotion back to the closet cloaked in shadows where it belonged. Out of the glaring brightness of disappointment.

Back at the house, light spilled from the corner of the boarded windows, illuminating the wooden panels at odd angles. Brightness shone from Josh's house too. Everyone must still be up and awake. Should she share the news of Cammie's improvement or keep it to herself? Just to make sure they weren't crushed with disappointment later.

The door of the house opened as Maggie approached.

"How's Mama?" Wrapped in a pink leopard-print fleece robe, Dahlia stepped onto the porch.

Behind her, Josh stood with J.D. snuggled close to his shoulder, the boy's eyes barely open. Josh's penetrating gaze and serious expression held the same question Dahlia had just asked.

"She's good. I saw the doctor, and your mother's improving."

"Like how?" Dahlia's big brown eyes searched hers, likely looking for some kind of miracle. Maggie knew that look. Had lived that look.

"She feels a little better." True enough.

"God's taking care of her. And you." Josh wrapped an arm around her niece. He kissed her head. "Goodnight. See y'all tomorrow."

Of course, he'd keep reminding her.

Quietly, with light steps, he came off the porch but paused by Maggie. "I'm here for you." His blue gaze intensified with the words.

Warmth spread through her at the simple phrase. How long had she waited for those words?

Too long.

Chapter 13

"Sure, Angie. I'll take care of them for the weekend. My little buddy and I will come up with something good." Josh said goodbye, ended the call, and laid his phone on the coffee table. He and J.D. had gotten dressed for the day and had been talking about making an early morning trip to the grocery store. What would Dahlia and Ruth want for dinner Saturday and Sunday? A more frightening question was what would Maggie have to say about the assignment? Angie insisted that Maggie had agreed to let the church bring dinner, but that didn't mean Maggie would be expecting him and J.D. to be the first official deliverers.

"Who was that, Daddy?"

"Miss Angie wants us to make dinner for Dahlia and her family tonight. What do you think would be good?"

J.D.'s face lit up, eyes wide. "Captain cereal with bananas. That's got fruit, so it's healthy."

"Enough with the cereal ideas." Sweeping his son into his lap, Josh tickled J.D.'s ribs. "We need a good hearty supper that'll put some meat on their bones. Like right here." He dug in just hard enough to make him laugh without hurting him.

Giggles poured from J.D., bursting through Josh's trepidation about the dinner like sunshine in the midst of a hail storm.

"Stop, Daddy." More chortles. "Stop."

"Okay." He stopped, set J.D. on the floor. "So do you have a better idea than cereal now?"

"Um, you could make boiled strimp and batatoes in the big pot."

"Mmm. Good one, buddy. So we'll skip the grocery and get a few things at the seafood market." He wasn't really in the mood for a big shopping trip, anyway. Josh stood and grabbed his keys from the coffee table. "Let's shove off."

Forty-five minutes later, J.D. had examined all the crabs, oysters, and shrimp, and they'd picked out what they needed from behind the counter and stood in the long line to pay. Now that he'd loaded up the seafood and veggies, he should let Maggie know. He punched out a text while he waited.

Shrimp boil at my place tonight.

All he had to do was see if she answered. No stress.

A couple squeezed past him to get near the front cooler. Boy, business was hopping. Apparently plenty of residents were staying in town despite the possible storm. So far. Josh held out his card to the cashier when it was his turn. Once he took this food home, he'd go by the bakery. Maybe he'd pick up some beignets and take them to the antique store with some good coffee. That might sweeten the deal about the dinner assignment. Pastries and helping with the store so Maggie could make the lunch visit with Cammie.

When he finished the transaction, he scooped J.D. up to his hip, propped the bag of food on the other arm, and headed out to the car. "Let's get underway."

"Aye, aye, captain." J.D. squeezed both of Josh's cheeks. "It's going to be so good. We'll make 'em spicy, right?"

"So hot, it'll burn their nose hair."

"That's gross, Daddy. No."

They reached the truck, and Josh strapped J.D. into the seat.

"Okay. We won't burn their noses, but hot enough to make

their eyes water, at least, right?" He tweaked J.D.'s chin and waited for an answer.

"Yeah. A little bit of burning is good." His son's lips poked out as they curved upward. He couldn't get much cuter if he tried.

"Joshua David Bergeron, you know what?"

"What, Daddy?"

Josh pressed a kiss on J.D.'s forehead. "I'll love you longer than the Mississippi River and wider than the Gulf of Mexico."

"I love you bigger than the world." His small hand, which had that little bit of baby plumpness still filling out his fingers, rubbed the place Josh had kissed. "You have scratchy kisses, Daddy."

"I can't help being manly." Nuzzling close again, Josh mussed J.D's hair. "You complaining?"

"No." Another giggle rolled out. "But, Miss Maggie's kisses are soft."

A memory of her breached the walled-off places in his mind. Sharp and explosive, the pain hit.

He'd held her in his arms, saying goodbye to her before he'd left for Kings Point, New York. She'd kissed him at least a hundred times—sweet, soft, and breathless, promising she'd wait for him. If only he'd known the monster lurking in the deep, he might've made other plans. He might've waited a year to start the maritime academy. But a couple of months changed everything. Maggie'd been okay with his plans to become a pilot until…August twenty-ninth, 2005.

He sucked in a gulp of air and moved to the driver's seat. His knuckles whitened on the steering wheel. Maybe he should've come back, given up the appointment and helped Maggie and her mother. But Mr. Marovich had been so proud of Josh's acceptance to the academy. Said he loved him like his own son, and that love had spurred Josh with the determination he needed to follow in the man's footsteps.

"Are you crying, Daddy? Your eyes are wet." J.D. called from the backseat.

Sniffing, Josh smeared his hand across his face, sweeping away any trace of moisture. "I'm thinking about those spicy shrimp tonight." He pressed on a smile for his son and slipped on his sunglasses. He'd wash his face and shave before going to Cammie's store. No sense letting Maggie see that he'd been blubbering like a baby.

Josh checked his phone once more before turning the key. No text from Maggie yet, but she might still be busy with customers. Or she might be ignoring his messages like she'd done years ago.

Except that one time. That one time, she'd emailed. *You know what I've asked. Don't call again if nothing's changed.*

~~~

The powdered sugar of the beignet melted on Maggie's tongue, no doubt before going straight to her hips. Oh, how that man knew her preferences. There was nothing like the sweetened fried nuggets of dough and a cup of stout coffee.

"So you're okay with me making dinner? Angie said you were open to accepting the help." Josh interrupted her confectionary bliss of sugar and fat. He reached toward her cheek, but hesitated. "You got some right there."

Maggie swiped at her face, feeling for what was probably a mess there. Beignets were impossible to eat without getting doused in the white sugar.

His blue eyes twinkled with mischief. "That made it worse." He grabbed a stack of napkins off the checkout counter and stepped closer. Too close. "Let me."

Though her heart thrummed in her chest at his proximity,

she held still. If she ate another one, she'd do so in the back room like the kids and Aunt Ruth had. Out of sight.

"This feels familiar. You were always a bit untidy with these. Remember our trips to New Orleans?" Josh's mouth twitched as if he were holding back a smile. He tossed the napkins in the trash can under the register.

Of course she remembered riding over to Louisiana, sitting close to him in his truck. Warmth flooded her chest. They thought they were so grown up walking on the river front, listening to jazz, stopping in at Café Du Monde for coffee.

Finally, clear of food and Josh, Maggie pressed sanitizer into her hands and wiped them with another napkin before returning to her open laptop next to the cash register. "Are you going to make fun of my untidiness if we eat with you tonight? I mean boiled shrimp have to be peeled."

"Probably. I'll make sure I have a lot of paper towels. Or I can peel them for you, ma'am."

He still loved toying with her. And she wanted to love it, too, still. Angie's assessment of long-held bitterness came to mind. Could she let that go? Her mom used to say to take a step in obedience, and the emotions would follow eventually. Would that work for all the hurt she'd pent up? "That won't be necessary."

"But you're okay with the idea. Angie said—"

"I forgive you." Blurting and getting it over with seemed easiest. Now to see if her mother's advice would ring true.

Blinking, Josh cocked his head, his features softened. "What?" His voice was barely a whisper.

"I forgive you." Her nose stung. Her eyelids, too. She wouldn't cry. She'd done too much of that lately. "For not coming back to help. Angie said I hadn't…that I was bitter." She swallowed past the tightening in her throat. "She was right,

I guess… We can be sort of friends, like adults, Christian adults, should do."

Moisture welled up near Josh's lower lashes, breaking a wide crack in Maggie's defenses. She pressed her thumb into her palm.

"I'm so sorry, Maggie." His hand rested over both of hers. "I hurt you. I didn't know how much back then. I was young, and you're right, I was stubborn, and I didn't realize what you were going through. I'm really sorry."

The words seeped in and covered some of the old wounds like a salve, smoothing a bit of the jagged edges of the scars. She would let him help, and she would try to be friends. Until this mess sorted out. The anger she'd been clinging to had been using up emotional energy. She could see that now. And they were supposed to be grown up Christian adults.

The intensity of the moment overwhelming her, she stepped toward her computer and moved the mouse, awakening the screen.

Josh stepped next to her to look over her shoulder. "Not looking at the weather?"

"Already checked." The variabilities crowded her mind. "The storm strengthened to a category two but made a turn toward Texas. Who knows?" She sure didn't, but she kept praying the beast away. Not that she wanted the western state to be hit either. "I started looking at business plans for antique stores and other ways to increase Cammie's income. I'm working on a list of ideas to run by her."

Leaning closer, Josh squinted at the screen. "Sell more volume of smaller, lower priced items. Local pottery. Working with a decorator and a local artist." Smiling, he bumped her shoulder with his. "Look at you. Not just a weather girl. I like it."

"Thanks." His praise shot heat to her cheeks. Why did everything Josh do bring about such intense reactions? "We'll see what Cammie thinks about my ideas to raise the profits."

"She'll love that you're taking an interest. Like I love that you're taking an interest in J.D."

His kindness floated over her, soaked her with sweetness. She wished it could last. Yes, she forgave him, but it didn't mean she could give her heart to a pilot.

Chapter 14

Now she'd pretty much have to invite Josh to Thanksgiving lunch, with him fixing dinner and helping at the store. Maggie grabbed her purse and shut off the lights behind the cash register.

The key stuck in the deadbolt, so she gave it a good jerk. Finally it clanked into the lock, and she walked quickly to the car to join Dahlia and Aunt Ruth.

"All done." Maggie slid her seatbelt on and clicked it into position. "I don't know about y'all, but I'm ready to get home."

"Me, too. Can I see your phone?" Dahlia held her hand over the seat.

A small chuckle slipped out. "Yeah, but no texting pretending to be me."

"Okay." The word drew out into two long syllables. "It was one time." Dahlia produced headphones and plugged them in her ears.

"That I know of," Maggie mumbled. Dahlia had heard the text inviting them to the shrimp boil earlier and had been about to answer Josh's message before asking for permission. *Note to self*, number thirty-one, *never leave cell phone unattended with a ten-year-old girl in the room*. She'd have a whole book of anecdotes by the time this mess cleared up.

If it cleared up.

It had to.

After she made the night deposit at the bank, the darkness deepened, causing the hour to feel more like midnight. Maybe she could fix a plate and bring it back to the house, claiming fatigue. Which would be true. Having dinner provided for a while would be nice. She wouldn't have to think about what to feed Dahlia and Aunt Ruth, could rest a bit, then go to the hospital for a visit. As long as Josh wasn't the one to deliver every time. Just because they were trying to be friends didn't mean they had to be around each other constantly.

Along the short drive, white lights sparkled from branches of the live oaks and swayed in the wind. The business district glittered with the illuminations year round, but a few residents must've gotten into the Christmas spirit early. Good grief. It was still the Saturday before Thanksgiving. Why did people get in such a hurry? Plus, it seemed silly to decorate when the storm would likely rip off both branches and trimming.

Cars lined the curbs on Aunt Ruth's street. Families visiting loved ones already. No one seemed to be evacuating at all. Of course, hurricanes this late in the season were rare, and the new trajectory aimed the storm westward. But still.

Most years, Cammie, Dahlia, and Aunt Ruth spent Thanksgiving Day at Maggie's house in Jackson. Then they'd rush home to work at the store on Black Friday. Not this time. She'd be the one manning the shop.

Lord, I wish things were back to normal.

An unwanted vision came to mind. The lonely Thanksgiving evenings after her family left. Watching old movies or reading. Volunteering to work the rest of the holiday so other Weather Service employees could spend time with their families.

Aunt Ruth's driveway came into view. Next door, the front porch lights shone at Josh's as if he were welcoming them home. Her stomach growled. A hot supper waiting for her after work was a nice treat. And rare in her world, except for an occasional invite from a coworker or church family. Most of the time, she ate out with a friend or had a bowl of cereal at home. Alone.

"Here we are." Ignoring her seesawing emotions, Maggie pressed on a smile as she slowed to a stop and put the car in park in Aunt Ruth's drive. "Want to go get the food at Josh's before we go home?" Speaking his name so casually still stung, even with her new determination to move past all the negativity.

"Sure," Dahlia said, "I'm starving."

"My phone." Maggie held her hand out.

Dahlia took off across the yards as if she hadn't heard a word.

Wind caught Maggie's car door, tore it from her grasp, and swung it open wide. Springing out, she slammed the thing and hurried around to help her elderly aunt on the passenger side. They didn't need two people laid up. Maggie grabbed the handle and made sure the door opened slowly. She'd get the phone later.

"Take my arm, Aunt Ruth. A gale is ablowin'." Without thinking, she'd mimicked her father's playful banter again. This place was taking over her brain. No telling how bad the habit would be by the time she left.

Aunt Ruth patted Maggie's hand. "Isn't it sweet how little Josh and his son are making us dinner?"

"He's not little. He's over six feet." Even taller than when they'd been in high school.

"I love a spicy shrimp boil. He's a fine man. A good daddy."

Oh, yeah. Sink the dull knife deeper into her heart. Maggie carefully led her aunt over the wet grass.

"That darling J.D. needs a good, loving mama to be there

for him. A small child needs a maternal figure in his life." Aunt Ruth stopped and gave Maggie a pointed look.

One that split her in two. "I don't know what to say to that."

"Actions speak louder than words, dear. Listen to your heart."

This conversation was quickly becoming a greeting card commercial. A clichéd one at that. She led her aunt forward and onto the steps.

The door swung open, and J.D. ran onto the porch, his bare feet patting the concrete. "Miss Maggie! Come eat the strimp I made you."

How precious. "I can't wait to try it. Thank you for cooking dinner for us." A mother might tell him he shouldn't come outside barefoot in November, though it was still in the upper sixties. But she wasn't his mother.

Once she and Aunt Ruth made it off the top stair and onto the porch, J.D.'s fingers caught hers. "You sit by me."

So much for taking the food back to Aunt Ruth's. Garlic and cloves and red pepper mingled with the aroma of the seafood, filling the house with that delicious scent she'd grown up with. Inside, the table had been set for five, including place mats and folded napkins. A sort of paper turkey served as a centerpiece, made from what looked like a toilet paper tube and cutouts of J.D.'s handprint. They'd gone all out.

"Did you do that?" Pointing at the lopsided bird, Maggie smiled at the adorable child.

His head bobbed. "I made it at school. My hands make the feathers." He held up and wiggled his fingers.

"It's very good. I like turkey, and it makes me want to gobble, gobble." She pretended to nibble his hand.

Giggles filled the air as she nuzzled him close. "No. Miss

Maggie. My fingers aren't turkey, silly."

"What's going on in here?" Josh entered, grinning and carrying a bowl of steaming shrimp, potatoes, and corn. "Sounds like a flock of seagulls fighting over a piece of bread."

"Miss Maggie tried to eat my fingers, Daddy." Giggles still laced J.D.'s voice.

"I better hurry up and feed her, then." He set the bowl right in front of her and winked. "She's pretty scary when she's hungry."

Why'd he have to act so familiar? As if nothing about her had changed in over a decade.

"Y'all have a seat." Once everyone complied, his gaze traveled around the table. "Looks like the gang's all here. I'll say the blessing."

"Can I say it, Daddy?" J.D.'s little hands were already folded.

"Of course." Pride and love shone in Josh's gaze when he looked at his son. That much was obvious. He'd achieved his goals—a pilot and a good father.

Though bowing her head, Maggie couldn't help but turn J.D.'s way. His earnest expression along with the way his eyes were squeezed shut made her want to snuggle him in another embrace.

"Thank you, God, for the strimp and botatoes and corn. Help it make us big and strong. God bless Daddy and Dahlia and Aunt Ruth. Please help Miss Cammie get well. Thank you for Miss Maggie. She makes really good boats. And hugs. In Jesus' name, Amen."

"Amen," the others echoed.

Except Maggie. Her throat had constricted too tightly to speak, and her eyes stung. She reached for the empty glass in front of her and stood.

Josh noticed and motioned for her to sit. "I forgot the ice and the tea. I'll get it."

"I can." The words squeezed out, and she hustled past him.

But he followed her into the small kitchen. She stared at the ice bucket and pitcher.

"You okay?" The slight touch of his hand on her shoulder only added to her churning emotions.

She nodded, hoping he'd drop the subject. "A lot on my mind."

"You want to talk about it?"

About as much as she wanted to launch a boat in a storm. "I'm good."

If only that were true.

~~~

Josh forced his hand back to his side. If Maggie didn't want to talk now, fine. But at some point, she needed to hash out some of the enormous issues going on in her family's life. Her heart, too. They both did. A private moment with the woman without her stomping off would be nice.

"I'm thirsty. The strimp's spicy, Daddy."

But that moment would have to be later. He picked up the ice bucket, and Maggie grabbed the tea. "Coming, son."

He dropped a few cubes in J.D.'s glass while Maggie waited beside him to pour. Her watery brown eyes met his for a moment and flitted away.

A private moment alone with her might be his undoing.

J.D. guzzled the drink and started peeling more shrimp. The kid might not be able to say the word correctly, but he could peel as fast as any processor on the wharf. Josh finally sat down to his own plate and dug in. Enough cayenne pepper to clear his sinuses, but not enough to make him cry. Perfect.

"These are delicious." Ruth wiped her chin with her

napkin. "I'll have to fry y'all some oysters tomorrow after work, Joshua."

Dahlia paused her peeling and licked one finger. "Tomorrow's Sunday."

"Perfect." Her aunt held up one finger. "After worship service."

"Will Aunt Maggie be carrying us to church? Or Josh? Or what?" Dahlia shot a look over at Maggie.

"What?" Maggie seemed to be caught off guard. "I hadn't thought about it."

"We could ride together, Miss Maggie. My daddy knows the way." Expressive brows lifted above J.D.'s vivid blue eyes.

"So y'all actually go to the same church now?" Maggie's forehead crinkled above her adorable sloped nose.

"Duh. Why else would we ride together?" Dahlia's tone wasn't really appropriate, so Josh stifled a laugh.

"Enough with the *duhs*, young lady." Maggie huffed. "And I thought Josh was filling in with the dinner because it was too short of notice for Angie and Cammie's church to get something together."

An honest mistake. Josh bobbed his head. "It made sense to keep J.D. going to the same place when I'm in town. Consistency and all, you know."

"Oh." Maggie's full lips circled, capturing his attention. "Okay. But I better take my car, so I can make it to the lunch visiting hour."

"Why can't I see Mama yet? Isn't she getting better?" Dahlia's voice cracked and her eyes pleaded.

"She is, sweetie." Maggie stood and went to her niece, wrapping an arm around her shoulder. "The doctor wants to make sure she rests and stays away from germs."

"Achoo!" J.D. sneezed loudly.

"Cover your nose with your napkin, buddy."

J.D. complied, but three more times, he let sneezes rip.

Not the best timing.

"Is he getting sick? Angie said her son had caught something." Worry carved hard on Maggie's face. She seemed to shrink back.

"I'm not sick. Daddy burned my nose hairs with the strimp." Pinching his nostrils, his son let his head fall back. "I tell him not to, but he didn't listen."

Chuckles circled the table. Thank goodness. His timing might be pretty good after all.

When they finished, J.D. dragged Dahlia to his room to play. Despite her curt replies lately, she was still a sweet girl and likely pretty anxious about her mother.

While Ruth finished her tea, Maggie helped clear the table. She rinsed the dishes and placed each one in the dishwasher in a meticulous fashion.

Josh stood back and watched. No doubt, she'd hate to see the way he haphazardly threw them in.

"I'll walk Aunt Ruth home and come back for Dahlia soon." Maggie found the dish detergent in the cabinet above the sink and started the wash cycle. She'd already caught on that he had to store cleaning products up high to keep his three-year old out of them.

"Works for me." After covering the bowl of leftovers, Josh carried it toward the refrigerator.

At the same time, Maggie stepped toward the archway to leave the kitchen. Their shoulders collided. The bowl jostled in Josh's hand, and Maggie grabbed for it. Her fingers landed on his.

After the bowl righted, her hand recoiled as if struck by lightning. "Sorry."

"My fault." A lot like the elevator incident at the hospital. Couldn't they move past this?

"Be back soon." She all but ran to shoo out Ruth.

Nope. They might be *friends*, but they weren't moving past the juvenile behavior, yet.

Chapter 15

Once more the desire to pack her bag and run home overwhelmed Maggie. With a careless brush of Josh's hand, her heart leapt to her throat. Somehow she had to convince her family to head north, away from the Coast. Away from the worry about the weather. Away from the memories flooding her of life on the Coast. Away from memories of being in love with Josh Bergeron.

Maggie held her aunt's arm as they traversed the yard and climbed the porch steps. If Cammie improved, surely they could transfer her to a hospital in Jackson. There were plenty of doctors in the state's capital. Rehabilitation centers, too.

Aunt Ruth hobbled back to her bedroom to change into her loungewear, as she called it, so Maggie took a minute to do the same. She slipped on her favorite black yoga pants and a long Weather Service T-shirt. There was nothing like yoga pants to help one relax. Whoever created them deserved an award. Now where were her cushy flip-flops? Her feet were killing her from standing around the store for hours. And she'd thought sitting at a desk was hard on a person's back. How in the world did her elderly aunt keep going? They sure did make people sturdy in her day. Once she'd located the shoes, Maggie padded down the hall to her aunt's room.

"Knock, knock." She didn't feel right leaving without explaining where she was going, in case Aunt Ruth hadn't heard her plan. "I'm walking next door to get Dahlia."

"Oh, okay. You did a good job at the store today."

"Thanks. It was pretty busy. What do you think about having Sylvie Daigle help out there?"

"I think it's great. Y'all could hire her to take my place."

"What?" The shock of that statement stunned Maggie. "You always said you'd never retire until you…" Saying *kicked the bucket* seemed wrong. Like the words would invite more trouble.

"We all say stupid things now and then." She chuckled and winked at her. "You should know."

Nice. Her aunt hadn't lost her sense of humor. "Are you sick?"

"Nothing like that. Some of my friends at the senior center are going on those Caribbean and Alaskan cruises." Aunt Ruth's wrinkled lips twitched into a one-sided smile. "It's a thing now for people my age."

"A thing, huh?" Dahlia and Aunt Ruth were rubbing off on each other. "I think you should go for it, then."

The front door opened and slammed shut, and Dahlia jogged down the hall.

Maggie turned to face her. "I was going to get you and walk you back."

Lines crinkled Dahlia's forehead. "It's right next door. Besides…" Her voice lowered. "Josh insisted on standing on the porch to watch. Like I'm a baby."

"Good for him. Want to play a game or something before I go to the hospital?"

"I recorded a show I've been dying to watch. Oh, and J.D. wants you to read him a story." A slight smile crept across her lips. "I told him I'd send you right over."

"I don't know if that's a good idea. And what show? Is it age-appropriate?"

"Mama lets me watch it." She lifted one shoulder. "Poor

J.D. He'll probably cry himself to sleep if you don't go."

That stinker was trying to set her up. "You people are all alike."

"Like you, Aunt Magnolia." Dahlia giggled and turned back toward the living room.

Groaning, Maggie trudged down the hall. She didn't mind reading to J.D., in fact, she relished the idea. Too much. That was the problem. The delightful child oozed sweetness, and he was entrenching himself in her heart.

~~~

"The end." Josh sat on the edge of the twin bed in J.D.'s room. The story finished, he fingered the last page before closing the book. Maybe J.D. would go on to sleep. If Dahlia remembered to tell Maggie about the reading request, he'd be surprised. Really shocked if Maggie came.

"What do you want to read next, captain?"

"Umm." J.D. chewed his lip and pointed. "This one."

"*Green Eggs and Ham.* Going with a classic, huh?"

"Uh huh. Saving the boat book for Maggie."

Josh's stomach dropped like a man overboard. Already, his son would be disappointed, and it'd be his fault. It was one thing to let his own heart be tossed at sea like a piece of driftwood. It was another to set his little boy up for a heart-breaking goodbye. What an idiot he was being. Hadn't his own little-boy heart been shattered when he'd been abandoned by his father? He knew the kind of wreckage that left.

"Am I too late?" Maggie poked her head in.

His stomach dove deeper. So she'd come. Right when he'd decided it was a bad idea. Josh set the book aside and leaned his elbows against his knees.

"Miss Maggie, I saved my favorite book for you."

"Oh, let me see." She wandered around to the other side

of the bed. *"Theodore and the Tall Ships.* What a surprise." Her smile tightened.

Obviously, Maggie wasn't happy with the nautical selection, but she covered well. She took the book and began reading.

Josh leaned against the doorjamb and watched her.

Dressed casually in T-shirt and gym pants, wearing the longest part of her hair secured in a clip while the rest of the dark curls cascaded around her shoulders, Maggie looked a lot like she had the summer after they'd graduated, the summer he'd had to report to the academy. The summer before the hurricane. Nights spent walking on the beach under a blanket of stars. They'd chased ghost crabs with their flashlights, used their flip-flops to touch the glowing jelly fish that washed up along the shore. They'd kissed. Oh, how they'd kissed. Always waiting for real intimacy, because they'd both had no doubt they'd marry. The thought blasted warmth through his chest and to his cheeks. Tugged on his heart, too.

When Maggie finished reading, she rumpled J.D.'s hair. "Goodnight, pumpkin."

Scrambling up, J.D. flung his arms around her waist. "Goodnight. Love you bigger than the world."

The same hug and the same words J.D. said to Josh every night.

The bombshell had Maggie blinking. She returned the hug, a mix of astonishment and amazement written all over her face. "Love you, too, J.D."

Josh's throat seemed to close off, locking the air in his diaphragm. Yep. He was an idiot. Both he and J.D. would suffer for it when Maggie abandoned them. With a quick push of a button, he turned on the sound machine, and rolling waves played from the speaker. "Go to sleep so we can get up for church tomorrow."

"Yes, sir. But you didn't say it, Daddy."

"Love you as long as the Mississippi River and as wide as the Gulf of Mexico." He kissed J.D.'s head and moved to the light switch. "I'm going to turn the light off, so Maggie can see the stars now."

"Okay. Love you bigger than the world."

He flipped the switch, which allowed the glowing constellations on the ceiling to make themselves known. What would she think of that?

"This is amazing. Like being on a real boat in the Sound." Maggie's voice wobbled. "See you tomorrow at church."

"See you later, gator."

Josh smiled at his son. "You go on to sleep while I walk Maggie out."

Her steps were sluggish as he followed her, and she seemed deep in thought. What he wouldn't give to know what was going on in that beautiful head. He stared at the black curls. And he'd really love to sink his fingers in her hair.

Talk about heartache and bad ideas. He balled his fingers at his sides, commanding them to stay put.

At the front door, Josh stepped ahead of her and put his hand on the knob. "Can we talk on the porch for a few minutes?"

Her teeth caught her bottom lip, and she turned away from him and then back. Twice. "Okay. But I have to leave to see Cammie soon."

He followed her out and leaned beside her on the wooden railing. "I know being home and the accident's gotta be stirring up a lot of hurt." It was for him. "How are you holding up, really?"

The Gulf wind whipped, and Maggie shivered. By reflex,

he wrapped an arm around her. "Cold? Or worried about the storm?"

She shook her head and didn't recoil. "I love that little boy already, Josh. Blast it. What's it been…a few days?"

What did that mean for them, if anything? "He's easy to love."

She covered her eyes with one hand and massaged her forehead.

Was she hiding? Crying?

"Maggie." He nudged her chin toward him, but she wouldn't meet his gaze. Fine. He could say this to the top of her head. "How do you think I feel? I love you and your whole crew. Always have. Now you're here and my son… I feel like I'm living in a dream, but I'm going to wake up one day, and you'll be gone. And we'll be… I'll be…abandoned… like always. J.D. will be hurt. I'll be torn apart. Again."

Her head jerked up. Jaw squared and stormy eyes flaring, she shot him a hard look. "Me leave him? You leave him every two weeks, and every time you do, you could very well not come back."

"I always come back. I'm a pilot. It's what I do." Why'd she have to be so stubborn? "You can't ask me to give up everything that makes me who I am because you're afraid."

"Don't you see?" Her head gave the slightest shake. "Piloting is not who you are. It's a career. It's not what I fell in love with. And you don't have to be like my father to make anyone proud."

At least she'd said it. The L-word. That was something. "Okay. You're right. But Maggie, you can't live in fear. Storms find you, whether you're inland or on the Coast. What's next? Are you going to live in a tornado shelter? Or build a house twenty feet in the air in case of a flood? Are you preparing for earthquakes? I mean you can't tell me you feel alive living the way you do. You're more than that."

Her gaze dropped. "So what if I'm careful—prepared? I am alive. I'm happy enough."

Every molecule of his being told him otherwise. She'd shut herself off. Partly his fault. Maybe a lot his fault. Part of it was simply life in this temporary and imperfect world. Bad things happened, and way too often, they happened to good people. But surely God intended Magnolia Marovich to be fully alive and engaged. And the Coast had been as deep a part of her as it was of him. Before Katrina had washed that life away as if it were a child's sandcastle.

Josh pressed closer, holding her face with both hands, breathing in the view of the girl he'd loved since childhood. The woman who'd landlocked herself out of grief and devastation. "Maggie." His breath hitched. "You're more than what you've become."

Liquid filled her already glistening eyes. "You don't know me or my life. I—"

"Kiss me, Maggie. Then walk away like it meant nothing. Prove to both of us once and for all that you're alive and fulfilled up there in Jackson. Not just playing it safe. Prove you don't need me or anyone else."

"I don't have to prove anything to you." Defiance laced her voice.

"Of course you don't. Prove it to yourself. Afterward, say the word, and I'll take J.D. out of town as soon as you can get someone else to fill in at the store. We'll get out of your life. I'll put my house on the market. Prove it, and I'll do everything in my power to lessen the chances of you ever running into me again."

Her jaw tightened, and from the looks of it, she gritted her teeth. "You... You are so maddening, Josh Bergeron."

"Yep."

In one quick motion, she raised her gaze. Her mouth captured his. Caressed his skin with enough power to capsize him. She cupped the back of his head with her hands, teased his neck, sending shockwaves through his entire body. The power and intensity of her kiss crashed over him with more force than any hurricane ever could. He lost himself in the strength of it, drowned in his love for her. His fingers found their way to her hair and roamed through the ocean of soft curls.

With a sudden gasp, she pushed him away and pressed her fingers to her mouth.

Josh's vision blurred as he stood dazed. Like a dream of another life had come true. For one second.

"I have to go." Maggie turned and fled, running toward Ruth's house.

He should have known better than to give her such a stupid and painful and intoxicating challenge.

Chapter 16

How she'd gotten to the hospital, Maggie had no clue. She was so flustered, yet here she was, waiting to enter the ICU. Fire still lingered on her lips, Josh's kiss branded deep into her skin. And beyond. How was she supposed to think, much less function?

She shouldn't have accepted his dare. She knew better. But he'd always been able to push her buttons, goad her…provoke her into some kind of crazy action. The image of the dazed expression on his face when she'd left slipped through her mind. A bitter chuckle shook her chest. He'd likely gotten more than he'd bargained for this time, too.

Good. Maybe he'd let her be. That would be the best thing.

The nurse appeared and motioned her through. Maggie continued her foggy procession until she reached her sister's bedside.

"Oh, wow." Cammie's eyes widened. "Tell me everything."

"What?" Her sister could read people faster than a card shark. "How are you?"

"The same. And you can't fool me—I know that look. You kissed Josh. Now spill it."

Less than a minute and Cammie had nailed it, the same as she had when they were in junior high, the first time Josh had kissed her. That night circled round to front and center in her mind. They'd been sitting on her parents' porch steps. That night he'd professed his love for the first time, too. His lips had been soft and sweet then, barely a hint of beard compared to tonight's masculine scruff. He'd been lanky and thin, but now he was a grown man, muscular and broad. His arms firm and strong around her waist. The kiss passionate and fervent, drinking her in, engulfing her. Maggie's midsection fluttered and swirled as if a swarm of dragonflies hummed inside her.

"I *do not* wanna talk about it." And she shouldn't think about it anymore, either.

"Hmm." Cammie's mouth twitched into a sarcastic smile. "I'll wait to hear more. But not too long. Tell me about something else first—the store, Aunt Ruth, and Dahlia. The weather even."

Relief replaced the angst saturating her. Cammie was giving her a pass—for once. Maggie briefed her sister on anything and everything else she could come up with until the visiting time passed. "I better go. I have to follow the rules and let you rest."

"Coward." Cammie rolled her eyes. "Since when are you a rule-follower?"

"Since your doctor said—"

"Did someone call for a doctor?" And there appeared the neurosurgeon, the friendly Dr. Castro. He couldn't have timed it better. In fact, he seemed to be here pretty often, checking in on Cammie.

"I'm about to leave, but is my sister healing?" She'd stay long enough to get his report and then go, fully accepting her sister's assessment of her lack of bravery.

"Still improving in small increments. I'm hopeful."

Hopeful? A lump rose in Maggie's throat. She didn't see much potential in *hopeful*. She'd been down that dead-end road before.

~~~

Fatigue tugged on Maggie's eyelids as she exited the car the next morning. "Do you need help, Aunt Ruth?"

"Go on. I'm powdering my nose. I'll be along in a minute."

Maggie shut the door and stepped up the curb and onto the sidewalk leading to the church. At least they had a great parking place. She squinted in the glare of the light bouncing off the gray concrete. She returned to the Acura and reached in for her sunglasses. Could she wear these in church, too? Stupid puffy eyes. After the intense scene with Josh, she'd spent all night punching her pillow instead of sleeping. Reliving the moment a few times too many, in between the tears that had drenched her sheets.

The intoxicating kiss the night before also left little doubt in Maggie's mind that Josh was partially right. She was missing something in her life. Maybe a lot. She'd grown used to being alone...untouched. But despite having involved herself in ministries and thrown herself into work, Josh's insistence that she wasn't really living—that she was meant for more—rang with a chord of truth.

Being around him now renewed the connection they'd always shared. The way they'd helped each other out the last few days reminded her of all she'd lost, all she'd never found again. She was missing her partner in life. Josh had been her other half until Katrina. Maybe her whole. What he knew, and what she'd ignored, was that she'd closed off her heart— barricaded it to real emotions, to love.

And especially to Josh. Had she blocked out others, too?

"Miss Maggie!" J.D. barreled toward her, his loafers slapping the pavement.

"Wait!" Josh gave frantic chase and swept the boy up in his arms as a minivan slowed behind them. "You know you're supposed to stay by me and hold my hand near the street, son."

"Yes, sir." His chubby fingers held Josh's cheeks, and he pressed his forehead on Josh's. "But I want to sit with Miss

Maggie."

She couldn't imagine a more adorable picture. Warmth spread through her, drawing out a tenderness she'd never imagined she'd have for any child other than Dahlia. How quickly she'd developed an affection for J.D. "He can sit with me."

Aunt Ruth and Dahlia joined them on the sidewalk, shielding their eyes with their hands in unison. So much glare today, and not a cloud visible. So far.

"We can all sit together." Josh cut his gaze Maggie's way, as if waiting for approval. "You don't want me to sit by myself, now, do you?"

They were friends. She could do this. "Sure." The single word squeezed between her lips.

"Let's go, or I'll be blind as a bat out in this brilliance." Aunt Ruth took an unsteady step forward, and Maggie clasped her elbow.

"Need my sunglasses?" Maybe no one would notice the puffy eyes. She often cried in church anyway. Something about the emotions that a worship service churned up, especially since Mama had passed away. A fight between joy and pain, it seemed.

"Lead the way, darling. Those big glasses would make me look like a cicada shell."

"Okay." Nice. Was that what she looked like in the shades? Inside the red brick building, Maggie lifted the sunglasses, paused, and blinked a few times to rid her vision of the dazzle from the sun. If she was having a hard time adjusting, she could only imagine what her aunt was going through.

"Let's sit near the back," Josh whispered near her ear, "in case someone gets restless." He nodded toward J.D. who was still in his arms.

"Of course." The warmth of his breath and a cinnamon aroma ignited a memory of the previous evening, but Maggie quickly tamped it down. They were in church, after all. She led Aunt Ruth to an empty pew four rows from the back of the auditorium and waited for her to take a seat. Dahlia walked off to sit with a friend, leaving J.D. and Josh sitting only inches from Maggie.

J.D. quickly scrambled into her lap and caught his fingers in her hair, twirling a curl. "They don't have children's church because of Thanksgiving, but next time you could come with me. We get to have animal crackers and yellow juice there. This one doesn't have snacks." His lips poked out as they pressed together. "Oh. Sometimes they have real small red juice and white cookies for the big people, but not for kids. I tasted one time." He shook his head. "It wasn't sweet."

A laugh worked its way past the awkwardness of sitting beside Josh. Kids did have such an innocent view of life. She ruffled his hair and smiled. "I'd like to come with you sometime."

The hard look Josh gave her as his head spun her way caught her off guard.

"What? I can't go with him?"

Josh's forehead formed a firm crease where his brows met. "He'll remember what you said, and if you don't..." His jaw hardened. "Kids expect adults to follow through—to be there."

The broken expression on his face sent a tsunami of understanding and empathy over her. Poor Josh. He'd never gotten over his father leaving them. That loss had bled away his trust in people. A lot like she'd never gotten over her father's death. They had more pain in common than she'd realized. Plus with J.D.'s mom gone...

A tall bearded man greeted the crowd, and then a singer began a poignant melody. The worship song eliminated the need for her to think of a way to respond. The words and tune inched into the cold and fearful places of her soul, soothing away a bit of the worry over Cammie and the storm. J.D. snuggled closer, resting his head against her shoulder, his chest rising and falling against hers.

The minister took the podium. A slide on the screen behind him read: *Have you been disappointed in God?*

Air caught in Maggie's lungs, and her ribs tightened against her midsection. What kind of lesson was this? It almost seemed blasphemous to say such a thing.

He asked everyone to turn to John 11. After the rustle of pages quieted, he read the story of Lazarus' death, stopping where Martha and Mary each approached with a lament.

Lord, if you had been here, my brother would not have died.

It was as if Maggie had been turned inside out in that moment. Hadn't she felt that very same way about her parents? Where had God been in the hurricane? Where had God been while cancer ravaged her mother?

The minister went on with the story.

Jesus was deeply moved and troubled.

Jesus wept.

Jesus could've kept Lazarus from dying. He could've healed his friend, even from afar. He'd done it before in the Scriptures. But He chose not to.

His friends had been hurt. Disappointed in Jesus. Disappointed in God.

Maggie swallowed at the thickness clogging her throat and forming a chokehold. Her anxious fingers made circles on J.D.'s back, and his breathing slowed. She looked down as his long lashes fluttered and then closed.

Tears blurred her vision. Why did God answer some prayers and not others?

God had answered their church's prayers when her friend Jane's daughter had been born premature. Not even two pounds at birth, the infant hadn't been expected to live, but the beautiful child not only lived, she flourished. Her brain sharp, her body perfectly formed and healthy.

Another woman from the church had a tumor disappear, never to return.

Moisture dampened Maggie's lashes.

No miracles had happened for her family. Time and again she'd prayed. And the answer had always been a solid no.

The Gulf stole her father. Cancer stole her mother. Life stole Josh. Now her sister...

The preacher's volume increased. "God isn't caught off guard when disasters and tragedies assail us from all sides. He is not shocked."

Maggie's attention turned back to the sermon.

"Jesus himself quoted the Psalm, 'My God, my God, why have you forsaken me?' Isaiah says 'He was a man of sorrows, acquainted with grief.' He understands pain and disappointment. He understands having His best friends abandon Him when He needed them most."

A single tear rolled down Maggie's cheek, and she swiped it with her free hand before it could land on J.D.

"The eyes of the flesh can't see God's plan, but know this"—the pastor seemed to look right at her—"God loves you. He has a purpose for you."

Hadn't her soul whispered that this was true? *God loved her.*

But what was His plan, and why couldn't she feel loved?

"It takes very little faith to trust when all goes right in our lives. How much more faith does it take to trust and love Him

151

back when life doesn't go like we want it to go? Being a Christian doesn't disqualify us from heartache. Isaiah 43:2 says, 'When you pass through the waters, I will be with you,' Being a Christian means we have a Comforter and a Savior who walks through our floods alongside us."

Had God been with her through the flood of pain and grief? Maggie rummaged around her past for an answer.

J.D.'s head popped up, and he stared at her as if orienting himself. "I gotta go potty," he whispered loudly.

Josh's elbow nudged her. "I'll take him."

"I want Miss Maggie to take me." Louder whispering came from J.D as he slipped to the floor.

"God has a purpose for your pain. Your pain can become your platform. Trust Him." The minister's voice slipped back into Maggie's consciousness. "Death is only a change of address. Eternal life starts now. It starts when you begin a new life in Christ."

A platform of pain? Eternal life now? She stood beside J.D. "I got him." She'd done the bathroom chaperoning a few times now and was getting accustomed to the task.

"What is it that's dead in your life? What is it that's past hope?" The preacher was hitting a little too close to home anyway. Maybe Cammie was right calling her a coward, in more ways than one.

J.D.'s small hand took hers, and they slipped out the back of the auditorium.

~~~

The sermon's words permeated Josh's being, flooding him with gratitude for all that the Lord had blessed him with. God had stood by him more times than he could count, starting way back when his father left. God had provided Mr. Marovich. When the appointment to Kings Point came through, Josh had felt God's leading. So many days at work, in the beauty he encountered in creation, he saw God's hand. Piloting on rough seas, God kept him safe. In the hard nights since the divorce, the Spirit of the Lord had been a comfort. Verses and worship songs had lifted his face to the Giver of Life during the loneliness. And precious J.D. had been the ultimate gift, aside from Christ's sacrifice.

Josh's gut twisted. He hated that Maggie had walked out before the message was over. She needed to hear these words more than he did. Did she even go to church anymore? He wasn't sure because she exuded such despair. The minister ended, and a worship song began. Maggie still hadn't returned. He hoped they were okay out there, but he would resist the urge to check on them.

Finally, the benediction came, and Josh led Ruth out to the foyer, her hand tucked in the crook of his elbow.

"Wasn't that lovely." The elderly woman squeezed his arm. "The perfect message at the perfect time, don't you think?"

"Yes, ma'am." He tried to keep his tone positive.

"She heard enough to get her thinking. Don't you worry. The good Lord's working on that girl."

The women in this family seemed to read his thoughts fairly often. "Hope you're right."

"Trust me. I'm right more than I'm not, didn't you know?" A cackle followed her self-assessment.

"I should by now." Winking at her, Josh smiled. Trusting came with work when it involved people.

"Daddy!" A push against the back of Josh's legs turned his head.

Maggie and J.D. had slipped up behind him. "There you are, son. I thought you fell in, you've been gone so long."

Giggles tumbled from J.D. "Gross. I didn't fall in the toilet.

153

We looked out the window at some birds."

"Are you sure? Let me see if you're wet." He ran his fingers around J.D.'s midsection, earning more laughter.

"Stop tickling me, Daddy."

"Sure is bright out there still." Maggie was suddenly the focus of his attention, her brown eyes staring at him and J.D. "I need to scoot if I'm going to make the afternoon visit."

He hadn't noticed the dark circles under her eyes before church. Obviously she hadn't slept much. Neither had he after being blasted with that kiss. Knowing she was right next door had kept him tossing and turning under his ceiling fan all night.

"How about I take everyone home and use the leftover shrimp to make etouffee while you go visit. When you get back, I'll have some saved, and maybe we could all ride out to the harbor or the beach for a walk."

"The beach? The harbor? Really, Josh?" The fierce look she harpooned him with could've scared off a great white shark. "That's the last place I want to be with a storm in the Gulf and all the…memories."

"We won't be getting in the water. I know there could be a rip current." He softened his tone. "I thought Dahlia and J.D. would enjoy getting outdoors, stretching their legs awhile. You and Ruth, too. A little of God's creation and some vitamin D?"

"You can take them home for lunch. I have vitamin supplements, and we can walk in the neighborhood." Maggie bent down to press a kiss on J.D.'s head. "See ya later, pumpkin."

"See you, Miss Maggie."

"Bye, Aunt Ruth." Maggie took a step away, then paused and turned back. "I'll let Dahlia know who to ride with. Does J.D feel warm to you?" She blinked a few times and shrugged. "Not that I know anything about kids. I'm being ridiculous."

Josh pressed his palm to J.D.'s forehead. "I don't feel fever if that's what you're asking. And if not the beach, maybe a nature hike near the bayou—"

"Not today. I need...I need some space." In an instant, her back was to him and she marched away.

Chapter 17

Maggie pushed her sunglasses over her eyes and took another cautious step in the sand. Her sister always seemed to get her way lately. She couldn't believe she was standing on the beach when there was a hurricane out there somewhere past the blue horizon where water and sky met. Already a headache wrenched around her forehead. But she wasn't doing this for Josh. Cammie had insisted she go along with his insane idea, saying Dahlia didn't need to be taught to fear the Mississippi Sound. Maggie's teeth caught her lip. That wasn't what she was trying to teach Dahlia. Or anyone for that matter. She wanted people to be careful. Prepared. Educated on the risks.

The images of this beach inundated with the storm surge during Katrina engulfed her, stealing her breath. The mounds of trees, boards, and wreckage scarring the land. The topography of the terrain made it vulnerable to mass flooding, laying waste to homes, businesses, and government offices all the way from the shoreline to Interstate 10. Whatever had been left intact had needed to be gutted due to the mold that set in before owners could even get to their property. No one who'd not seen the aftermath of the debris field could imagine the ravaged landscape here years earlier.

A shiver scampered across Maggie's shoulders. She wanted to believe she could move past all those memories, but so far, it hadn't happened.

"Take your shoes off and let the sand get between your toes, child," Aunt Ruth called from her perch in the lawn chair

Josh had set up for her. "It's like riding a horse. You get right back on."

"I don't ride horses." The Keds on Maggie's feet had pretty much filled with sand. She might as well go barefoot. She slipped off the sneakers and dropped them to the ground. The beach had warmed, at least, from the intense sunlight.

"It's like riding a bike then. You like bike riding."

"Okay." She did love the feel of the breeze ruffling her hair, a lot like when she went cycling at home on the trails near Jackson. She should've brought a ponytail holder, though. Her curls would be tangled into a rat's nest by the time she left.

About twenty feet away, Josh crouched over something on the ground and seemed to be explaining whatever it was to Dahlia and J.D. The light reflected off the waves behind the three, sparkling and shimmering. The rays glistened on Josh's blond hair, too. A detail she didn't want to dwell on. What was he showing them, anyway?

J.D. waved wildly. "Come see, Miss Maggie. It's a mermaid's purse."

A memory rushed into her mind—her father squatting down, showing her, Cammie, and Josh the same sort of black, square shell with spikes on four sides. Daddy's quirky smile as he teased her and Cammie about getting them a new handbag for school. Squealing, Cammie had recoiled and pretended to gag at the thought of a stingray egg sack being any part of an ensemble.

But she and Josh had fought over the chance to hold the biological wonder. Even pushing each other a few times until her father had given a stern command to halt. An unexpected sigh passed through Maggie's teeth. If not for the storm, her plan had been to study marine biology. The hurricane had left nothing in her life untouched, including her career choice.

157

"Come on, Aunt Maggie. Quit standing there like a knot on a log." Dahlia's chin jutted out, and she rolled her eyes.

Again, her niece's expression was like looking in a mirror. How scary. "Coming." Maggie shuffled toward them.

What would it be like to have children of her own? An enormous responsibility, one that was causing her a good bit of worry right now with her sister's situation. She prayed Cammie healed quickly. Her sister had taken to motherhood from the first day like a pro. None of those new-mommy jitters for Camelia Marovich.

Maggie kneeled on the sand next to J.D., doubting she'd have the same maternal gift as her sister. But it wasn't like kids were on the horizon anyway.

"Miss Maggie, do you want my daddy to tell you how this was made, too?" Cobalt blue circled the azure of J.D.'s irises, and the sun reflected from the corners of his eyes. Excitement lifted his brows, and his lips parted, waiting for her to respond. Ten miles past adorable.

She'd play along. Unable to stop her smile, she lifted her gaze to Josh. "Enlighten me, Joshua."

The same circles colored his eyes, but lines crinkled his temples when he grinned back at her, knowing she was being sarcastic.

"Mr. Marovich taught Maggie, Cammie, and me about these, so she knows as much or more than I do. Maggie had a shell encyclopedia, and she loved to gather what she found out on the barrier islands and look them up in her book." His Adam's apple bobbed as he swallowed. "Speaking of barrier islands…"

No. Maggie let her head drop forward. Everything between her temples ached, and she didn't want to go there right now. "Don't bring that disaster up."

"Now you have to tell." Dahlia stood and punched her fists to her hips. "Spill it."

Yep, like looking in a mirror. "Josh brought it up. Not me."

"Let's walk and talk." Josh motioned everyone forward with his head and began a leisurely pace eastward. "It was the day after Cammie graduated. We thought it would be a good idea to take the *Cajun Princess* out to Horn Island."

"The *Cajun Princess*." Maggie scoffed. "We all hated the name of that boat. Daddy thought it was hilarious. He'd tell people 'I'm taking out the *Cajun Princess* today.' And they'd say 'Which one this time,' acting as if we were all spoiled, Mama included." Well, maybe they had been. The man had doted on each one of them when he was home, trying to make up for lost time after two weeks out. He took them to dinner, shopping, fishing, boating…quality time, as they say. He'd always been bigger than life. A booming voice, enormous arms that would catch them in big off-the-ground hugs whenever he came home, and the tales her father told. He spun yarn like a sailor for sure.

"Anyhow," Josh continued. "Maggie and I, plus Cammie and her friend, set out for Horn a little too late in the day. Without checking the weather, either." He pointed a stare Maggie's way. "Apparently, before your aunt was into all that meteorology."

"Wait. What happened was not my fault." Maggie's spine bristled. "You and Cammie's *friend* came up with the idea in the first place." The guy with Cammie had been another loser. For a sweet, smart girl, her sister had made more than one bad choice in dating. Cammie'd given up the whole activity after Dahlia was born, claiming she didn't want any weirdos around her baby girl.

Josh's mouth pulled up on one side. "So we got to the

island and set out a tent, which would've been a good thing because it started hailing. But there was also lightning striking down to the ground, and we got nervous that the metal poles of the tent would attract the electricity. We pulled the poles out and lay flat on the ground huddled beneath the tarp."

Sniffling, J.D. rubbed his nose and tugged on Josh's shirttail. "Were you scared, Daddy?"

Maggie made a mental note to stuff a few tissues in her pocket for J.D. Josh was a good father, but men didn't tend to prepare as well for those kind of issues, it seemed.

Mischief lit Josh's eyes, and they sparkled even more, if that were possible. "A little scared of Maggie. Part of the time, she called out commands like an angry pirate, the rest of the time she used me like her human shield from the balls of ice pelting us. Not to mention the lightning. She acted like we were doomed if we didn't follow her orders."

"I did not." Maggie's mouth fell open. She remembered the situation very differently. "I may've yelled to be heard over the storm, but someone had to come up with a plan. And human shield?" There may've been a bit of cuddling close beside Josh, but she'd rather not go there. A brief flash of that memory zapped her with a current about as dangerous as the lightning. "I—"

"Puppies!" A shrill cry rent the air, and J.D. took off at a sprint down the beach.

Josh passed the mermaid's purse to Maggie and followed his son toward a blue pickup that had parked, unloaded a kennel, and set up a small playpen. A handmade sign read *Free to a Good Home.*

Gloom weighed down Maggie's shoulders. There was no way J.D. could have a dog with Josh gone all the time. But little boys loved puppies. And J.D. looked so excited. Dahlia's steps quickened, and her face brightened to the perkiest Maggie had seen since arriving. What would Cammie think about a pet? They were at the store so many hours, plus Aunt Ruth might trip over a small dog. Her aunt would never see something low to the ground like that. Maggie's abdomen locked up, jarring the air and the fear trapped there. If Cammie stumbled… Or would Cammie ever walk enough to worry about falling over an animal?

She strode to catch up with the kids. Already J.D. held a fat, black puppy with short floppy ears and a white belly, and he giggled when it licked his cheek.

"He likes me." More giggles floated along the briny Gulf breeze.

A middle-aged man in a red T-shirt and jeans offered Dahlia a slightly larger dog, muddled brown and white with floppy ears, one of which stood up while the other hung low. With lopsided ears and a smashed-looking nose, the dog wouldn't be winning any best-in-show awards. Her niece scooped the pudgy animal into her arms like a newborn baby, and the dog lay back, pink belly up, enjoying the attention.

"You kids look like you'd be good pet owners." The man eyed Josh and then Maggie. "With your parents' permission, of course."

Another steaming tide of anguish crashed over Maggie, shredding her heart. Again. How many people would assume she and Josh were a couple? A family even? She covered her mouth with her fist to keep from making a sound—or saying anything at all.

Shaking his head, Josh lowered his gaze. "It's not the right time for us to make a commitment."

Disappointment instantly shaded both kids' faces.

"What about you, Aunt Maggie?" Rotating Maggie's way,

Dahlia gave a pleading look. "You're alone all the time. You could get a dog, and maybe you could share it with me. Like on holidays and in the summer."

Temporarily mute, Maggie stared at her niece. She shuffled through possible responses to such a blunt assessment of her life.

"Please, Miss Maggie." J.D. joined with a begging pouch of his lips. "I could babysit him for you."

Now she was sniffling and wishing she could make things better for both of the children.

~~~

He needed to come up with a distraction. And quick. Josh scrambled to find something to say. Poor Maggie. The mortified look on her face melted his heart.

Her brows jerked up and down, and she blinked at least three times in rapid succession. "I'm...not home all the time because of my job, and puppies need training. I...I mean if I were going to get a pet, it might be a cat. They aren't as much work."

Both of the kids slumped, and their faces fell.

"Can cats ride in a boat?" J.D. rubbed his cheek against the pup still wriggling in his arms.

Dark curls cascaded over Maggie's shoulders when she shook her head. "Not so much. Cats and boats don't really go together."

He had to dig them out of this hole quickly or he'd end up with a kitten running between his and Ruth's houses. And cats weren't his favorite. A wild feline had jumped out of a tree and onto his head once as a boy, and he'd never trusted the beasts since. "Let's play with the puppies a minute and then see what other exciting discoveries we can find down the beach. I think I can make out a sailboat."

The boat caught his son's attention, but not Dahlia's.

"Aww." She sighed. "She's so cute, and she needs someone to love her." Her lower lip quivered a little before she caught it in her teeth.

"Sir, can we get your number?" Maggie stepped closer to the puppy peddler. "If something works out, we'll call you."

The man scrambled to jot it on a scrap of cardboard.

Was it even legal for the guy to be out here? The unexpected development irritated Josh about like a sea nettle sting. "Let's put the puppies down without making me jerk a knot in your heads, and I'll take y'all for frozen yogurt on the way home."

Hesitantly and with downturned lips, both children complied. They all started back down the narrow stretch of beach toward where a sailboat floated not far from shore.

Josh gave Maggie a playful nudge. "I wouldn't really jerk a knot in their heads, you know."

"I figured." Her voice came out soft and somber, tightening a noose around his chest.

The beach was supposed to cheer everyone up, not churn around more misery. Josh breathed a heavy sigh.

"Mr. Josh?" Dahlia cocked her head, gazing at him with huge brown eyes. "What does a ship pilot do?"

"I'm what's known as a bar pilot. We approach larger ships in our boat. I climb a ladder onto their deck and take the helm. I bring the vessel through the narrow, shallow, shifting channel of Southwest Pass. Sometimes the ship's headed inbound into the wide, deep Mississippi River, where a river pilot will take over. Sometimes, the ship's headed outbound, and I take over from the river pilot and guide her out to the deep waters of the Gulf of Mexico."

"How do you take over? Do you steer the ship?" Dahlia

asked.

"I give orders to the helmsman, like degrees of angle and direction of the rudder or compass headings to steer. The helmsman is the guy actually steering the ship." He studied her posture and body language. She twisted the ends of her hair. What was going on in her mind? "Why do you ask?"

J.D. scampered after a crab, and Maggie jogged to stay close. She didn't let him out of her sight for much. She'd make a good mother. Wistfulness crept into Josh's mood now, too.

"My grandfather was a pilot, but no one talks about it much." Dahlia's tone gripped his heart and squeezed like a bowline tangled around a cleat hitch at the dock.

Pausing in his tracks, Josh struggled to get his bearings. The girl resembled a younger version of Maggie grappling to comprehend her past. Something in the air today seemed to be stirring up all sorts of ancient debris. Maybe even a storm of another kind, which, it seemed, they were all running into headlong.

Was there any way to reverse their course? "Yes. Your grandfather was a pilot. He's the reason I wanted to pursue this career, my life's work."

Maggie's head pivoted his way. She must have the ears of a bobcat. Probably the claws, too. But the sea and water glistening behind her profile made her look more like a blissful dream. He could still hardly believe she was here.

"Did you ever go…on a rescue?" Dahlia treaded tenderly around the question. She'd surely heard the way her grandfather had been lost at sea.

A quick, honest, and short answer seemed best. "Yes, several."

"What were they? Did the people make it?"

He eyed Maggie, and her face contorted. "They made it."

"What happened…?" Dahlia stared toward the water. "I mean—"

"Daddy, I don't feel good." A nasally whine tinged J.D.'s tone. Not a good sign.

Maggie lifted him and headed their way. Her lips pressed against his forehead, and her eyes rounded. "He's burning up."

Chapter 18

The last thing they needed was for one of them to get sick. Fatigue weighed down Maggie's shoulders like four feet of sand. A tension headache throbbed against her forehead and behind her eyes.

She pressed the back of her wrist against J.D.'s forehead for the fourth time since they'd taken a seat in the plastic chairs of the walk-in clinic. Feeling even hotter, the child leaned against her arm while Josh parked the truck behind the building. They might as well have everyone checked out. Dahlia and Aunt Ruth sat on her other side, both staring at copies of *People Magazine*.

Today was Sunday. *Lord help us*. That only left them four days to make sure Dahlia was well enough to visit with Cammie on Thanksgiving without spreading some dangerous illness. Ragged-looking children and adults fidgeted in seats nearby. If they weren't sick already, they would be by the time they left.

"This is not good at all. What are we going to do?" Maggie spoke into the air, not really expecting an answer.

Aunt Ruth patted Maggie's hand. "Child, you could worry the whiskers off a catfish. The baby may be ailing, but most likely the rest of us are fit as a fiddle. I feel great after sitting out in the sun awhile."

Maggie prayed Aunt Ruth was right. But already her worst nightmares seemed to be coming true. With J.D. running a temp and all of them in such close contact *every single day* since she'd arrived, there was a good chance she had already spread it to Cammie. Of course, Cammie had been keeping the child even before that.

Winded, Josh rushed in. "Did you have to fill out papers?" He pulled his wallet from his back pocket and removed an insurance card.

"I signed in, but I didn't know the answers to all those questions." She nodded toward the clipboard in the empty chair on the other side of J.D. "And I'm wondering if we should all get an appointment. Or do you think the doctor could check everyone out at once?"

He sat on the edge of the chair, quickly filling out the paperwork, line by line. "Doubtful. They have to have a form for practically every tongue depressor."

"What ever happened to a family doctor?" She smoothed her hand over J.D.'s damp head, and he curled in closer to her side with a shiver. "Poor baby. Should we get him something to drink?"

Twin lines formed between Josh's brows as he looked up. "Yeah. I should've thought of that. I have water in the truck. I'll be right back." The clipboard clattered on the hard chair, and he was out the door in a flash.

A few minutes later, he jogged back in, five bottles of water in his arms. He passed one to Dahlia and Aunt Ruth but kneeled in front of Maggie and J.D. "Here you go, buddy." He unscrewed both the caps off two bottles and held one out to J.D. "You need to drink. Miss Maggie is smart about these things." His blue gaze met hers and flickered. "You're good at this…a natural parent."

Something cracked open inside, releasing a mingled torrent of warmth and ache. Rawness covered her throat, and the ache in her forehead pulsed harder. No words came. How many times would this scenario crush her beneath its cruel heel?

Exhaustion pulled at her emotions, and her eyes stung.

"Joshua Bergeron?" A nurse in pink scrubs called from a cracked hallway door.

"That's us." Dahlia stood and tapped Aunt Ruth. "Let's go back."

Josh held up the paperwork. "I'm not finished."

"You can do it back here," the nurse answered.

Shifting her weight, Maggie scooped the boy into her arms, and J.D. leaned farther into her shoulder with a slight groan. She pushed to her feet, ready to carry him. *God, please let this sweet boy feel better.*

"So I guess we're all going back then." Josh shrugged and waved them on.

"I have to know what's going on. It's urgent for all of us so we protect Cammie."

~~~

Josh stifled a sigh. Maggie was right, of course, but the doctor was going to be in for an interesting afternoon with the Marovich women. Josh let them lead the way back to the exam room, where they lined the wall of the small space, Ruth and Dahlia each taking one of the two chairs. The nurse made an abrupt double take when she looked up from the chart she'd been studying and scanned their gang. Maggie's chin jutted out, as did Dahlia's, both giving hard looks that dared the woman to ask them to leave.

The medical professional schooled her features as best she could, which wasn't very well. "Let me get our boy's temperature."

Never moving from his spot against Maggie's shoulder, J.D. allowed the nurse to place the thermometer into his ear without a fuss.

Josh swallowed back his surprise. Going to the doctor had

never been this easy with his son. A memory washed up of the time when they'd needed to take blood from J.D.'s finger a few weeks after Trisha had left them. The child had sat on his hands, refusing to obey. Josh shook his head. When he'd finally forced J.D.'s hand out for the prick, he'd been squeezing too tight, so they'd had to repeat the horrible process on the other hand. That had been one of his worst days…and parenting fails.

Of course, Trisha hadn't been any better. Okay, she'd been worse. She usually tried to put off any kind of pediatric appointments until he was up from the river. If J.D. was really ill and couldn't wait, Trisha asked Mom to go with her. Or asked Mom to take him while Trisha was out on her important socialite business. Whatever that was. Bitterness hit the back of his throat. How had he not seen what kind of woman she was?

"One hundred and three," the nurse announced, matter-of-factly. "I'll go ahead and do a strep test and a flu swab, to rule those out."

J.D. whimpered. "No."

"It's okay, baby. I've got you," Maggie crooned. "I won't let go. You mind the nurse so we can make you feel better."

"I don't want to." Panic laced his son's voice.

Josh readied himself to take over.

"I'll let her do it to me first. Okay?" Maggie held open her mouth wide toward the poor nurse.

J.D.'s eyes widened, as did the nurse's.

Closing her mouth, Maggie nodded. "Go ahead. Test me. My sister's in ICU, and I need to know if I have something contagious." Her mouth opened again. "Aaahh."

"You're going to have to fill out some paperwork once I finish."

Maggie's head bobbed again, and then the nurse stuck the swab in and circled. Maggie's eyes watered, but somehow she kept herself from making a sound, even smiling when it was over.

"Your throat is pretty raw. Whatever it is, you probably have it too."

"Really?" Maggie blinked hard. "I thought I felt bad because I was near Josh."

A loud laugh erupted from Dahlia. "Aunt Maggie. Talk about rude."

Realization lifted Maggie's brows, and she turned Josh's way. "Sorry. I didn't mean that like… You know… Not how it sounded."

The nurse's expression spoke total bewilderment, but she held up another swab. "Now the nose for the flu test."

Maggie squeezed her eyes shut tight. "Boy, that tickles."

"All done with Mama." The nurse opened another packet. "Your turn."

Josh's heart squeezed. If only…

His son stared at Maggie and she stared back. What were they thinking? She opened her mouth wide again and nodded. "Like this, J.D." Her voice garbled as she tried to talk with her jaws that way.

The awkwardness brought a small smile to J.D., and he complied. Before he could change his mind, the nurse tickled his throat with the swab, bringing up a gag and a cough.

"Good boy." Maggie kissed his head.

"Now the nose."

His son's body flinched, but he allowed the test. That had gone well enough. Josh released a pent-up breath. Somehow Maggie gave J.D. confidence.

Josh blinked hard. Too bad she didn't send any his way.

And oh, how he hoped they didn't have to draw blood.

"I'll take these to the lab, and Dr. Collins will be in soon." The woman left carrying a tray with the specimens.

"Lord, let it be something simple." Josh spoke the prayer out loud, turning all eyes toward him. "I'm really sorry about this. I had no idea he was sick."

"Children get sick, Joshua." Waving him off, Ruth clucked her tongue. "We can't live in a bubble. We work with the public, go to restaurants, not to mention the hospital…" She shook her head. "Hospitals are full of sickness."

"I hope Mama doesn't get worse." Dahlia's voice wobbled. "I haven't even gotten to visit her yet."

Ruth wrapped an arm around the girl. "God's in control, darling, don't you worry. Like the minister said today, there's no panic in heaven. The Lord's not caught off guard by this."

Wise words from the elderly. Josh nodded. "That's right." If only he knew what the plan was or understood it a little better. Was Maggie sick, too? Or was it fatigue? How would they manage if she was? She'd likely blame him if anything bad happened to Cammie.

Silence fell in the room like a dense fog of apprehension. Only the sound of Dahlia playing with Ruth's phone penetrated the quiet.

After what seemed like an hour, a knock sounded on the door. "Good afternoon, guys, I'm Dr. Collins."

Josh shook the man's hand. "I'm J.D.'s father."

"We ruled out flu and strep, but let me take a look and listen to our boy, and we'll go from there."

Maggie stepped to the exam table. "Can I hold him while you check him?"

"Sure, have a seat up there, and then, J.D., you lean forward so I can listen to you breathe in and out. Okay?"

171

The paper on the table crinkled when Maggie scooted on. "I'll be right here, pumpkin. Lean toward Dr. Collins so he can listen."

His son obeyed, and after a few breaths, the doctor put the stethoscope to the front of J.D.'s chest. When he finished, the doctor kept going with his examination, and J.D. submitted willingly. It seemed as long as Maggie held him in her arms, the boy could handle it all. Must be nice.

"I'm hearing a little rattle in his chest. There's a bug going around the state called mycoplasma, commonly known as walking pneumonia. I'll need to do a blood test to confirm."

Josh's abs tightened. Not only about the test, but also about the word pneumonia.

Chapter 19

No one could make this stuff up...all the unfathomable storms that seemed to rain down on their family.

Walking pneumonia? It couldn't be. A tremble shook Maggie's shoulders. Was fever causing the shiver, or just plain fear? They'd all taken the miserable blood test, not without a few tears from J.D. Dahlia put on a brave front, but that finger prick had hurt. At least the doctor had accommodated their unique situation. Now they waited for the results and filled out paperwork. For thirty more minutes.

A moan slipped from J.D.'s lips, and Maggie brushed a lock of golden hair from his forehead. "We need to get something to bring his fever down." She stood and walked to the exam room door. "I'm going to get that doctor to give him Tylenol or Motrin, whatever they give little kids. This is crazy."

Josh stepped in front of her. "I'll do it. You're right. I was lost in thought about the situation and how to handle our schedules." The back of his hand caressed her cheek. "You may need some too. You said you felt bad." His blue gaze searched her face, his features soft and caring.

She filled her lungs with a large gulp of air. "I'll wait until we get home, but get him something right away."

"Yes, ma'am. I'm on it."

Before he could exit, the door opened, and the doctor appeared. He stopped abruptly, and his brows raised. "Sorry for the long wait. Were y'all coming to find me or giving up and going home?"

"He needs something to bring his fever down." Maggie tried to keep her tone in the polite range, but her patience had faded twenty minutes ago.

"Of course. I'll have the nurse bring a dose of Tylenol right away." He typed something on a tablet. "But first what pharmacy do you use? I'll send the prescriptions out."

"Prescriptions? Everyone's sick?" A wave of nausea flooded her.

"Not yet. Only you and the little man have walking pneumonia. I'm not surprised because there's been an outbreak. The two of you will need to steer clear of the rest of the crew for a couple of days. Close yourselves in a separate room, watch some movies. After that, if you're fever free, you can join the family again." He looked at her then Josh. "Though Dad didn't test positive, there's a slight possibility he has it, too. Especially if you've been in *close contact*." He raised his brows to drive home his point. "He might need treatment before he visits your sister. Or he could wait it out a week or so."

"I'll take the medicine just in case." Josh ran his fingers through his hair. "We don't want to take any chances."

Yep. They'd been in close contact. Maggie swallowed hard at the memory of the kiss. What a mistake. Now neither she nor Josh could visit Cammie for several days. That left her aunt, who really didn't need to be driving and navigating the hospital three times a day by herself. What in the world would they do? They couldn't leave her sister there alone.

Once J.D. received a dose of medicine and they paid, Josh drove to the pharmacy. From the front seat, Aunt Ruth pointed across the parking lot to a smoothie shop. "Oh, that's exactly what we need, a nice cold slushy."

"Smoothie, Aunt Ruth." Dahlia corrected her. "And I want

chocolate peanut butter cup."

"Me, too." J.D. suddenly raised his head in the car seat. The fever must've been lower. "I like chocolate."

"They have strawberry banana, mate." Josh chimed in. "That would be better for you. I'll get it as soon as I finish in the pharmacy."

"I'll go," Aunt Ruth offered.

"No." Maggie wouldn't chance letting her aunt cross the pothole-filled parking lot. "I got it."

"Maggie, are you well enough?" Josh studied her.

"Yes, and I'll hold my breath carrying them back."

He opened his wallet and offered a few ten dollar bills.

"I don't need money, but you'll need my insurance card for the prescription." Maggie dug through her purse to find her wallet. After shuffling through at least fifty shoppers' reward cards, she found what she was looking for.

Josh took off toward the drug store, and Maggie held up her phone. "I'll make a note of your orders. My brain is tired. I know what Dahlia wants, and J.D. gets what his dad said, right?" She looked at Dahlia to confirm that was how things worked.

Dahlia's head bobbed.

"But I want chocolate." J.D.'s lips poked out in a pout.

"I'm going to get strawberry banana, like you. That flavor is good for sick people." She didn't need an argument right now. "Aunt Ruth?"

"I'll have what you and J.D. are having." Her tone was flat. No doubt she'd rather have chocolate, too, but was taking one for the team.

"I'll be right back." Maggie trudged across the parking lot, fighting the headache hammering her skull. Outside, she sucked in the humid air, which stirred up a cough. A hard throaty cough.

Nice. My head just might explode if anything else goes wrong.

Inside the cool store, she placed the order and then held out the phone to type a text to Angie. Maybe their nurse-friend could go talk to Cammie and explain the situation. The sound of the mixer whirling sent another wrack of pain, this time down the tightening muscles of her neck. Mid-text, the phone chimed. She didn't recognize the number. It might be the hospital. Her heart rate accelerated as she accepted the call. "Hello."

"Miss Marovich?"

"Yes, who's calling?" This better not be a sales call, or someone was getting a dressing down.

"This is Dr. Castro."

"Oh, crud. She's got it, too, doesn't she?"

"I'm sorry. What's going on?" Confusion laced his words.

"The little boy Cammie babysits and I have some mycoplasma pneumonia. We left the doctor's office and are getting a special antibiotic."

"Oh." After a deep breath, the line fell silent for a long moment, ramping Maggie's anxiety higher. "That could explain your sister's fever. I'll treat her accordingly. At least we know what we may be dealing with." He expelled a breath.

Fear waged war with Maggie's faith. She let her eyes close. "Lord, help us," she whispered.

"Miss Marovich, I'm praying for your sister, too. I'll stay with her and watch her. When I have to leave for surgery, I'll make sure the staff is attentive. Don't worry. You give yourself at least forty-eight hours or so on the antibiotic and get some rest before coming back. This is my personal cell. Call or text me anytime."

Unshed tears stung the backs of Maggie's eyelids, burned

her nose. She wouldn't lose hope. Not yet, at least. "Thank you for taking care of her."

"We both want her to recover fully." Something in his tone piqued her curiosity for a second, but she was too over-whelmed to follow up on it.

"Number twenty-five, your order is ready," a voice called from behind the counter.

"I'll let you get back to work, then."

They ended the call, and Maggie collected the sack of icy drinks. A shiver ran through her. Maybe she had a fever after all. She hadn't had time to think about anything but Cammie and the kids. And the store and Aunt Ruth. And the storm. And Josh.

~~~

Josh made it back to the truck as Maggie handed out the smoothies. A cold drink would be great right about now.

"What kind did you get me?" He glanced at the empty cup holder then looked to the backseat.

"Oh, shoot." Maggie pressed her palm against her forehead. "I don't know what I was thinking. Sorry. I'll go back."

"No. I didn't want one, really." Not much, anyway. He cranked the truck. "We need to get y'all back to rest. Oh, and the pharmacist said this antibiotic is hard on the stomach and not to be surprised if you taste metal for a while."

"Great." Maggie's tone said anything but.

Should he pitch his idea yet? Or should he wait until they got home? He backed out of the parking place and shifted into drive. Better to throw it out there. He cleared his throat. *Some help here, Lord, would be good.* "So. Maggie. You and J.D. could room at my place, and I can sleep on the couch at Ruth's. She and I, with Dahlia, of course, can run the store. That leaves checking on Cammie. I texted Angie and updated her on the situation. She said her son has this stuff, too, but she was well, so she'll check on Cammie." Now to wait for a reaction. He held his breath.

Other than the hum of the motor and some loud slurping from J.D. and Dahlia, the truck fell silent. For a long minute.

"Okay." Maggie's one word answer almost made him pull over. Nothing was that easy with her. Something else had to be going on.

Worry rained down on him, needling him the rest of the way home. But he wouldn't question her in front of the kids.

After parking in his driveway, he grabbed the bag from the pharmacy and then opened the door for Maggie. She stepped out and turned to unlatch J.D.'s car seat.

"Maggie, let me—"

"You need to stay well. I'm depending on you."

Her words and tone spoke volumes, piercing him. She'd needed him before, and he'd let her down. Now he might have indirectly caused her sister to get ill. "I'm sorry. About everything."

No answer.

Ruth and Dahlia continued into their house while Josh followed Maggie into his. "Let me change the sheets on my bed and grab some clothes, then I'll be out of your way so y'all can rest."

"I'll read J.D. a story in his room." She cradled his boy like a baby. And J.D. let her. His son was wiped out, and Josh's heart squeezed. He hated not being the one to care for J.D.

Fifteen minutes later, he had the bed made and had packed a folded stack of clothes in his travel bag. He'd savored the echo of Maggie's voice reading to his son, but the house had become quiet now. Maybe they'd both fallen asleep. Should he leave? He lingered in the living room, toeing the hardwood floor.

"Hey," a voice whispered from the hall. Weariness weighted Maggie's lashes halfway over those dark pools that drove him mad.

"Hey." A stupid thing to answer, but it was all that came to mind.

She took a hesitant step closer and stopped. "Cammie is sick, too."

"No." His stomach lurched. "This is all my fault."

"You weren't driving the truck that hit her."

"I shouldn't have moved here."

"Too late about that, and I need you to run the store until I get well, so you're stuck. For now."

What did that mean? Did she want him to leave once she was well? He wrestled to think of what to say next.

"I actually have a pretty bad headache, so I'm going to lie down." Her phone chimed, and she quickly answered. "What's going on?"

Swaying, Maggie mashed her eyes shut as she listened. "Yeah, sorry. I can't leave now, and I have pneumonia. I hate letting y'all down, but we'll all have to deal with what we got." She ended the call and opened her eyes. "That was Steve from my office. I think my friend Jane gave me the crud, because she's out sick, too. You're off the hook. And…" Her chest lifted as her chin jutted out. Never a good sign. "The hurricane turned back our direction."

Chapter 20

"I'll get us ready for the storm. Don't worry. I have everything we'll need to prepare. Even a generator." Josh's tone sounded so confident, almost compelling Maggie to believe him.

Almost.

"Thanks." What more could she say? She still hoped they would evacuate. Maggie wrapped her arms around herself to fight the chill creeping over her and then turned back down the hall toward his bedroom.

His bedroom. His bed. Her neck muscles wound into tighter knots, if that were possible. When she reached the spotless room, the covers had been folded down on one side. Swallowing hard at the lump in her throat, she slid between the navy-blue sheets. Cool and soft, they wrapped around her like a wave, warming the ache that seemed to come from every part of her body and soul. She let her eyes close and hugged the pillow, fighting the urge to pretend she was holding Josh Bergeron.

~~~

A ball of heat pressed against the small of Maggie's back. Her eyes opened to dim light, and she slid her hand around to touch the source. Had someone's cat gotten into the house?

Soft skin and cloth met her fingertips, along with what felt to be a little arm. *J.D.* Warmth for the sweet child engulfed Maggie's chest. Cautiously, she slipped over an inch or two and then rolled to look at him.

Long blond eyelashes lay against the tops of his lightly

freckled cheeks. A lock of golden hair curled at his forehead. His skin shone a milky pink and so perfect. What an angel he looked like when he was asleep.

A rattle came from outside the window. Josh must finally be covering them, probably more to assuage her fears than his own worry about the storm. Something about pilots seemed to make them immune to fear of storms on land. Maybe because they'd survived so many squalls at sea. At least, most of them survived.

She scooted to the edge of the bed and touched her feet to the cool floor, then she grabbed her phone from the nightstand. At some point, she'd need her computer and clothes from next door. Seemed like now was as good as any while the little man was still asleep. She made stealthy movements toward the door, quiet like she'd seen Josh doing.

"Miss Maggie? Where ya going?" Almost to the hall, the small voice caught her. A cough and a sniffle followed.

Josh's technique surpassed hers apparently. A cough tickled her own chest, taking hold of her body as it wracked her shoulders. She covered her mouth in the crook of her arm until the spasms subsided. Goodness, she sounded like a ninety-year-old man who'd smoked for eighty years.

"You can keep resting, pumpkin. I need to get clothes and my computer from next door so we can have a spend-the-night party."

"My nana has parties with me, and I get to have Mickey Mouse waffles for breakfast." The sheets swished as he glided across them and dropped to the floor.

"That's really sweet. She must be a great nana." Josh's mother had been a good parent, despite having had to work so many hours to make ends meet.

"I don't want to stay and rest in the bed. It's too alone."

If that hadn't melted her heart enough, J.D. caught hold of her fingers. They took small steps down the hall.

"Can you make waffles into animals, Miss Maggie?"

"Not unless your dad has a special griddle to cook them on. Has he ever made them?"

"Just Nana." Disappointment laced his words.

"If there's pancake mix, I bet I can make a fun-shaped pancake in a skillet. My dad used to do that." She hadn't eaten pancakes in a long time, and a sudden memory returned of her father holding a spatula on Sunday mornings. The image brought a smile and a tender ache. It had been his routine for the weekends when he wasn't on duty.

"Okay. I want that." He halted in his tracks and squeezed her fingers. "Can you hold me? My legs are swimming."

"Aww." Heart squeezing, Maggie pocketed her phone and held out her arms. "Poor pumpkin, come here." She bent down to lift him, and her vision spotted black-and-white as though her brain hit the backs of her eyeballs. Teetering, she managed to get him to her hip. Squatting might be a better tactic next time. "We'll give your dad a grocery list. Let me take a quick peek in the fridge."

"Like peek-a-boo with the fridgerator?" He giggled at his own joke.

She tweaked his nose and twisted her lips into a lopsided smile. "You play that, too, don't you?"

His nose scrunched. "No, silly. Daddy has a safety on it."

Blinking, Maggie rounded her mouth. "Oh." Right. The refrigerator could be dangerous. "I hadn't thought of that one. I hope I can get it open." After making her way into the kitchen, she spied out the Velcro latch near the top of the appliance and breathed a sigh. "Not a problem." Velcro strap she could do, especially after her skirmish with his car seat.

Now for pen and paper, or, if she could manage to be coordinated enough, she'd text a list. Shifting J.D.'s weight, she dug her phone from her pocket. She sent a grocery list to Josh and another list to Aunt Ruth's phone containing the things to pack in an overnight bag for her. Maybe Dahlia would hear the text. No way was she letting Josh sort through her unmentionables, as Aunt Ruth had called them. Josh could bring everything over at one time, though.

"I'm thirsty." J.D. let his head nuzzle next to her neck.

"You probably need Tylenol or something, too." But how much? And what should he drink? There were so many things to learn about children. She might as well step out back and ask Josh. The texting was requiring too much concentration. "Let me set you in your chair and ask Daddy."

Once she had him safely settled, she crossed the kitchen. The door creaked when she pulled it open, and the porch lights flickered. "Hey, Josh. I need the dosage for Tylenol."

"I wrote it on the prescription bag. Give him a bowl of chicken noodle soup, crackers, and apple juice before the next dose of antibiotics, too." He twisted one more screw into the window cover and headed their way. "I got your text. I'll hurry to the store. I have plenty of MREs and canned food in my emergency pantry, but it's not much in the way of culinary fair. Mostly ravioli, canned meats, and canned fruit. Stuff to get by on, if needed."

Her stomach churned. "Oh man, I was sick of ravioli after Katrina. We cooked so many cans of the stuff on the grill or over a fire while the power was off." A shudder ran through her. "Although we were fortunate we had it, the taste still reminds me of those days."

His gaze dropped. "Sorry." He toed at the earth. "Maggie, I should've come back...been at the memorial—helped you

183

all. I see that now. I could've still become a pilot through a route other than Kings Point."

His eyes rose to meet hers, with a pitiful stare.

Not that it made up for much, but the apology was nice enough—until he got to the still being a pilot part. "You can leave our things on the front porch and text me. No sense getting too close with germs and all." She rotated away from Josh and the hurt his words stirred up, but paused. She turned back. "On second thought, bring my stuff over before you go to the store. I want to check my laptop to see if there are any evacuation orders planned." One could hope.

"Okay, but my sources say only a curfew Tuesday night and Wednesday."

His sources. Huh. Doubtful they were meteorologists. Probably other stubborn pilots.

"You know, Josh, you could take Aunt Ruth and the kids and get out of here."

"Angie said they aren't evacuating the hospital, so I think we should all stay together."

Fire lit in her midsection. He sounded exactly like her father had during Katrina. She turned and stomped back into the house without responding.

In the kitchen, she prepared J.D.'s food and dosed him with the appropriate meds. When Josh texted, she waited five minutes to make sure he was gone before she went out to retrieve her computer. Soon, she had J.D. set up in the king-sized bed to watch a cartoon like the doctor suggested, and she opened her laptop. A look at a few of the forecasts indicated that there would be no mandatory evacuation. Her heart thrashed in her chest. She'd promised herself she'd never ride out a hurricane, no matter the category. Not even a tropical storm. At that moment, J.D. nestled in closer beside her, and his fingers made circles around a piece of her hair.

If Josh wouldn't leave, that meant J.D. was stuck down here, and it wasn't like she could steal J.D. away if she left with Dahlia and Aunt Ruth. She wouldn't want to leave that baby. And what would Cammie want her to do?

Her stomach plummeted a few fathoms. But she knew. Cammie would want her to keep the store open as long as possible and stay put if there were no evacuation orders.

With a deep sigh, Maggie soaked in the view of the little boy at her side.

Looked like she'd be breaking her promise about riding out storms.

~ ~ ~

Josh set the items Maggie needed on the porch and sent her the requested text. Her avoiding him was more than just to keep the germs inside, no doubt. He'd blurted out that apology at an inopportune time, like an idiot. He hadn't planned to say any of it. The realization of what he'd done had smacked him, and he'd spilled it out.

He should go, but his feet stayed glued to his porch. Everything he ever wanted was inside that house, just beyond—that door. Pretending the life he longed for was possible bordered on insanity, but he couldn't stop the thoughts pounding in like rough surf. Him and Maggie and J.D.—a family, maybe with a little curly-headed daughter, too, someday, one with big brown eyes. Maggie would be chiding him about something, and he'd tease her, like they'd always done, a dance they both had known and loved in the past.

The woman would run a tight ship at home, he'd wager, but she'd give those children a love that ran deep and strong and wide. A small chuckle made its way out. Long as the Mississippi River and as wide as the Gulf of Mexico. He hated not saying goodnight to his boy, but Maggie would take care of him. Already, she'd shown a strong maternal instinct, even to a child that had been born to him by another woman.

A clatter sounded near the door, and regret razed through him. He'd better go. Maggie didn't want him here, and he kept stirring up more trouble and pain for her. After Thanksgiving, Mrs. Daigle had said she could help with the store. As soon as the storm passed, he needed to start that search for a nanny and a new place to live. Maybe he'd go ahead and email his real estate agent tonight and scan a few websites. It wasn't like he had much else to do.

Chapter 21

The next afternoon, the phone's chime broke into Maggie's nap, and she scrambled across the bed to grab the thing before the sound woke the little man. She'd given up trying to get him to sleep in his own bed. After punching the *Accept* button, she tiptoed out of Josh's bedroom before speaking. The number read *Angie*, and a knife of anxiety plunged into Maggie's gut.

"Hello," she whispered.

"Maggie?"

"Yeah, sorry. J.D. is asleep. I wanted to get to the kitchen so I wouldn't wake him." The evidence of their morning pancake fest still covered the table. She'd been too tired to clean it up once they'd finished.

"How is he?"

"We both hacked all night. Those cough syrups don't do much for this."

"Sorry. It's hard when the mo…caretaker is sick and the child, too. I'm bringing supper for y'all tonight."

"You don't need to." And Angie's slip hadn't escaped her.

"Everything's already in motion. Graham is making gumbo. Mrs. Daigle's cooking homemade chicken soup and cornbread for you tomorrow."

A sigh slipped passed Maggie's lips. "I hate for everyone to bother, and I thought you said only a few nights a week?"

"This is what a Christian family does. We care for each other."

Their situation had swirled into such a challenging

predicament, she'd allow herself to be taken care of, if only for a short while. She lifted the dirty skillet with her free hand and set it in the sink.

"You haven't said how Cammie is. You saw her today, right?" Keeping her voice steady required patience she didn't have right now.

Angie's quick inhale sounded through the phone. There was something the nurse didn't want to say.

"Angie, I need to know."

"She's very weak. On oxygen. But fighting. Dr. Castro is staying with her almost around the clock, except for when he checks other patients."

Maggie's throat tightened. "I should be there."

"She's in good hands, and I asked her if I could put her on the prayer list at church. She said yes. I hope that's okay with you."

"Sure." Anything was worth a try. But she knew better than to hope.

"Both Dr. Castro and I will be on duty when the storm rolls in, so please rest until it passes."

Like that was possible.

~~~

Air hung heavy and foreboding while Josh double-checked all the windows one more time at both houses. The generator was ready, and he'd pulled his boat out of storage and parked it in the driveway, in case they needed it if the situation went south.

Lord, please let this one weaken. For Maggie. Her family needs a break right now. We'd be thankful for no storm surge. No tornadoes.

Maggie wouldn't like seeing the vessel here. Plus the name. Would it be dumb to pray that Maggie didn't notice? *Cajun Princess II.* What had he been thinking when he'd named the thing eight years ago? Three gallons of crazy in a two-gallon bucket.

But he didn't have to question his reasoning. He'd been thinking of her. Thinking he'd figure out how to win her back. Thinking she'd eventually forgive him.

A 4Runner slowed, then stopped on the street in front of Ruth's place. Looked like Angie arriving with their dinner. Josh's stomach rumbled at the thought of his partner Graham's gumbo. The man could cook a mean batch, and it would be chock full of all the best seafood. They'd spent plenty of days fishing together. A little toasted French bread, and they'd dine like kings while the storm passed.

A gust of wind whipped up as he made his way through the yards to the SUV. They'd be fine. He'd been watching the same models from the National Hurricane Center that Maggie had. Some high winds maybe, but these houses had endured that before.

"Hey. Let me help you." He stepped close to the front door where Angie struggled to get out with a large stock pot.

"Sure. Take this." She held out the gumbo. "I've got the soup from Mrs. Daigle, too. She didn't think she'd be able to get over tomorrow because of the curfew. You can freeze the leftovers if it's too much." Angie opened the back door of her car and heaved up another large plastic container and a bag of pistolettes.

"Never too much gumbo." The aroma of the bread and spices swirled in another gust of wind, and Josh breathed in the succulence. If this didn't make Maggie feel better for a second, nothing would. "How's Cammie?"

Angie's lips twisted and twitched. "I'm not going to lie. It's serious. Pneumonia in her already precarious position is dangerous."

Suddenly not hungry, Josh mashed his eyes closed. "I don't even know what to do."

"Pray. Be supportive. Listen when they want to talk." She stepped closer and nudged him with her elbow. "Being here helps."

"I'm not so sure. My presence keeps splitting open old scars."

"It can't be that bad having an extra set of hands to help."

But he had an extra little one to watch. "I—"

"Hey, Daddy!" J.D. clung to Maggie's hip outside his front door, where she stared up at the sky, likely assessing the atmospheric conditions.

"Hey, mate! We're gonna eat good tonight." He raised his brows and shot a smile at his son. "Mr. Graham's gumbo."

"Is it spicy?"

Chuckling, Josh nodded. "Oh, yeah." He sobered when another burst of wind blasted past. "Maggie, don't you think you two can come back over to Ruth's? We've been on the antibiotics twenty-four hours already. I'd feel better if we were all under one roof tonight."

Her dark eyes scanned the horizon. "I just hope we have a roof."

~~~

The hot, spicy liquid of the gumbo warmed Maggie from the inside out but did little to calm the flutter of her heart. The wind thrashed small branches against the roof. Or maybe it was hail. Josh had insisted they come over, but she and J.D. were staying back in the bedroom. While J.D. worked on a puzzle on the floor beside her, she refreshed her computer screen over and over in some vain hope of staying in control of the situation. They'd been blessed to have dryer, cooler temperatures move in, along with a good bit of wind shear.

The combination was breaking the storm apart, but still, they were in for high winds, possible tornadoes, flooding. And who knew about the storm surge?

After an hour or so of games and more puzzles, J.D.'s eyes grew heavy. Unfortunately, the clatter outside wasn't conducive to sleeping. At least not for her. The child wobbled up and climbed on the bed. "Can you read me a story now?"

How blissful it must be to sleep in the midst of a storm.

Like Jesus had. *Oh, ye of little faith.*

The verses about Jesus calming the storm popped front and center in her mind.

"Lord, I know you can…but will you? Please?"

"Miss Maggie, we can say our prayers together." The sweetness in J.D.'s voice curled around her heart, calming the wild beating a bit. Had the wind actually quieted, too?

"Okay, pumpkin." She stood, crept onto the covers, and snuggled close to him, sweeping his hair from his forehead. "You want to say something to God?"

"Uh huh." Eyes closed, he bobbed his head. "Dear God, thank you for Miss Maggie coming to take care of me. Thank you for her curly hair. Thank you for her calling me pumpkin."

Tears pressed hot behind Maggie's eyes.

"Thank you for the roof still being on our house."

She never should've made that stupid comment earlier. Boy, she needed to be more careful.

"Thank you for spicy gumbo when I'm sick. Thank you for Dahlia and Aunt Ruth and Daddy being well. Please, help Miss Cammie get well. Keep all the animals safe in the storm. And the people."

From the mouth of babes.

"Amen." He rolled to his side and let out a long breath. "Oh, and could I have a puppy, God?"

Aww, she wished he could. Maggie pressed a kiss on his forehead. "Do you want me to pray, too?"

"If I forgot something."

He'd covered the bulk of it, so she sat quietly beside him, debating whether she could sleep at all tonight. Oh, to have the trust of a child.

Maybe she'd tiptoe to the kitchen for some hot tea. Cammie kept chamomile in the canister beside the coffee. It was supposed to be calming. What she really needed might be a sedative. But J.D.'s prayer had been soothing.

As she crept down the hall, light shone on Josh and Dahlia's faces from the TV in the den. She waved as she passed and kept going. The germ-thing still worried her. When she turned the corner, Aunt Ruth stood inches away, drinking her own cup of hot tea.

"We had the same idea." Maggie neared and grabbed a mug from the cabinet.

"Heavens." Her great aunt dribbled tea and wiped her mouth. "You scared me again."

"Sorry." That hearing-aid appointment would need to be soon.

"No apologies needed, child." Aunt Ruth handed her a tea bag. "You're likely terrified of this storm. Are you making it?"

"Yes, ma'am." What else could she do *but* make it? Although curling into the fetal position had crossed her mind a couple of times. "How do you handle life so well?"

"In the eye of the storm, He is my anchor."

"Yeah, but sometimes ships sink. People die."

"In the Bible, Job said, 'Though He slay me, yet I will trust Him.' Shadrach, Meshach and Abednego facing a fiery furnace said that the God they served could save them, but *even if He didn't*, they would not serve another god. When Wilbourn and

I married, we wanted a big family. We prayed earnestly for children. Time after time, I miscarried. It was hard. Then he got sick, so young, too. I became a widow."

"I'm really sorry." How did she not know about her aunt's life?

"I had to wake up every day and decide whom I would serve. Did I trust that the Lord loved me and had a plan for me? Your mother and father always treated me so well. And there was you and Cammie. I loved babysitting you girls, watching you grow up. Then more storms hit this fallen world we live in. I needed you girls, and you needed me. Turns out God gave me the children I'd asked for."

"I'm glad you're a part of our lives."

"Me, too." Her aunt cocked her head and gave Maggie a pointed look. "But there's more you want to question, right?"

How wise the elderly could be. "Where was God in Katrina? Why would he allow that kind of devastation to our homes, our lives?"

"This is only our temporary home. And God was here during that storm. I saw Him in the faces of the volunteers from all over the country who removed debris and hung sheetrock. I felt Him in the hugs and prayers of strangers. He fed us through the churches that set up food tents for months on months as the Coast began to rebuild."

The realization and truth in Aunt Ruth's words struck hard, bringing the sting of tears. Her aunt was right. The Lord had shown up in big ways after the storm. He had been relentless showing His love in small ways, too. A policeman had found the Bible she'd received at her baptism, virtually intact, and returned it to her. A friend whose house had miraculously come out unscathed shared clothes with them. So many other memories of small miracles came to mind.

193

God was here now with a bowl of soup from friends. He'd provided her with this sweet aunt who'd always been there for her. And He'd shown up in the prayers of a little boy.

Now she just had to trust like those believers of old. *Though He slay me...* Could she ever have that much faith?

Chapter 22

Dahlia's TV show finished, and she left Josh alone in the living room. He closed the laptop where he'd been continuing his fruitless search for a nanny, and stood. He wouldn't leave J.D. with just anyone. That's why the arrangement with Cammie had been so perfect. Pacing now, he tried to squelch the urge to find out what Maggie was doing in the kitchen. She'd been in there a long time. He lingered near the archway and strained to hear the voices of her and Ruth, to no avail. The television still droned on, but cutting it off would be too obvious.

"What are you doing?" Maggie's voice nailed him as she plodded around the corner. "Eavesdropping?" Her fingers wrapped a mug of something steamy, and her eyes looked like wet glass, as if she'd been crying.

He couldn't cut and run. Being honest might buy some favor. "I tried to hear y'all, but the TV was too loud." He gave her his best pouty look.

Shaking her head of curls, a small smile lifted one side of her lips. "You."

"Yep. Me." He grinned at her, relieved that he'd skirted a possible battle. "Can we sit and talk a while?"

Her eyes narrowed.

"I mean, we're going to be hunkered down for the night. I'll stay up to monitor the weather. The outer bands are starting to come through, so it'll be a long one."

Features softening, she gave a tiny nod. "You're going to keep watch for us?"

"Of course. You need rest to get well. My phone is charged, and I have all the weather sites saved. We have batteries for the radios and everything we need."

Relief seemed to flow over her. She sank down onto the couch and set her mug on the coffee table. "Thank you."

He took cautious steps to the other end and sat.

"What did you want to talk about?" Her fingers massaged circles on her forehead and temples.

His mind scrambled. What did he want to say? He'd simply wanted to be near her…to know what she was thinking, but that wouldn't fly. "How are you holding up?"

Her eyelids closed and slowly opened. "Only tired, mostly."

"You don't have to sleep with J.D., you know. He'll be fine on a pallet."

"It's not him that keeps me awake. It's my wretched nighttime cough. As soon as I lay down—"

The howl of the wind outside curtailed her words. Her shoulders hunched forward, and she hugged herself as the whistle and moan of the gale continued. She was like a clam in a shell, quickly closing at the first sign of danger. Closing tight and wanting to shut the world out, him included.

Josh's midsection tensed. He'd heard gales much noisier, but seeing the fear oozing from her every pore broke his heart. If only he could hold her, but that wasn't going to happen. "Can I…help somehow? Tell you a story, be quiet, something in between?"

She sucked in a breath. "I'll make it. Katrina was a lot worse."

"Want to talk about it?"

Her gaze stared at a distant place he couldn't see. A place he should've been.

"It was so quiet beforehand. The birds and insects seemed to know more of what was coming than the meteorologists." The tendons of her slender throat worked hard to swallow. "Then the wind screamed, and the booms began—one earth-shattering crash after another as trees fell and shook the hotel we were staying in. The carnage went on for hours, and we had no power, no phone, nothing."

"That had to be horrifying."

"It was, but opening the door when the storm finally ended was worse. I'd say the Coast looked like a war zone, but that would be an understatement. It was more like Armageddon—landmarks obliterated, no street signs left anywhere. We didn't know where anything was, not that we could get far. The ground was piled with layers of peeled shingles, leaves, and debris. Trucks and trains lay mangled and out of place, propelled for miles by the tremendous storm surge. I can't begin to make anyone understand who didn't see it firsthand, and most of the coverage had shifted to New Orleans when their levee broke. We felt forgotten here." She cradled her face in her palms.

Josh scooted closer and placed a hand on her knee. She'd felt forgotten by the world and by him. "I'm sorry." He'd say it a thousand times if he thought it would make her feel better.

She didn't move away or cringe at his touch. A good sign.

"Finally, the drone of helicopters, chainsaws, and generators began. An endless parade of dump trucks hauled away the mangled remains of everyone's lives. Search lights scanned for the injured. We were lucky our hotel didn't crumble and the surge hadn't reached us. Others lived in tents and cars, scavenging for food. Someone delivered MREs, and people were so thankful."

"You know it's bad when those taste good."

She paused and stared at him. "Life was more than bad. It was surreal. Terrifying. We didn't have any way to find out where anyone was…our friends and neighbors…we didn't know who had left, who had stayed, or what happened to them for months. And my father. We couldn't—"

His phone rang, interrupting at the worst possible moment. He kept eye contact with her, ignoring the wretched sound. "I'm not answering." He pressed the button to end the call.

Her gaze fell. "You know the rest. He was never found."

The ringing began again. *Shoot. Not now.*

"Go ahead and answer it."

Josh knew the ring belonged to his boss. Sighing, he answered. "What's up?"

"Need our best pilot for a rescue."

Maggie stared at him as if everything between them hinged on this phone call. And maybe it did.

Guilt weighed him down. Answering yes would kill any leeway he'd made with her, plus Maggie really needed him. Answering no left some poor souls in a dangerous situation.

But he wasn't the only pilot in the world. Someone else would have to step up. Maggie needed him, and he couldn't let her down again.

"Josh? You there?" His boss's voice boomed through the connection.

"You'll have to get someone else."

"Not everyone has your skills."

"What kind of vessel?"

"A small cargo ship."

That type of ship meant less passengers. "Sorry. I really can't go out this time."

"Got it." The call ended.

Maggie stood and gave him a stare that scorched his soul. "This time. But next time there's a terrible storm, you'll go, right?"

"Maggie…"

He thought she'd be happy with his decision.

"I'm going to lie down with your son and try to get some sleep."

As he watched her disappear into the darkness of the hallway, a cold weight pressed his chest. Maybe there was no way he could ever make Magnolia Marovich happy.

~~~

Outside, the winds moaned and whistled while rain pelted the old roof. Maggie's heart raced in her chest and ears, rivaling the rattle of the constant thunder against the windows. She curled around the extra pillow on the queen bed and squeezed her eyes shut.

She'd given up watching the weather over an hour ago. There was nothing to be done now but wait. The governor had declared a state of emergency and a mandatory curfew, citing the possibility of tornadoes and flash flooding. Of course, her cough had finally stopped, but now she couldn't sleep for the fear gnawing at her nerves. Getting up wasn't an option. She wouldn't leave J.D. alone for a second. Plus Josh was sitting up in the living room. At least he said he would be.

Trusting him to watch out for them came harder than she'd thought it would. She couldn't help but remember her father's memorial. Sitting on that stiff bench beside her weeping mother, believing that Josh would find a way to come to them from New York. He was just late. Maybe a plane delay…car trouble.

A fool's dream.

The phone call Josh had received during the storm had

been another too painful reminder of the hazards of his profession.

He'd made his choice years ago. Though he didn't go out tonight, it was probably only to prove a point. There would come a time when he'd choose the water over her.

A small, warm body rolled over and scooted close to Maggie's side. The toasty snuggle from J.D. melted away some of the churning emotions. Somehow, the child soothed her like not much else could. She took a deep, cleansing breath.

God, I may not trust a man, but I want to trust You to take care of us. I want to trust like this little child.

~~~

"Miss Maggie?" Fingers pulled open the lid of her left eye. "Are you awake?"

J.D.'s adorable face stared at her from about two inches away.

"I am now." She couldn't help but grin. "Good morning, pumpkin."

"Good morning. Are you making pancakes?"

A laugh rumbled through her chest, forcing out a little cough. What time was it? She reached one arm toward the nightstand for her phone. "Ten o'clock? Good grief, we slept late." She scanned the ceiling for water damage. "The house is still standing. That's a good sign. Maybe I can make breakfast, then." Her head finally felt clear of the crud, and she breathed easy.

If she had no fever, she could see Cammie today. And Josh could go back to his own house. It would be so much easier on all of them.

"Where's the house standing?" Wide-eyed, J.D. looked around.

"Oh, the same place. Miss Maggie was being silly." When

was she going to learn to be careful what she said around children? She didn't want to scar J.D. and Dahlia for life. "Let's get our thermometers and see how we're doing." Josh had a special toddler gadget—a gift from his mother—so they hadn't had to worry about cross-contamination.

Sitting up straight, J.D. cocked his head over and tugged on his ear to open it wide.

"You are good at that, but I don't think you have to pull that hard." Another chuckle slipped from her lips. "Just a second." She opened the drawer to the nightstand, grabbed the thermometer, and covered the probe with a lens filter. "Here it comes." Gently, she placed the device inside the canal and pressed the button. A chirp sounded, and she removed it to check the reading. "Normal. Yay."

"Now it's your turn."

"Yep." She traded for the cheap oral thermometer she'd found in Cammie's bathroom and stuck it under her tongue. While she waited for the beep, those big blue eyes stared at her, melting more of her heart.

The beep signaled her to remove the instrument. "No fever for me either, and I feel good." Except for how her stomach ached after she took the awful antibiotic. They'd need more yogurt when they went back out. One could never have too much yogurt. That was her theory, anyway. "Let's go to the kitchen."

"Okay." He slid down and waited for her.

A strand of blond hair stuck up near the crown of his head, and she smoothed it down before taking a step into the hallway.

Aunt Ruth met her in the hall. "There's the sleepy-heads. Glad y'all got some sleep."

"Yeah. Sorry."

201

"Now, don't apologize. We all need a Sabbath rest, and it doesn't always happen on the weekend."

"True." But resting with all they had going on seemed like too much of a luxury.

"Josh made pancakes earlier and left some in the microwave for you." Aunt Ruth motioned toward the kitchen.

That had been a little bit sweet. J.D. was expecting shapes, though. "Is he in there?"

"He and Dahlia are outside gathering limbs into a pile. I don't know how he's still going. He stayed up all night. I checked on him a few times, but he said he was fine."

"I'm fever-free now, so he can go back to his place and sleep."

Her aunt leveled a stare at her above her reading glasses. "What's the rush?"

"I'm just saying he can sleep in his own bed." A cup of coffee would be nice before she continued this line of conversation. "J.D.'s hungry, so I'll get him fed." With that, she continued past her aunt and down the hall.

In the kitchen, the aroma of good coffee delighted her nose. A pot steamed on the counter as if someone had just made a fresh one. She soaked in the blessed savory smell. If she were honest, she could get used to having someone getting coffee ready for her in the morning. But… "I'm going to pour a cup of coffee real quick." Her fingers grasped a mug, and she filled it with the warm liquid. One sip, and she would take care of the boy's plate.

"Can I have some?" He smiled up at her.

"Not until you're twenty-one."

His cheeks dropped, taking her heart with them. How did parents say no to such cute faces?

"It's not good for growing boys, and I know you want to

be big and strong. Let's get the pancakes Daddy made and some milk."

"Will that make me strong like Daddy, so I can steer a boat?"

"I think so." And it crushed her to imagine that scenario.

"Okay." He ran to a chair where Josh had attached a booster seat and started climbing.

That didn't look safe. "Wait. I'll help."

"I can do it myself." He kept scrambling.

Tendrils of anxiety tightened around Maggie's chest. "I don't want you to fall." Maybe if she spotted him. She placed her hands behind him without touching. "Does your father help you?"

"I do it myself."

Finally, he reached the seat, and she grabbed the straps. "Let me buckle this."

"I can do it—"

"Yourself. I know. But I'm doing it so I can hurry to get your pancakes. Yum. Yum." She pushed the lock together. "Phew." Coffee would have to wait until she got him settled.

She wiped perspiration from her forehead. At the microwave, she pulled the handle. What met her there took her breath away as though she were flailing on rough surf.

All the pancakes were in the shape of hearts.

~ ~ ~

Perspiration clung to Josh's brow despite the fact that the temperature had dropped significantly after the storm and most of his body was soaking wet from the continued showers. He wiped his feet before heading inside to clean up. The dozens of limbs and hundreds of sticks had been piled high near the end of the drive and away from the drainage ditches. Keeping the culverts cleared of debris was critical to keeping the yards free from flooding, though, so he'd done the best he could, worked until he'd run out of daylight. Dahlia had been sweet to come out in her galoshes to help.

Maggie, on the other hand, had avoided him all day, despite the fact that she'd declared both herself and J.D. fever free. Not that he wanted her to come out in the wet weather, but whenever he'd come in for lunch or a snack, she'd completely ignored him. She and J.D. sat on the floor of his son's bedroom.

"I'm back inside, going to take a shower," he called from the hall.

"I texted the doctor," Maggie answered, her back to him. "He said I can visit tonight, so I'm going home to change." She gave J.D. a hug and marched to the door of the bedroom. "Bye, pumpkin."

"Is the curfew lifted?" His brows knit together. It still seemed too soon for her to be out.

"They still say no nonessential travel, but this is essential."

"What about the flash flooding?"

"I know the roads, and I checked with the highway department."

Her mind was set. Nothing would keep Maggie away from her sister any longer. "Tell her I said hi, and I'm praying for her."

No response, no eye contact.

She practically clung to the other side of the wall when she skirted past him. Probably because of the stupid breakfast he'd made.

The pancake idea had become another blundering debacle on his part. Obviously, J.D. had eaten his fill, but he doubted Maggie had eaten a bite. A slew of pancakes had still stood stacked on the plate covered by foil next to the sink at Ruth's when he'd made lunch for Dahlia. He'd started to throw the stupid things in the trash, but being a single parent, prudence stopped him. Instead, he found a plastic storage bag and salvaged them. They saved pretty well in the refrigerator.

He had no inkling of what to do about him and Maggie.

After his shower, he baked a frozen pizza. He'd left the gumbo and soup leftovers next door, so this would have to do. He fed J.D. and bathed him, then wrapped him in a towel and marched down the hall. When he set J.D. on his feet, he tousled his son's hair. "Let's get your PJs on, buddy."

"Is Miss Maggie going to read me a story?"

"Daddy's reading tonight." Josh opened the drawer and fished out the latest favorite pajamas.

Face scrunched, J.D.'s lip poked out. "I want Maggie to read."

Josh's stomach took a plunge.

Poking his lips out, Josh pretended to cry and rubbed his eyes. "You hurt my feelings." Then he lifted his head and grinned. This tactic worked on occasion, though he tried not to use it often. Tonight he was a bit desperate. "I've missed my sailor."

A smile returned to lift J.D.'s cheeks. "Okay. You read, Daddy."

Josh dressed him and read until J.D. fell asleep, relishing every moment. Too soon it would be time to go out on the boat, and they'd lost a few nights of their precious time together. The thought reminded him he needed to make a plan. He stalked to the living room to grab his computer and return to his bedroom. He had to know within a week who would care for his son.

The bed had been made with fresh sheets. His heart both raced and broke as he imagined Maggie sleeping here. He ran his fingers across the comforter, and he sucked in a deep breath, hoping to find a hint of sweet perfume lingering.

It was missing. Gone. Like she would be soon enough.

Regret swarmed over him. Life was so messy in the first place, but he seemed to keep making his into a landfill. He opened the computer and waited for it to boot. The file with a list of babysitter and nanny recommendations was still in his documents. He'd email his real estate agent about finding a house and then set up appointments for nanny interviews starting Monday.

His phone vibrated with a call. The number wasn't in his contacts, but it could be important. "Hello."

"Joshua, this is Sylvia Daigle. Ruth gave me your number. She said Maggie had gone to the hospital."

"Yes, ma'am. The soup you brought was delicious. Thank you."

"Oh, good. I was glad to help. My grandmother swore by that recipe. Said it would cure most ailments. It's a special recipe."

"Everyone seems to be feeling better." He waited for the purpose of the call, if there was one.

"Before I forget, what time do I need to be at the store on Friday for the sale? I've cleared my schedule after Thanksgiving, and I'm ready to work for as long as Cammie needs me. Or Maggie, I should say."

What time would they open? Some stores had early hours for Black Friday. "We haven't discussed it. I wonder what the other businesses on the street have planned. Cammie would probably follow their lead."

"I'll look at the ads and send you a text. Oh, and will there be refreshments? Most of the stores on the street will offer them for shoppers."

"No clue. I—"

"Don't worry about a thing. I know the wife of the owner of the bakery across the street from the shop. I'll call her and set something up. It'll be fine. You take care of that precious little boy, and I'll take care of everything."

"Thanks."

They ended the call, and he tossed the phone on the nightstand. Maggie had some good help now. She might not need him at all.

~~~

"We're here." Maggie parked in the hospital lot, white-knuckling the steering wheel before exiting. She'd barely slept the night before, and today she was apprehensively making good on her promise to bring Dahlia and Aunt Ruth for the Thanksgiving lunch and a visit. The sight of Cammie so weak the night before had left Maggie's fragile faith in tatters again. The oxygen mask wrapped around her sister's face, her pale complexion. As if Cammie hadn't looked bad enough before the pneumonia.

"I can't wait to see Mama." Dahlia's sweet face looked hopeful, despite the heart-to-heart they'd had before leaving the house. The ten-year-old had taken the news hard when she and her aunt had explained Cammie's condition more fully.

Maggie bit her tongue. She wouldn't dampen her niece's hope, but she continued a somber trek inside the building.

Lord, I could use some help with Dahlia today.

At least, J.D.'s prayers had been answered about the storm. The hurricane had weakened to a tropical storm, only flash flooding near drainage ditches and branches covering the ground. Things could've been so much worse.

Maggie clasped Dahlia's hand as they entered the ICU. Dr. Castro led them back with his usual warmth, encouraging

Dahlia not to worry. But from the looks of it, the man hadn't slept since Cammie'd arrived.

As they entered through the glass door, Cammie smiled. The oxygen mask had been removed, and Cammie held out one arm to her daughter. "Come give me a hug."

Hesitant, Dahlia approached slowly. "I don't want to hurt you."

"Pull up a chair and hold my hand if you feel more comfortable."

Once Dahlia sat, Cammie directed her gaze to Maggie. "Can you give us some time alone?"

"I'll be in the waiting area." Should she have that mask off? Had she removed it to make Dahlia more at ease?

Back in the very-familiar lounge, a few families huddled in various corners. The Thanksgiving Day parade captured Aunt Ruth's attention. She smiled when she noticed Maggie taking a seat beside her. "How's our girl?"

"She wanted to talk to Dahlia alone."

"Needed to be done. Sweet Dahlia."

"Yeah." How hard would that conversation be? The situation was difficult enough on the adults. Kids shouldn't have to go through tough times like these. Maggie's mind traveled to J.D. How had Josh explained when the adorable child's mother had left them? The child had to have asked for his mother. It must've been heartrending for Josh.

As if summoned, the man appeared with his son wrapped in his arms.

"Miss Maggie!" Struggling to get down, a sweet smile lit up J.D.'s face. Once free from his father's arms, he ran to her, stopping at her knees. "Where's the turkey?"

Josh didn't look her way but stood just inside the doorway, his attention focused on the giant floating bird on the TV screen.

"Well, happy Thanksgiving to you, too." Rumpling J.D.'s hair, she flashed a smile. "The food will be here soon." She hoped, for all their sakes, since they had nothing else prepared. The savory aroma drifting through the hospital seemed promising, though. Much better than the normal smells here.

J.D. scrambled onto her lap and curled a strand of her hair around one of his fingers. He had her heart wrapped in a similar fashion. Only with a tighter grip. "What are we gonna do while we wait? Go to the store?"

Of course, he remembered her buying things to occupy him from the gift shop last time he was here. "It's closed for the holiday. Sorry." She motioned toward the TV. "There's a parade on. They have a ton of really neat floats people make with lots of huge balloons."

He focused his attention on the screen. "Is that Snoopy?"

"It is."

"Wow." Entranced, he slipped from her lap and walked closer to the TV.

Would Josh get annoyed that she'd started the preoccupation with the show? She had no idea whether he limited television watching or allowed the indulgence, but the distraction worked at the moment.

"Josh." Aunt Ruth's voice wobbled. "Don't stand there like a stranger. Come sit down and join us."

Blast it, if her aunt wasn't going to start the matchmaking again.

The door swung open to the waiting area, and Dahlia ran out, tears streaming down her face.

Josh stepped toward her, and Dahlia went to him and threw her arms around his waist. Her petite shoulders shook. Poor baby.

Maggie rose, but Josh caught her gaze and shook his head. "I'm going to take Dahlia for a walk. You got J.D.?"

"Sure." Dahlia had run to Josh instead of her or Aunt Ruth. Maggie glanced at J.D., still staring at the parade. He'd taken to her, too, though, even saying he loved her. The children seemed to look for a piece that was missing from their lives that they craved. J.D., a mother, and Dahlia, a father.

And where Josh could never force her to unlock the bars around her heart, J.D. had barreled through. Barreled through and latched on as much as if she'd given birth to the child.

As she sat staring at the beauty that was J.D., the realization dawned. Even though she craved a father to replace the one she lost, she hadn't allowed God to fill that void. Though she'd served God, she'd not trusted and really loved Him as she should have since her father died. She'd become even more distant from God after the loss of her mother. If someone else she loved died, would she lose her faith as well? Another painful lash, and she might close the door forever.

But yet, here she was. Cammie injured, Dahlia hurting, Josh lonely, and a little boy needing her as a mother. A scripture sprang to her mind.

In this world you will have trouble. But take heart. I have overcome the world.

Take heart. The words her mother had said. The truth stared her in the face. Take heart. Not hide heart. Was that what she was supposed to do now?

Take heart.

A rolling cart rumbled through the door, and two ladies dressed in white unloaded trays.

"Can I help?" Maggie rose and made her way over. "Or I can move and let you do your thing. Your call."

"You jump on in with both feet. The water's fine." One of

the cafeteria workers grinned, revealing a gold tooth with a heart in the middle.

Good one, Lord. Stifling a chuckle, Maggie pitched in as every few moments, more deliveries arrived. It was a feast to be thankful for.

~ ~ ~

Was he being selfish with his career choice? Holding Dahlia's hand, Josh walked back toward the ICU waiting area. He'd been able to comfort her a bit and pray with her. But she needed a parent. Needed her mother to get well. Needed a father. Family needed each other to be there.

Maybe that was why Trisha had left him. His weeks away on the boat.

No. Trisha left J.D., too. His ex-wife had deep issues. But still. He'd never considered giving up piloting. Until all this. Between going over a list of childcare workers and scouring the internet for a new place to live, the thought had crossed his mind. Maybe he could teach at one of the piloting schools. He could work tugs in Gulfport. He'd still work some nights, but he wouldn't be out for two weeks.

Back in the waiting area, the aroma of turkey, dressing, and trimmings seemed to perk Dahlia up. She released his hand in favor of admiring the dessert table. If only food could lift his spirits that way.

Medical staff and a few other tired-looking families milled around.

"If everyone would gather in a circle and take hands, we'll say a prayer and get started with the feast." A man with a cleric collar stood, arms stretched. "If you have a specific prayer request, speak up."

For a moment no one spoke, and an uncomfortable silence descended.

"I do." Maggie's voice was soft, and the dark circles under her eyes pricked Josh's conscience. He'd added to her burdens by being here. "I'd like you to pray that my sister, Cammie, regains use of her legs and that the pneumonia is healed."

The priest nodded. "Indeed, I will."

Emboldened by Maggie, others added their concerns, a few even more tragic than those of the Maroviches'.

Sniffles travelled the room as the prayer ended. This would be a tough holiday for many families.

Dahlia reappeared at his side. "Want to go through the line with me? Looks like J.D.'s going with Aunt Maggie."

"Sure. I'm with you, kid." He gave her a smile and tweaked her nose.

A young doctor stood with a girl Dahlia's age near the table. The dark-haired man turned to face them. "Dahlia, I'd like you to meet my daughter, Anna."

The girls exchanged shy smiles and hellos.

"Anna's in fifth grade. I thought you might like someone to talk to other than us old folks."

A slight interest lifted Dahlia's gaze. "I'm in fifth grade, too."

"Where do you go to school?" Anna asked.

The girls began chattering, so Josh turned his attention to Maggie. His son hung from her hip, talking nonstop, and she somehow filled plates for the two of them. Women were naturals at multitasking. Like they had two brains and octopus arms.

"I'm Dr. Castro." The doctor extended his hand.

"Josh Bergeron." Josh gave him a firm shake.

"Josh, are you related to Cammie?" Dr. Castro's focus was intense.

"A longtime friend of the family, and Cammie babysits my

son while I'm working. Well, she did."

"Ah." Something akin to relief lifted the doctor's lips into a smile. "Single parent?"

Quick deduction. Josh nodded. "Part of the club."

"Me too. I get it. What do you do for a living?"

The question he normally loved answering. But at this moment... "I'm a ship pilot."

"Fascinating career and a hard one to break into. What's it like out there on the water every day?"

That peaceful feeling he always got when he visualized his boat washed over him, the sea, the sky, the wind on his face. "Some days and nights it's so beautiful I can't believe I get paid to do what I do. Out on the Gulf, dolphins play in the ship's wake. So much wildlife—sea turtles, huge jumping manta rays, sea birds like pelicans, gulls, osprey. I've seen unbelievable meteor showers and full moons. All types of interesting vessels, including the most modern passenger ships, vehicle carriers, and warships. I've piloted sailing ships and ships that can submerge themselves to carry other ships or oil platforms aboard for transit. I meet people from all over the world."

"Sounds amazing." Dr. Castro bobbed his head. "There's got to be a downside. I mean, I love what I do. The human body itself is a miracle, and trying to save people or help them walk again, it's certainly fulfilling. But..." He glanced at Dahlia and Anna. "Some days tear my heart out."

Josh's stomach took a dive. Yes, he understood what the doctor was saying. As wonderful as the job was, there was an ugly side to the sea at times. The part that Maggie hated. "Yeah. I've searched for bodies from sunken vessels. Been in fog where I couldn't see my hands in front of me and storms so rough, I thought there was no pay worth being out there. A bad day at my office could end up on the news."

"Sounds akin to what it's like for me, but on a grander scale."

"Luckily, I haven't had a bad day like that. Let me rephrase that. Thank God I haven't had a day like that."

Sadness lined the doctor's face, aging him. "Happens all too often here."

Worry for Maggie and her family took hold in Josh's chest, and he pivoted to look for them. Dark eyes met his as Maggie stood only a foot away. When had she walked up? A pained expression tensed her lips. Had she been listening to their conversation? She'd never wanted to be around him in the first place, much less hear about piloting. Everything he did seemed to make life worse for her.

"J.D. needs a bathroom, and I didn't know if you wanted to or I…"

"Got it. Thanks." He searched her face for some clue as to what she'd heard and what she was thinking.

"Daddy, I hafta go."

"Okay, son." He took J.D. from her arms, never breaking from her gaze.

As soon as they finished with the luncheon, he'd pack their things, and they'd get out of Maggie's way. Somehow he'd find a new place to live and someone to watch J.D. He'd caused Maggie enough pain for a lifetime.

Chapter 23

Hearing Josh describe his job to Dr. Castro—the look on his face, the passion in his voice, the picture he created—cut a gash in Maggie's heart. She'd listened to the same sorts of stories from her father. As if the Gulf was in their blood, as if life was monotonous without at least half of their days spent on the sea. Maggie understood. She'd loved the water, too.

Before.

The feel of the hot sand shifting under her feet, the wind whipping her hair when they sailed out to the barrier islands. Josh's tanned arms around her.

No. She had to stop this train of thought or the emotion clogging her throat would engulf her.

Sure, a part of her missed those days in the sun… understood her father and Josh's love of the Gulf. But the other part couldn't forget the sheer devastation of the storm surge that had ripped through their town then carried homes and lives back out to sea. The wreckage, the chaos…the funerals. She hadn't been the only one to give up on the area for good.

Josh emerged from the restroom with his son, and realization poured over her as she watched him give the boy an aye, aye, captain salute. The truth was that Josh would never be fulfilled if he gave up his career. Especially if he gave up piloting because someone, like her, badgered him into quitting. Her gaze traveled out the window to the skies, blue now. But only a couple of days ago, the gusting variable winds had made havoc with the branches of the nearby trees.

Another truth nagged Maggie. Dr. Castro had been so excited about the small bit of progress Cammie had made. This was going to be a *really long* recovery. A leave of absence from the Weather Service wasn't going to cut it. And Dahlia and Cammie and Aunt Ruth needed their friends and the church community to help them heal. Maggie's breath halted with the realization. If she truly loved them, she had to give up the safety of Jackson and come take care of them all.

Lord, please give us two miracles. No, three. Let Cammie walk, heal her from the pneumonia, and give me the courage to move back here. For Cammie, Dahlia, Aunt Ruth, and J.D. They need me. And we all need You. Amen.

Maggie inhaled deeply. She could do this. Refocusing on her food, she nibbled at the turkey and savory dressing. The caterers had done well. Better than she would have at home. She could never get the turkey quite right, not like her mother had. Once she'd eaten a bite of each menu item, she stacked Aunt Ruth and Dahlia's plates with her own and crossed the room toward the garbage can. She eyed Josh, who was slipping out the door with J.D. Why was he leaving without telling them? After tossing the plates, Maggie strode after him. He and J.D. were halfway down the hall.

"Where do you think you're going?" Her voice came out sharper than she'd intended, but the pounding in her chest made it harder to control her tone. What would make him sneak away without saying goodbye? Had something else terrible happened? The food roiled in her stomach.

The crinkles in his forehead showed his surprise and confusion. And a flash of something else seemed to touch his gaze but disappeared before she could identify it. Fear maybe, or remorse? "Thought I'd scoot out with J.D. and pack up…take him on a trip to get out of your hair."

"Pack up? Get out of my hair?" No. That little boy had ingrained so deeply in her heart and her head these past few days. "You're kidding, right?"

"This was a bad idea. I'm sorry I…never should've moved next door to—"

"Oh, no, you don't." Now he was giving up? Desperation turned to a simmering steam of anger boiling through her whole body, and Josh had popped the cork. "You're not jumping ship. If you try to skip town, you're gonna find the full-blown wrath of Magnolia Marovich after you like you've never experienced before." How dare the man think he could desert them? Again. And this time there was a little boy in the picture. She'd be blown away in a hurricane before she'd let this sweet, blue-eyed angel suffer the consequences.

J.D. tugged Josh's shirt. "Daddy, are you in trouble?"

"Looks that way, buddy." He sent a weak smile to his son before raising a probing gaze back to her. "What are you saying, Maggie?"

"I'm saying J.D. needs someone to take care of him when you're off being a pilot. Someone who loves him. I'll find a new position here, whatever it takes." She forced out a huff. "Since I know you'll never leave this place, and he needs me. My family needs me."

Josh's brows drew together while he let that sink in. "What you're suggesting… It's a big commitment. A child's heart can be fragile when someone doesn't follow through." His lips pulled downward and a shadow of angst touched his tone.

Maybe it was the pain in his voice, or maybe it was the words themselves that stilled her anger. But in the space of that moment, the intensity of love she'd developed for this little boy pressed hard against her chest. She softened her tone. "I

217

understand that."

"Plus, you wouldn't only be taking care of him." He pressed on, as if he hadn't already driven his point home. "You'd have a ten-year-old, an adult with a spinal injury, and an elderly woman to care for." He gave a small scoff. "Oh, and a store. That's more than a handful."

"You don't think I can manage?" She met his gaze, raising her brows. "And do you really believe I'd change my mind once it's made?"

"If anyone can manage, it's you." A chuckle slipped through his lips, but it held no joy. "And I know better than to try to change your mind." His eyes seemed to glaze, and he blinked, then met her gaze with a direct intensity. "But they're not the only ones who need someone to take care of them…to love them."

Her chest locked up as if she were swimming over a jagged and dangerous reef. What did she plan to do about Josh? She hadn't gotten that far, but a stark awareness clamored and gnawed on her nerves. She'd be forced to come to terms with her feelings for him at some point. But she couldn't go there now. Not with Cammie and everything else weighing on her mind. "You…I don't know about. Yet."

"Yet." Josh's lips lifted a fraction, and a touch of hope lit his eyes. "I can take a yet."

Unable to validate his optimism, she dropped her gaze and scooped J.D. into her arms, pressing her forehead to his. "Would you want me to babysit you when Daddy's gone piloting?"

"Yes, ma'am." He giggled when she rubbed his nose with her own.

"All right, then, pumpkin. It's a deal." She scraped a smudge of sweet potatoes from the front of his shirt and pivoted her head toward Josh. "Daddy needs to get some stain remover on this tonight. And see if Dahlia and Aunt Ruth want to ride home with you. I have to speak with the doctor, and I want to visit Cammie again."

Saluting, Josh gave her a flirty grin, locking eyes with her for one last weighty moment. "Aye, aye, captain."

He wasn't going to make this *yet* easy on her.

~~~

"Come to Daddy, sailor." Josh held his arms out for J.D. "Let's invite Dahlia and Ruth to ride with us."

His son held Maggie tighter.

Man, didn't he know that feeling. "Maggie's coming after she talks to the doctor. You need to mind me now."

J.D.'s mouth twisted as he complied and switched his hold to Josh's shoulder. "Okay."

"That's not how we answer." Josh forced a stern look on his face, despite the way he wanted to smile at the connection developing between his son and Maggie.

"Yes, sir."

"Let's walk Maggie back in and get Ruth and Dahlia."

"Can Dahlia play with me?"

Josh lifted one shoulder. "That's up to her."

As they entered, the ten-year-old about ran over them. "Aunt Maggie, I've been invited to Anna's house with her and her grandmother. Can I go? Aunt Ruth said to ask you." Her expression was the brightest he'd seen all week.

Looked like J.D. was out of luck.

Maggie's brows lifted, and she seemed to contemplate the request. Her first of many decisions if she took all this on. "I need to talk to Anna's father and grandmother."

They walked as a group to the other side of the waiting room and approached the Castro family.

219

"Mrs. Castro?" Maggie placed a hand on Anna's grand-mother's elbow.

The woman had to be the doctor's mother. They looked so much alike, both with the dark hair and the exact same smile lines creasing their temples.

"Hi," Maggie continued, "Dahlia says she's been invited over?"

Mrs. Castro beamed. "We'd love to have her. The girls seem to have hit it off. I can drive her back this evening or she can spend the night."

"Will anyone else be at the house? Or just you and Anna?" Maggie twisted one of her many wayward curls around her index finger.

"Just us."

Both Dahlia and Anna stared at Maggie with pleading eyes.

"She can come for a while, but I'll pick her up myself. What's your address and phone number?" Once they'd exchanged information, she turned to the doctor. "I'd like to speak with you after they take off."

Josh had to smile. She'd done pretty well. Deciding who looked safe these days was no small feat. He'd love to be a fly on the wall when Maggie cross-examined Dr. Castro.

"So Dahlia can't play with me?" J.D. turned Josh's chin, forcing his attention to him.

"Nope. But Daddy can. You name it, and I'll play. Let's get Ruth, and we'll sail on out."

"Okay, but can Miss Maggie play, too, when she comes home?"

Those blue eyes had always tugged at Josh's being. Since the first day at the hospital. How Trisha could have left him, he'd never understand. But thank the good Lord, she hadn't taken their son with her.

"We'll see. Can't make any promises right now, though." His mind couldn't wrap around the fact that Maggie had really agreed to stay at the Coast. For good. He held in a sigh. For J.D. Not for him. The sooner he got that one straight, the better. But there was that *yet...* His heart wobbled at the possibility. This was gonna be agony.

Chapter 24

The families and medical personnel cleared out, and the culinary crew began to clean up. Maggie tried to collect her composure and sort through the heavy conversation with Josh.

"Can we talk?" Dr. Castro was at her side.

She hadn't noticed his approach, but maybe now was as good a time as any. "I wanted to speak with you, as well."

"Let's go to a meeting room where we can talk privately."

Fear spiked in Maggie's chest. "Has something happened to Cammie?"

"Oh, no. Sorry." He shook his head and lowered his voice. "It's of a personal nature."

Relief loosened her constricted muscles. Maggie matched his steps until they reached the end of the hall and entered a small room with a few chairs in a circle. She chose a seat near the door. "You first."

After a heavy breath, he sat a couple of seats away and rotated toward her. "This is awkward, and I apologize in advance. Are you a prayerful person?"

"Yes. Mostly." She tried anyway. Questions bounced around her mind, but she waited for him to continue.

"I am, too. And since the moment Cammie arrived, I've had the profound impression that I was meant to be a part of her life. It's bizarre. In all my years as a physician, nothing has ever happened to me like this."

A part of her life? "What exactly are you saying?"

"At first, I thought I was meant to save her and help her

walk again. Then Cammie and I talked, and there was this connection. After finding out we were both raising daughters the same age—alone—I figured friendship. When this is all over, of course. I wouldn't want to cause any appearance of a breach of ethics." He paused and fidgeted with his watch.

"But now?"

"I'd like to have another doctor take over her case."

A wave of anger crashed through her gut. This guy had a lot of nerve. "So you changed your mind and you're going to dump her on someone else because of some weird *impression* you had?"

"Oh, goodness, no." Twin lines formed between his brows. "Though it scares the life out of me, and I have no idea if she feels the same, I'd like to get to know her in a different way…if you know what I'm saying."

Whoa. *Huh.* Now she understood what he was saying. And he'd better not be some pervert. Maggie scrutinized the man. "You of all people know she might be permanently paralyzed."

"I do. And I'd love to tuck tail and run. But who better as a friend or partner than a man who's spent years studying the spinal cord?" He lifted one shoulder. "If she's even interested. Now isn't a time for her to make life-changing decisions, though. I'd keep our relationship in the friend zone. For as long as it takes."

A bit of the anger receded. "Who is this other doctor?"

"Dr. Lincoln. He's the best on the Coast. He's taking her on as a personal favor to me." His brows raised now, hopefulness covering his expression.

"I need to talk to Cammie. I have no idea what to say about y'all's business." She pinned him with her hardest gaze. "You know I'm doing a background check on you now?"

"I don't blame you." He dropped his head in his hands and

massaged his temples. "I'm sorry this is so unprofessional."

Having a doctor in the family could come in handy, though, with their history. She allowed a small chuckle. "Don't be so hard on yourself. I can't imagine there are many men who'd meet a woman who can't walk and has a kid and think, man, I want to ask her out."

He peeked over his hands at her. "Thanks for saying that."

"I still might be hiring a private detective to check you out."

"I would, too, in your shoes."

"Cammie didn't have her oxygen on when Dahlia came in. Is she better? She looked so weak last night."

"She was breathing easier this morning. I'll examine her latest stats and shoot you a text."

Maggie pushed to her feet, and the doctor followed.

"How long will you be able to stay down here, Maggie? What about your job?"

She felt her pocket for her phone. "I'm thinking I'll look for a job here after Cammie is released for rehab. If she…"

Dr. Castro stepped in front of her and leveled a warm gaze her way. "Cammie will get out of here, but her recovery might take a while. She's lucky to have you."

"You, too." Her mouth quirked as she turned away. "I think."

"Check me out all you want. I'll give you any information you ask for." His chuckle drifted behind her.

She would. And she wanted to see Cammie, but right now she'd call the office and update them on her situation, see who had drawn the short straw and had to work on the holiday. After pulling out her cell, she pressed the number and added the extension for the meteorologist in charge.

"National Weather Service, Steve."

Not him. Maggie groaned into the phone. Randy must be off. "It's me. I was looking for the boss."

"Hey, *you.* Great to hear your voice, Mags. Still at the Coast?"

No one called her Mags. "Yeah, and I only have a minute. Make that a second. I just wanted to speak to Randy."

"I know you were glad that hurricane downgraded to a tropical storm. I heard landfall centered on Bay St. Louis with torrential rainfall, five inches where you were, sustained winds of forty mph and gusts to fifty-five mph, but not as bad as it could've been. You still have a wet and soggy Black Friday forecast and the rest of the weekend."

That was more than a second. "Yeah." But a little rain never sounded so good.

"So when will we see your pretty face again?"

Never, if she could help it. She wasn't about to get into her personal life with him. "Gotta go, Steve." She cut the connection. The jerk hadn't even asked about her sister. She'd email her boss to let him know that she was moving down here. He probably wouldn't be in until Monday anyway. Maybe he knew of some employment options for her. Now, on to visit Cammie.

Through the glass door, Cammie smiled at Maggie's approach. "Guess what?"

Had the doctor already asked her out? "I don't know, but you look happy."

"I am. I don't need the oxygen mask today, and my leg itched a minute ago, and the nurse scratched it." Cammie's eyes sparkled waiting for a response.

"Okay." There had to be more than that.

"Don't you get it? I could *feel.* She poked around after that, and I felt it every time."

A swarm of relief drenched Maggie, like buckets of cool water on a sweltering day. "So what does that mean? Can you try to walk now?"

"The nurse paged Dr. Castro to tell him."

And the man appeared in the door, grinning. "I heard. This is fantastic news, Cammie. Recovery is more likely if movement or sensation starts to return soon after an injury."

"Isn't this wonderful." Cammie mirrored his grin, holding his gaze.

Maggie clapped her hands together. "Thank God. Three miracles in the works already."

"What were the other two?" Cammie turned her attention away from the doctor to Maggie.

"You're breathing well, and I'm staying here. For good. To take care of J.D. and whoever else—"

"You and Josh?" Cammie's brows shot up.

That *would be* her sister's first response. "Give the *me and Josh* obsession a rest. In fact, don't worry about anything but getting better."

"Okay, for now, but I want to know more. Soon. And please open the store tomorrow. And Saturday. Has it been busy so far?"

"It's been fine. I'll open your store. Rest now."

~~~

"Ruth, I was wondering about that big chest in the back of your store. The one with the box Maggie used to make J.D. that ship." Josh held the elderly woman's arm as he walked her across the rain-sodden driveway to her door.

"Big chest? You mean the armoire?"

"That's it. The piece is like the one Maggie had in her room growing up. She loved that thing. I'd like to buy it for her as a Christmas gift. Unless Cammie ordered it for someone else."

Mouth gaping, Ruth stopped and stared up at him. "Cammie bought that armoire from a dealer because of Maggie. She thought Maggie might want it. Maggie always loved the one she'd had and spoke of it often. Cammie just wasn't sure if Maggie would be happy or grieved with the find and the memories attached to it. The truck had just delivered it when Cammie was hit. I guess the driver miscalculated his turn and backed up to try again."

"Oh, man. I didn't realize." Strange how one moment could change the whole course of so many people's lives. "Do you think Maggie would want it if she knew?"

Ruth's wrinkled hand squeezed his. "Sometimes what we want and what we need are not the same thing."

A laugh worked its way through his soul. "Don't I know it."

"Maggie thinks memories are too painful, and she's locked them out. She's wrong. Pain is as much a part of this life as joy. Through pain, we learn to depend on the Lord."

He'd experienced that first hand. "You're a smart lady."

"There's a few marbles left up here." She winked and pointed to her silver-haired temple. "I'll give you the key to the store. You can get the armoire while Maggie's at the hospital, so you can surprise her. I'll tell her we sold it." She chuckled. "Which will be true, of course."

"I'll write you a check and call a buddy of mine to help get it loaded in the truck." From the looks of the gray sky, he'd better hurry.

"Leave J.D. with me. It won't take long, I bet."

Once he'd led Ruth and J.D. inside, he called around until he found a semi-willing volunteer only a few blocks away to meet him at the store. Together they made quick work of hauling the huge piece into his truck. The only problem was where to hide the armoire once they had it inside his house. With no better ideas flowing, he pushed it into the master bathroom and shut the door. He'd share the restroom in the hall with J.D. for a few weeks. They'd survive. He just hoped Ruth was right about the purchase. And the memories.

~~~

A large cold front kept the showers in a holding pattern. Maggie sank back into the pillows on the bed at Aunt Ruth's as rain pummeled the rooftop again. Standing all day and helping customers left Maggie's feet aching. She'd been accustomed to sitting at a desk, staring at computer screens. The wet weather lingered after the tropical storm with such a deluge that they'd had fewer shoppers this Black Friday than in past years, according to Aunt Ruth, but it was still busy enough. Thank goodness Mrs. Daigle had taken care of the Black Friday festivities at the store and was working full-time with them. Their mother's old friend had been a godsend.

With help over the last few days, Maggie'd had the freedom to go to the hospital as needed, even taking Dahlia every night. Both the old and new doctors looked to be legit, and Cammie was more than happy to be friends with Dr. Kyle Castro. Even their names sounded cute together. Cammie and Kyle. Maggie smiled and shook her head. Who would've thought her sister would meet Mr. Right by getting hit by a truck?

Maggie's phone chimed with a text.

J.D.'s asleep. Want to watch a movie?

She cradled her cell in her hands like a fragile bird. His offer was tempting. Could her own Mr. Right be next door? She'd always thought she'd prove everyone wrong when she left Josh and the Coast. She'd find love again. Move on. And she'd tried dating, but no one had measured up. No one had understood her like Josh.
~~~

No one had hurt her like Josh.

He'd found love and moved on. When the news came about his marriage, her heart died a second death. She'd secretly mourned for over a year. Wondered how he could've fallen for someone when she hadn't. Then insisted that no one update her about him or even speak of him. Her eyes stung at the memory.

Since their talk at the hospital, they'd shared meals, played games with the kids, and taken turns running household errands. As if they were a couple. Josh hadn't pressured her for more kisses.

Warring emotions tussled over that missing element. Was he giving her space? Or did avoiding kisses make it easier for him?

Because that one kiss haunted her day and night.

The phone sounded again.

I've got Elf or National Treasure.

That stinker. He'd picked two movies they'd first seen together, and he knew she'd loved them both back then. Still did.

Just like she still loved him.

The thought smacked her like a hard slap. She did love him. Of course. So how did that affect her answer now? Letting him back in her life in a romantic way would blast open the last bastion of this Pandora's Box, exposing her heart.

Her fingers hovered over the screen, at last pressing one letter before sending.

K

One letter. One letter that could shred her heart.

She slid off the bed and shoved her feet in her flip-flops.

When she passed the mirror on the dresser, she did a double take and groaned. "That will not do at all." Between the

229

humid air and wallowing on the pillows, her hair had formed a gigantic snarled beehive. She captured the disobedient mass and twisted until she had it tamed enough to fit in a clip.

Mashing her dry lips together, she grabbed a lip gloss and spread a shiny layer around. No sense looking totally gross. Mouthwash might help, too.

A few minutes and a tooth-brushing later, she sucked in a minty breath and ran across the sloshing yard, up the steps and onto Josh's porch. She tapped lightly on the door. She didn't want to wake J.D.

The precipitation had slacked enough for her not to be totally drenched, but her flip-flops and feet dripped from splashing through a puddle or two. She lifted each foot and shook it, as if that would help. What was taking Josh so long? Should she go on in? She stared at the rain flowing through the yards and streets. The scarred live oaks stood tall and strong, bearing the storm well enough despite their wounds. Much better than her scarred heart, which seemed to be beating out of her chest at the thought of simply watching an old movie with Josh Bergeron.

~~~

How hard was it to open a door? Josh steadied his shaking hands near the knob.

Just watching a movie with Maggie Marovich. No big deal.

But he still couldn't believe she'd said yes. Well, in not so many letters, but it was a start. He glanced around once more to make sure everything looked clean enough. Not perfect, but he'd hustled to sweep and dust the living room before he'd sent the text. Then he'd made popcorn. He reached for the knob.

Lord, help me to...just help me, please.

He opened the door to find Maggie staring up at the rain and the trees. The sight of her profile outlined against the downpour unlocked pain and hope and memories, punctuated by the scent of the salty Gulf air. "Hey, there."

The muscles in her strong, beautiful jaw ticked before she turned and offered a hesitant smile. "What took you so long?"

"Making popcorn with real melted butter to pour over the top. I seem to remember someone liking to drench her popcorn."

Her eyes flashed before she rolled them. "I gave that luxury up when I started sitting at a desk all day, or else my grand-mother's hips would show even more."

He couldn't stop his gaze from raking over her. "Your hips are fine. And please don't refer to them as your grandmother's. Ever."

A chuckle bounced through her, lighting up her entire face. "Sorry for the weird visual."

Not much could stop him from enjoying the picture standing before him. "I'll let you in anyway. So, no butter?"

One shoulder lifted as she strode through the door. "Go ahead and throw it on. I'm living dangerously already."

Boy, he liked the sound of that. "Have a seat on the couch. Greasy popcorn and Coke coming your way." In the kitchen, Josh dumped the snack in a big bowl and drizzled the butter around. How many times had they sat on her parents' sofa, snuggled as close as possible to watch movies? The memory made his hands and lips tingle, and he hurried back to the living room to plop down next to her. Not as close as way back when, but as near as he dared. "Here's your Coke."

Her brows scrunched together as she studied him and took the drink. "There's a whole couch here, you know."

"We can both reach the bowl this way."

"You only own one?"

"No, but—"

"Just hand over the popcorn." The slight smirk made her lips quirk as if she were trying not to smile.

"Figures you'd start hogging it already." He placed the bowl on her lap.

She huffed. "Because you eat way too fast."

"You're right." He winked and grinned.

"Of course, I'm right. Play the movie." She threw several pieces of the buttery snack in her mouth.

"Which one?"

"You know I like them both, so you pick."

He grabbed the remote and punched play. "In honor of the start of Christmas season, I put in Elf. J.D.'s not old enough for some of the plot yet."

The music from the previews blared, and he lowered the volume.

Maggie slowed her eating. "Probably not the best one for Dahlia yet, either."

"Especially with her questions about her father."

"Wait." Her head jerked toward him, and she set the bowl on the table. "Press stop and explain."

Complying, he rehashed the conversations he and Dahlia'd had recently about fathers.

Maggie shook her head. "So unfair."

Josh swallowed past the lump in his throat. "I'm sure J.D. will have the same kind of issues over his mother at some point."

"What's with his mother anyway? What happened? What's she like?" Maggie's arms waved around in her typical dramatic fashion. "I don't understand. She must've been nuts. Even with all my hang-ups, I'd never leave that little boy." She scoffed and nodded toward the window. "No matter what the stinking weather was."

"I know you wouldn't." And he didn't really want to talk more about his ex-wife. He wanted to talk about him and Maggie. "About not leaving… What about me? Have you thought more about us?"

"Josh, I was asking you about his mother. I want to understand. Is she anything like me?"

A bitter laugh slipped through Josh's lips. "She's a woman."

Her gaze nailed him. "I'm being serious."

Trisha. He might as well get this over with. But how could he describe his ex without diving into a deep black hole of anger. "Not like you. She makes a great first impression."

Maggie's brows scrunched, but she didn't say anything.

Way to flatter, knucklehead. "That didn't come out right. It's just she was quite a socialite. We met at the gym, and I ran into her a few times at events at the yacht club. She invited me to several high-dollar fundraisers for charities as her date." His jaw tightened. Why had he fallen into her trap? "I was lonely, I guess."

"So you married her because you were lonely?" Her head shook like that didn't compute.

"Well, she was attractive, too."

She sighed. "Attractive. Got it. Then what?"

Then the real Trisha surfaced. "She lived for the Coast society life. I mean, pilots make good money, but she could blow through our accounts fast. We had talks, more like arguments, about how I didn't believe in going into debt. I wanted to live within our means." He shrugged and clucked his tongue. "It never made any difference. The pregnancy came soon after we married and was an accident—she'd been on an antibiotic. I tried even harder to make things work. She wasn't happy about becoming a mother. While she continued to live at the gym, I worried about the baby."

"Oh, Josh. I bet you did." Her hand covered his, her warmth comforting him.

Was she actually sympathizing with him? Maybe they did have a chance.

"Once J.D. was born, she started traveling with single friends. Going to social events while I stayed home with J.D. It didn't take her long to find a new, wealthier husband."

Maggie shook her head, looked at their hands, and then met his gaze again. "I'm sorry for dredging this up. I just wanted to understand." She let out an extended breath. "At least I know the basics, not that I totally get it."

Neither did he. "That's the short version." In a way, it was good to get his past out in the open with Maggie. She knew him better than most, even though they'd been apart over ten years. Would she let him closer...let him back into her heart? "So?"

"What?" She cocked her head.

He inhaled a shaky breath. "I love you, Maggie. Always have. Could there be an *us* again? It'll be brutal being around you otherwise. Not that I wouldn't suffer through it for J.D.'s sake."

Mashing her lips together, she stared at the stilled image on the TV. "I don't know. If something happens to you out there while you're working, I just don't know how I'd go on if we..."

His free hand traveled to her cheek and caressed it with his thumb. "You can't keep your heart buried in the wreckage. Don't let fear chase your life away. You'll only end up alone."

Moisture gathered on her long dark lashes. "Josh, I do love you, but—"

The phone on the table broke the moment.

No. Not now.

It was the ring he'd designated for his boss. Maybe it wasn't a crisis, but with the rain, the cold front, and the likely fog at sea…

He stared at the aggravating invention.

"Just answer, Josh, or they'll keep calling like last time."

"Promise me you won't lose that thought. Except maybe you could forget the 'but.'" He grabbed the cell and accepted the call. "This is Josh."

"We've got an emergency. Need all hands on deck if you have someone to watch your son."

His chin dropped to his chest. "What happened?"

"Loaded cruise ship is in trouble. A lot of fog out there and shifting northwesterly winds. We really need you."

"Hold on." He glanced at Maggie and pressed mute. This would make or break things for them, no doubt. "A cruise ship in trouble."

Her mouth dropped open, and her hand slipped away from his, cool air replacing her warmth.

"I won't go if you don't—"

"Do what you have to do."

The thought of leaving split him in two.

Her gaze fell to the floor. "Do you have a will? Who's J.D.'s guardian?"

"Yeah, my mother. But, Maggie, nothing's going to happen."

"You don't know that. Just go do your job. I can't talk about anything else right now."

The phone weighed his hand down like an overfilled tanker, but he pressed the button to unmute it and lifted it to his ear. "On my way."

Chapter 25

Letting Josh walk out that door released a chilling fear deep in Maggie's bones. A fear that swept over her like a rip current grabbing hold and pulling her under. She struggled for air, anxiety locking down her lungs. It sent her sinking to her knees like a heavy chest plummeting to the bottom of the ocean's floor.

Tears flooded her vision, cascaded down her cheeks. She longed to beg and scream to God for Josh's protection, but she couldn't wake that sleeping angel in the back of the house.

Josh...so much like her father. Duty bound. Brave. Strong.

Her heart squeezed at the memory, and her chest shook. No longer able to keep the sobs inside, she rose, made her way to the front door, and stepped out onto the porch of Josh's house. Leaning over the railing, she spoke into falling rain. "Please, God, don't let his life end the same way as Daddy's did. Place your hand of protection over Josh. Still the wind and the waves at just the right time. God, J.D. can't lose him. I can't lose him."

More words and pleas and groans flowed from her lips toward the heavens. The harder she prayed, the more big fat raindrops fell, like tears from heaven.

"Maggie?" Above the downpour, a scratchy voice called from next door. "What are you doing out? You'll be sick again."

"Aunt Ruth?" Maggie turned and squinted to confirm she wasn't imagining things. Through her tears, she focused on the elderly woman standing in the entryway next door.

"Come here, child." Her aunt waved her over.

"I can't leave J.D." Her voice quivered. "Josh got called out."

"Just come to the porch, then." Aunt Ruth's fists went to her hips. "Don't make me walk over there."

A sigh worked its way through Maggie's teeth. "Just for a minute." What was so stinking urgent? Had something happened to Cammie? Or to Dahlia?

Cold and clammy, Maggie ran through the yard, sloshing water on her feet and legs. Breathless, she reached the top step. "What's wrong?"

"You need me."

"I need you?" Had Aunt Ruth finally lost it? Or was she sleepwalking?

"The Lord sends me nudges sometimes. I try to follow when He does."

Still not helpful. "Okay."

"I was snoozing in my bedroom with the TV on, and He nudged me. Nothing audible, but clearly I was to go onto the porch and help Maggie."

"A nudge?"

"That's what I call them. It's like an urge from above." Aunt Ruth held out her arms. "Come here, darling girl."

Her aunt hadn't ever been super affectionate or mushy— more a steady, comforting presence all their lives—but Maggie stepped closer. "I'm wet." She searched Aunt Ruth's face. Did her aunt see her swollen, red-rimmed eyes?

"I won't melt. Let someone comfort you."

Comfort did sound good. Shoulders quivering, Maggie moved into the embrace. Her emotions were too raw to hold back the tears, and they flowed onto her aunt's shoulder. Her nose stung, but warmth and love flowed back from the thin woman who had always been there for her family.

"Magnolia."

"Yes?" Maggie sniffled and lifted her head.

"Your faith can't keep tossing and turning with the wind." Aunt Ruth rubbed up and down Maggie's shoulder. "Sooner or later, you must decide, 'Though He slay me, still I will trust Him.' Know that He is with you when you pass through the rough waters of life."

"I know you're right, but I don't know how. It's so hard to let my heart hope."

"Let your hope be in the Lord. Let your faith come from knowing He loves you, no matter what kind of storm whirls around you."

Maggie swallowed the panic strangling her and allowed her aunt's words to seep into her soul. Everything her aunt said made sense. Maggie took a cleansing breath. Living out that kind of faith took such trust. A trust she would strive toward. "Thank you. Thank you for being faithful and listening for those nudges."

"You're welcome. I love you like a daughter."

"I love you, too. Like another mother." And she did. Maggie released her and took a step back. "Pray for Josh. And me. I need to get back inside. J.D. might wake up."

"I pray for you every day. Always have. I've been adding Josh and that sweet boy, too, for some time now." The door hinges creaked as her aunt pushed it open, but then she stopped. "Listen for your own nudges from the Lord, sweet Maggie."

"I'll try." The warmth of her aunt's words enveloped her as she splashed back across the puddles in the grass. Inside Josh's house, she shut the door against the wet, cold rain and shook off her flip-flops. Water dripped from her skin. She hadn't left anything to change into here, so she'd have to raid Josh's closet for a dry T-shirt and gym shorts.

Tiptoeing down the hall, she peeked in on J.D. The child slept curled in a ball, the nightlights revealing a sweet smile on his lips. He had no inkling his father was gone, possibly in danger. Maggie moved on to Josh's room and found one of his shirts, then slipped it over her head and snuggled under the covers. The sleep of trust. How she longed for that.

~~~

The cruise ship towered over the pilot boat like a dark, jagged mountain in the fog. It had been a long, wild ride out on rough waters, and transferring to the large vessel would likely be challenging. A ship this size would be difficult to control in heavy winds. They'd called out tugboats to assist, and even with the help, there would be a chance of losing control of her or having her break loose from the towing cable. In that case, she would be at the mercy of wind and seas and, in these waters, probably grounding or washing up on a rock jetty. With a full ship of travelers, Josh couldn't let anything happen on his watch.

Once Graham was safely aboard to pilot the lead tug and they'd confirmed the radio connection, Josh secured his harness to the railing and wiped the moisture from his eyes. Visibility wasn't zero, but it was bad enough.

Lights shone from the tugboats alongside and in front of the stranded vessel, but bobbed out of sight when the giant swells rolled between them. The engine fire that left the ship and its passengers stranded had been put out, and no lives had been lost. Yet. The violent wind and waves had come up quickly and pulled them into this quagmire, otherwise no pilot in their right mind would attempt to navigate the pass. Now they had no choice but to make the attempt. Tugging the ship into safe harbor would be hard enough without the monster waves crashing around them. Josh was well acquainted with the crew and captains on the tugs, though. Good, experienced men. And they all understood the risks.

A foaming swell crested and broke, pitching Josh's boat and sending him sliding across the deck. Angry water rushed at him, and his hip hit hard against the metal. Thank God, he still had on the harness, otherwise the assault would've sent him overboard. Maybe he should've taken up bull riding. It might've been safer.

The salty spray burned his eyes, and he squeezed them shut. A vision materialized in his mind, a beautiful picture of J.D. and Maggie waiting at home. She'd said she still loved him, but… He wanted more than anything to get back to continue that conversation. His grip tightened as another wave crashed over the deck. "Help me do this, Lord."

At the mercy of violent seas, he'd fail, but at the mercy of a good God, he had a chance to get himself and a few thousand vacationers through rough water and to safety.

He needed to concentrate. Josh looked up at the ladder attached to the cruise ship, tried to get a feel for the rhythm of the churning water, and then unhitched the harness. The boat pitched upward, and he flung himself toward the closest rung. A roller dipped them down into the swell, and his grip faltered. His hands scrambled to catch hold of anything solid.

Another breaker swept over him, and he plunged into the Gulf.

Chapter 26

The water-activated strobe light from Josh's vest flashed as he lifted, then immediately plummeted with the large swells. Everything else a blur, he tried to focus despite the frigid water chilling every inch of his skin. He needed to get his breathing under control. The crew should've dropped a life ring by now with a strobe of its own, and he had to find it before he was swept out to sea.

Swiveling, he scanned the undulating surface for his boat. He had to stay calm. The crew knew what to do. Salty water sprayed into his face, filled his mouth. A smell that reminded him of both home and fear—fear of being lost to the massive depths of the Gulf. Fear of leaving his son fatherless. Fear of never seeing J.D. or Maggie again.

He had to keep his head. He couldn't let the fear swamp him.

Help me, Lord.

The waves lifted him again, and he spotted his boat. Though a chill bit into his legs, he kicked hard toward it. He added vigorous strokes with his arms, fighting the currents. It seemed like the crash of the waves around him propelled him backward with every stroke. Still, he couldn't give up.

Fighting for breath, he peered up and spotted the glow of lights. One good thing about the cruise ship being disabled was that it wouldn't be making much headway either. Easier to try to stay close to…if that were even possible in this weather. The crash of the water filled his ears, making it difficult to hear if someone was yelling directions, but he shouted and waved both of his arms. "Here! I'm here!"

The pilot boat turned toward him and circled. They saw him, thank God. Now if they could get him aboard without crushing him against the hull in the wind and waves. "Lord, if you're willing, save me."

He stayed put as the vessel attempted to come alongside. One of the men stood on the port side and threw a blinking life preserver. Josh tried to catch it. He missed. He swam hard toward the flashing red strobe, the beacon that might be his only chance out of this predicament. The waves pressed against him. Time after time, he neared the blasted thing, but each time he was swept back before he could catch hold.

Come on.

He pushed himself to swim harder until finally, his cold, wet fingers caught hold of something solid. The needle in this haystack of water.

Thank you, God.

Josh pulled the ring over himself and tugged the line to let them know he was ready. The rope quickly yanked him close to the boat, and he prepared himself for possible impact as they tried to reel him up. The seas still churned, but maybe not as high. He thudded against the hull on the same hip that had hit the railing earlier. He groaned and grabbed toward the arms and hands reaching out to him. His body clipped the railing and then landed with a thud on the deck. Coughing, he laid his head back as the crew checked him for broken bones or other injuries.

Was he injured? He was so chilled, he couldn't tell.

He lifted each limb one at a time. All felt fine except for his bruised hip. "I'm good. Let me transfer to the other ship and get us out of here."

The crew argued to abort the mission, but he was determined, and the water seemed to be calming. He looked toward the clearing skies. Someone upstairs was answering prayers. "I can do this. Believe me, I won't slip this time." Despite the fact that his fingers were numb.

They lined up once again beside the cruise ship, and he caught the rung. Metal never felt so good in his hands. His legs seemed to have doubled in weight, but he forced them up, step by step, until he boarded the ship. Wide-eyed crewmen met him. Josh motioned. "Take me to the bridge, and let's get out of here."

~~~

Waking in Josh's bed might've been a long-denied dream of hers, but not the way it had happened so far on this trip. Those days when she'd been sick had been awful, but nothing like now, waiting while Josh ran off to save the world.

Maggie rolled over and turned off her alarm. She wouldn't need it. She hadn't slept much. As she'd done all night, she prayed again for Josh's safety before pushing her feet to the floor. At the closed master bathroom door, she stared at the *out-of-order* sign Josh had taped there. So weird. It wasn't as if J.D. could read. Was it a big mess in there, or should she call a plumber for him?

She'd figure that out later. Craving that black liquid that kept her going, she padded down the hall to start a pot of coffee. At J.D.'s room, she peeked in to check on him. The sweet angel still slept with the peace of the innocent. *Thank the Lord.* He hadn't even woken to climb in bed with her. Her emotions were in no shape to explain where his daddy had hauled off to, like there weren't enough able-bodied men to work the rescue.

Her aunt's words came back to her. "Your faith can't keep

tossing and turning in the wind. Sooner or later, you must decide, 'Though He slay me, still I will trust Him.'"

The thought hit her like a chunk of ice down her back. What had happened to her faith?

Had it sunk in the Gulf with her father? Had it been swallowed into the waters with their home?

She had still believed in God, but she hadn't understood Him. She hadn't trusted Him.

Why pray, if the prayers weren't answered? Why had He let her father die?

Take heart.

Her mother's words again. She found the filters, scooped coffee, and started the brew. "I'm trying to take heart, Lord. Trying to believe. Really." She spoke to the ceiling. She would try to cling to the fact that God was with her in the storm, not base her faith on whether her prayers were answered in the ways she thought they should be. After all, Aunt Ruth was right, faith was believing no matter what the circumstance.

"Though He slay me," she whispered.

"Miss Maggie?" A hand tugged on her T-shirt. "Who are you talking to?"

"Oh, J.D., I didn't hear you come in. Give me a hug, pumpkin." She lifted him up and closed her eyes, clinging to his warmth. "I love you."

"I love you, too, but you hug hard."

Maggie couldn't help but laugh. "Sorry. I didn't mean to suffocate you."

"Can we go eat captain cereal at Cammie's or have special pancakes?"

Maggie set him on his feet and shook her head. "I was thinking we should go back to having eggs like Daddy makes." Now that he was her responsibility, she'd study up on the best nutrition for kids. She was pretty sure protein for breakfast was a good idea.

"Okay." Not a super happy answer, but he hadn't put up a fuss. He made his way to the table and climbed into the booster. "I want them with orange cheese on top."

"Orange cheese, please?" If she was going to be taking care of him, she'd have to follow the manners protocol Josh was teaching him, too.

"Orange cheese, pleeeease." He smiled and drew out the word adorably.

Smiling, too, Maggie found a skillet and gathered the rest of the ingredients from the refrigerator. J.D. hadn't even asked where his father was. He must've been so accustomed to waking up with Josh gone. At least she wouldn't have to explain the sudden departure. But was it something she could get accustomed to?

Once they'd eaten and she'd dressed her little buddy, she carried him next door. The lights were still off, so she flipped the switch. Dahlia and Aunt Ruth must be still sleeping.

Maggie tweaked J.D's nose. "Can you look at a book while I get changed?" She didn't want to get him started watching too much television. Besides, she didn't know enough about children's shows to discern what was age-appropriate.

"What kind of book?"

Good question. She scanned the room for something to entertain a three-year-old. A shelf in the corner held old photo albums. "How about some picture books?" They had to be old since hardly anyone bothered to print their pictures anymore. And photos were the one thing her mother had been careful to take whenever they'd had to evacuate.

She stacked a pile of books on the floor. "See if you recognize anyone you know until I come back."

"Okay." He plopped down beside the mound of photo albums. "If I do, can I get a prize?"

"What's with you and prizes?"

"I like them."

Simple enough. "What kind of prize?"

His mouth twisted as he thought. "A sticker or coloring book. Or candy?"

"I think a sticker or coloring book would be fair." And it might keep him busy for a minute. "I'll try to pick one up later today."

The ring of her phone in her shorts pocket made her shoulders jerk. *Let it be Josh on his way home.*

She stared at the number. Angie? It was so early. A jolt of fear struck hard. Why would she be calling at the crack of dawn? Was something wrong with Cammie again? "Hello."

"Hey."

"Is everything okay? With Cammie? With Josh?"

"As far as I know. Graham was called out with Josh last night. I thought I'd snag J.D. before you get going with your day. He could come play with Conrad. Figured you wouldn't mind. Did you sleep?"

"Not really. How do you live like this? Your husband always in harm's way?"

"With my job as a nurse, I see plenty of sickness and accidents. Most aren't water-related. It's just part of life. It is what it is."

How could she see life and death as so cut and dried? "I'm sure J.D. would love to play with your son. Thanks."

"No worries. You've got a lot on your plate. I was excited to hear about Cammie's improvement. She said she'd be moving off the ICU floor into a regular room early this morning. That's wonderful."

So soon? "We are thankful." Maggie nodded, though no one could see her. She had to be more faithful in remembering to thank the Lord for every good thing. She'd been so caught up in the bad, she'd ignored the blessings around her, like Cammie's improvement. Like her aunt's love, and Dahlia staying well, and sweet little J.D.'s presence.

"Looks like our patient's got an admirer, too." Angie's smile could be felt through the phone.

A nurse was the perfect person to get the scoop. Not that Maggie hadn't been checking out Kyle Castro's background already, but nurses knew the lowdown on doctors' personal lives sometimes, too. "Yeah. I'd like to have a discussion about that."

Once she'd thoroughly grilled Angie—Dr. Castro's story seemed to check out—Maggie dressed in slacks and a button-down blouse, then went back to check on J.D.

Her eyes widened at the scene. Pictures littered the living room floor, and the plastic of many of the albums' pages were crumpled. Aunt Ruth and Cammie would kill her.

"J.D., let's put the pictures back in. They have to stay in the books to keep them nice." Another note-to-self about three-year-olds and supervision.

"But here's you and Daddy." He held up a photograph. "Is this your wedding?"

Maggie gulped and struggled to take a breath. "No. That's at the prom." What had she been thinking? A wave of memories assaulted her, clutched at her throat. The feel of Josh's arms around her, his goodnight kisses. That night had held so much promise for their future…all swept away a few months later.

"What's a prom?" His big blue eyes stared at her. So much like Josh's.

"It's a dance."

"But you're not dancing in this picture."

She couldn't look at that blasted photo a second longer. She bent down to stack the jumble on the floor. "We had to stop dancing to pose for the camera, pumpkin. Let's clean up." Hiding the mess in a closet and sorting through it later sounded like a better plan. Much later.

After Angie picked up J.D., Maggie dropped Aunt Ruth and Dahlia at the store. Mrs. Daigle had been waiting for them there. Another cause for praise. Maggie got things rolling, then set out to the hospital. A text from Dr. Castro gave her the new room number. He'd said Cammie was thrilled with the early morning move.

Inside the hospital, she followed the signs to the new ward. When she neared the open door, a giggle echoed from within, followed by her sister's voice. "Don't make me laugh, Kyle. It hurts."

"That's good. Means you're healing." Dr. Castro—Kyle—sat in a chair next to Cammie's bed. From the looks of the smile on her sister's face, the battle for her heart was good and won. The roses, gourmet coffee, and pastries from Cammie's favorite bakery had probably sealed the deal.

Maggie chuckled. The good doctor was...well, good. And by all accounts, a decent man. She knocked to get their attention. "Sorry to intrude. Y'all are sure chipper this morning."

"Come on in. We have good news." Dr. Castro stood and offered her his chair.

"No need. I'll take the other one." Maggie crossed the room to the sort-of recliner near the window. "What's the good news?" She sure relished the possibility.

"I'm moving to a rehab facility to start getting my strength back."

"When?" This was better than good news. It was a miracle.

"The day after tomorrow. I might even get a pass to come home for Christmas day if all goes well."

"Thank you, Lord." Now if He'd bring Josh home safe.

~~~

The bell on the door jingled again as Maggie checked out another customer. With the break in the rain before lunchtime, shoppers must've sprinted out of their houses and offices to start buying gifts this morning. All at once. Good thing Mrs. Daigle was at her side to help.

Maggie glanced up at the person heading straight toward the counter. "Angie?" Her fingers froze on the keys, and she craned her neck to search for J.D. "Why are you here without the kids?" Panic sucked the oxygen from her lungs, but she forced out words. "Did something happen to J.D.?"

"J.D.'s fine. My mother is watching both boys at the house. Can we talk in back or someplace?"

It had only been a few hours since Angie had picked him up. "You could've brought him here if you needed to shop."

"Maggie, I need to talk to you—"

"Oh, please, no." Fear seemed to drain the blood from Maggie's face. "It's Josh, isn't it?" Tears blurred her vision, but she staggered away from the register. "Mrs. Daigle, can you take over the front?"

"Of course, dear." Her warm hand patted Maggie's elbow. "Take as long as you need."

Moisture gathered on Maggie's upper lip, and she pinched the bridge of her nose on the way to the back room. "Tell me, Angie." She dropped her hand and spun to face the bad news head on. "Is he dead?"

Angie grabbed Maggie's forearms and squeezed. "No, no.

He's not dead. Sorry, I scared you. Graham called and said Josh is being observed in a Louisiana hospital overnight."

"For what?"

"Mild hypothermia and a couple of pretty bad bruises is all they've confirmed so far." Angie released her grip and took a step back. "Graham is there, but if you want to go to him, I'm here to help at the store. And my mom can keep J.D."

"Hypothermia?" A picture rolled through Maggie's mind of Josh being swept into the Gulf. Her nightmare had come true. "How did he…?" Realization swarmed her senses, lighting a fire in her gut. "He fell in, didn't he? Just like my father."

"Not just like your father." Angie gave a vigorous shake of her head. "Josh was rescued. He completed the mission and brought the cruise ship safely into port. He'll be fine, Maggie."

"This time." But what about the next? "I'm not leaving the store. Or Cammie and the kids. Josh knew the risks when he decided to leave. I promised to care for J.D. You can bring him here if you want to go visit Josh." Her fingers curled into a fist. She'd give Josh Bergeron a piece of her mind for scaring her like this when he got home. He'd better come home. Then she pictured him in a hospital bed and her heart pinched. "You said he's going to be fine, right?"

One side of Angie's mouth lifted. "You should go see for yourself. He's less than two hours away."

The woman was pushy.

"The store is busy. J.D., Dahlia, and Aunt Ruth need me. Cammie needs me, and I'm heading back to check on her again as soon as this rush of shoppers clears out. I'm not going to Louisiana. Really." Maggie pivoted and stepped back into the showroom. "Like you said, I have too much on my plate." Her feet led her back behind the checkout counter, but doubt followed her. Harassed her, really, churning her insides and her thoughts into one large vortex. The truth was, one way or another, Josh Bergeron would rip her heart out.

Chapter 27

There were too many voices in Cammie's hospital room. Something was up. Maggie hesitated at the cracked door. The aroma of food spilled from a passing lunch cart.

Dahlia shuffled at her side. "Are we going in or what?"

"Sure. I think I heard visitors." Inside, Angie and Dr. Kyle Castro and his daughter stood beside Cammie, who had devoured whatever was on her lunch tray already. "Angie, I keep running into you today."

Dr. Castro fidgeted with his watch. He seemed to do that a lot. His daughter smiled at Dahlia.

There was nothing fidgety about Angie. "I was telling Cammie about how Josh saved all those people on a cruise ship, but he is under the weather." Angie eyed Dahlia. "Dr. Castro has offered to take Dahlia home to spend the night with Anna, and J.D. can stay with my mother. I can help at the store…if you want to go visit him."

"Go, Maggie." Cammie waved a hand in a shooing motion. "What are you waiting on?"

"People in Jackson think I'm bossy, but obviously they don't know many people from the Coast." Overwhelmed, Maggie blew out a breath and turned to Dahlia. "What do you want to do?"

"I like hanging out with Anna, and Mr. Kyle's helping me get into her school after the Christmas holidays."

"He is, huh?" Maggie turned her attention back to *Mr. Kyle*.

He shrugged one shoulder. "The director is my second

cousin."

"You can be there in two hours if you leave now, Maggie." Cammie's hands started flapping again. "I already arranged for Mrs. Daigle to pick up Aunt Ruth in the morning and open the store." She batted her lashes and pouted Maggie's way. "Josh doesn't have any family here to look after him. He's all alone."

So much guilting. Maggie punched one hand on her hip, though the image Cammie had painted clogged her throat with emotion. "Angie said her husband is with him."

"That's not the same and you know it. Go." The set of Cammie's chin said her sister wasn't going to drop this subject. Or the quest to reunite her with Josh.

"Aunt Maggie, he'd love to see you." Dahlia joined the conspiracy. "I can tell by the way he looks at you."

A picture of Josh lying alone in a room much like this one filled Maggie's mind. Something inside her told her to go. Was this one of those nudges? "Angie, could you text me the hospital information? Please?"

Pivoting to avoid all the smirks, Maggie trudged back to the parking lot. She'd go, but it didn't mean she was committing her heart to Josh Bergeron.

~~~

Josh mashed his eyes shut as he readjusted his position in the hospital bed. The throbbing in his hip made it challenging to get comfortable, but he couldn't stay still any longer. Another rerun of *Everybody Loves Raymond* started on the TV. At least he'd found something to occupy his mind since Graham had gotten called away. His friend had been guarded about the reason. Hopefully, it was nothing serious, because he hated the thought of Graham having to drive all the way back here in the morning to pick him up. There was no reason for the doctor to keep him prisoner in this bed tonight. He should be home with J.D.

And Maggie, too, if she'd even speak to him. He'd been a coward and let Angie handle delivering the news of the mishap.

The door swung open, and as if the thought had summoned her, Maggie strode in. Was he dreaming? He didn't think he'd hit his head. The doctor might've been right to keep him for observation.

"So what happened? How'd you go overboard?" The vision's arms folded across her chest, and her eyebrows did that frustrated scrunching.

Josh stared.

"Did you bite your tongue or something? You're gawking at me." She walked to the edge of the bed and placed a warm hand on his forehead.

"Maggie? Are you real?" His confused brain churned.

"Last time I checked." A chuckle shook her shoulders and transformed her frown into a small smile. "Do you think you're hallucinating?"

"Pinch me." The real Maggie would. A second later, pain bit into his shoulder. "Ouch."

"Real enough?" Mischief danced in her dark eyes.

It was her. He rubbed his arm. "I should pinch you back. I'm in a hospital, you know." He tried to smother a grin. She'd actually come all this way to see him. Could there still be hope for them?

"I didn't think you'd been badly injured." Worry drew her lips together.

"A little chilled is all." He reached out from his cocoon of covers and scooted over, gritting his teeth to keep from groaning, and then patted the bed. "They say body heat is the best way to help patients with hypothermia. You could lie next to me." He raised his brows and gave a pitiful look.

"What?" She huffed. "Where is Graham?"

"He got called away, but he said he'd pick me up in the morning. I really didn't want him to snuggle up close to me, though."

"You." She waved her hands at him. "I don't think you're very injured at all." Her eyes narrowed, but her lips twitched as if she were fighting a smile.

"Tell that to my hip." He deserved a little sympathy after his ordeal. "Sit here and watch Raymond with me." He made his best puppy-dog eyes once more.

Almost growling, she sat and leaned back against the elevated mattress. "Don't look at me like that. You know I can't fight your pitiful baby blues."

"I should've tried being pathetic a long time ago." The warmth of her shoulder next to his spread through his chest. "Thanks for coming."

"Yeah, well, seems you have a lot of plotting fans. Graham included."

Disappointment welled a hole in his hopes. "So you didn't want to come?" He couldn't look at her face, or he might lose his composure. "I'm sorry they forced you into this. You don't have to stay."

"It's not that *I* didn't want to be here." Her fingers twisted the ends of her hair, and he wished he could touch it, too. "I didn't want *you* to be here."

Made sense. He didn't want to be here either, and she already had the tough situation with Cammie. "You have too much on you already. I knew that, and I made a stressful situation worse. I shouldn't have gone out. I won't do this to you again."

Her head spun, and she propped herself on one elbow, leaning over him to meet his eyes. "What are you saying?"

What was he saying?

Thoughts of J.D. and his conversations with Dahlia paraded through his mind. Thoughts of the water swallowing him into an early grave. He had a responsibility to parent his son, and if the only way Maggie would have a romantic relationship with him was if he gave up his career, so be it. "Maggie, you are my past, but you're my future, too. I'll find another job if that's what it takes to be with you." He lifted one hand from beneath the covers to touch her face. "To marry you."

Eyes welling with tears, she collapsed back against the mattress. She brushed at the moisture forming on her lashes.

What was she thinking?

Then she snuggled closer, her warmth spreading over him like the warm Southern sun. "We can't make those kinds of decisions today, so much is going on right now. Let's table this discussion until life evens out. Focus on getting you well for tonight." She took his hand in hers. "And being thankful you're alive."

She was right, of course. And she was here at his side. He would wait—as long as it took, because nothing had ever felt so right.

Chapter 28

The aroma of good coffee slipped into the bedroom. Maggie sucked in a large gulp of chilly air. She needed to turn on the heat. The temperature had dropped in time for Christmas. A whiff of something cooking made her stomach growl. Had Josh let himself in? Aunt Ruth hadn't touched the stove since Maggie had arrived.

She rolled over, blurry-eyed, to check the time on her phone.

Six a.m. Christmas morning.

The door swung open. "Miss Maggie. Can we open presents now?" The bed bounced as J.D. climbed up next to her. His fingers went immediately to her hair and twirled a strand in little circles.

So, definitely Josh cooking down the hall. "Good morning, pumpkin." She pulled him into a soft hug. "I'll have to ask Daddy first and wake up Dahlia and Aunt Ruth."

"I'll wake them." Sliding from her arms, he took off, scurrying on the hardwood floors toward Dahlia's room.

She kicked away the cotton blanket and pivoted to her feet to search out the source of the delightful aroma. Her robe hung from the quilt rack near the door, and she grabbed it on the way and pulled it around her shoulders.

Once she reached the archway into the kitchen, she halted. The sight of Josh's profile hovering over the stove took her breath away. Tall, strong frame. That sandy hair. The image that illuminated her past. Possibly her future. What would it be

257

like to wake to this vision for as long as they both should live?

Since she'd stayed with him that night at the hospital, she couldn't imagine going back to her life the way it had been before—living alone, coming home to an empty house, waking up alone. She'd put off the conversation he'd started, hoping to wait until things settled down. Had they settled yet? At rehab, Cammie was improving daily.

Josh caught her staring at him like a teenage girl with a crush. Maybe she still was.

He flashed a grin, his blue eyes twinkling.

"Merry Christmas." He set aside a pair of tongs and locked his gaze on her.

"Merry Christmas." It felt as though her whole body smiled back, and she couldn't stop her feet from stepping toward him.

Reaching out, he caught her in an embrace and brushed her forehead with a kiss.

Warmth enveloped her, flowed over her with the intense draw and peace of home. His chest rose and fell, and she buried her face in his shoulder, squeezing him closer.

"I woke everyone, Daddy. Can we open presents?" J.D.'s cute voice added to that peace. Dahlia and Aunt Ruth stood behind him.

Maggie lifted her head and gazed at Josh's face. "What do you say, Daddy?"

"What do you say, Maggie? Cammie's not here yet."

Why was Josh asking her? She waited for him to say something else, but he didn't. "J.D. and Dahlia can open their presents from me. And I have one for you and Aunt Ruth. We'll have breakfast and wait for Cammie before opening the rest."

"Good plan." Josh's lips brushed her cheek. "I've got

beignets made. Shrimp and grits in the oven."

"Beignets! My favorite." J.D.'s eyes widened as he scanned the counter for the squares of fried dough and powdered sugar. A temporary distraction from the gifts.

Maggie couldn't help but grin. "My favorite, too."

Rays of light from the window filtered through and danced in Josh's eyes. "I remember."

The warmth she'd felt earlier surged to a blaze. Maggie shifted her gaze to the table and pulled out a chair. Josh had even set out the dishes already. "If they're done, let's enjoy them."

Aunt Ruth shuffled toward the table while the kids scrambled around her to take their seats. Josh carried the food and set it before them.

He sat beside her and held out his hands. "Let's say grace."

Maggie laid her hand in his, and his warm fingers closed over it. Dahlia's feathery grip held her other.

"Dear Father." Josh's voice exuded strength and humility. "Thank You for Your bountiful blessings and presence in our lives. On Christmas, we are reminded of all You gave up for us because You loved us so. You were willing to send Your Son so we could be with you. We praise you. Thank you for this family you've put together here, Father. For J.D. and Dahlia and Ruth and Cammie." He squeezed her hand. "And for Maggie coming to take care of us all."

Joy filled Maggie, flowed over her like a warm, gentle wave.

"Amen." Josh finished, and the others echoed. "Let's dig in." He passed Maggie the tray. "You first, since I know you're dying for one of my treats." His smirk couldn't get much more mischievous.

After devouring her share of the sugary delicacies and the grits casserole, Maggie wiped the powdered sugar from her fingers and mouth. "That right there was all the present I needed. Thank you, Josh."

A satisfied smile lifted his lips. "Glad you liked the food, but I have a real present for you." His brows lifted and lowered. "Later."

What did that look mean? She'd bought him an antique compass and spyglass from the store, but who knew if he'd like it? Oh, and a brass barometer, thermometer, and hygrometer for staying alert to the weather. And a parenting book.

"I'm finished now." J.D.'s big eyes pleaded his unspoken request.

After checking his plate to make sure he'd eaten more than the beignets, Maggie stood and held out her arms. "All right. Let's go to the living room, and I'll let you and Dahlia open your gifts from me."

"Gifts?" His voice excited, J.D. latched arms and legs around her.

"Well, I wrapped them individually and put them all in one big bag. Come on, Dahlia." She tweaked her niece's nose and smiled.

Once she'd situated J.D. on the couch by Dahlia, Maggie picked up presents and handed one to each child and to Josh and Aunt Ruth. "I can't wait. I hope you like what I bought. I'm not the best at picking out gifts."

Dahlia shook her head. "She's really not."

"She tries, and it's the thought that counts." Aunt Ruth's attempt at scolding Dahlia only confirmed Maggie's insecurities.

"Dig in. I saved the receipts so you can return them." At least this would make whatever someone else gave them seem like a great gift. She took a seat on a nearby ottoman to watch.

Aunt Ruth opened her present and gasped. "Maggie, you

shouldn't have. A cruise?"

"I made a few calls to the senior center to find out which one."

A second later, J.D. dumped his bag over, spreading the contents onto the floor.

"That's one way to do it." Maggie laughed. "A man after my own heart."

"What's this?" J.D. held up the first package he'd unwrapped.

"That's a weather kit that you and I can play with together."

"Oh." His brows scrunched together.

Dahlia scoffed. "I get one every year. Get used to it, J.D."

"What? Not every year, and it'll be fun, but there's more. Open that." Maggie pointed at another good-sized package.

He tore through the paper. "A firetruck!"

"You like it?"

"Yeah." He ripped the cardboard holding it in place.

Maggie eyed Josh for a reaction. "He can at least consider other careers."

Josh rolled his eyes. "Because running into burning buildings is so much safer."

"I meant a career in meteorology."

"Right." He shook his head. "Did I get a weather kit, too?"

Oh no. Could she grab his present and ditch half of it? Her eyes shifted to his gift.

"You did, didn't you?" Chuckling, Josh took the package and split open the paper, then held up the instruments and the parenting book. "Actually, I like all of these a lot. Very nice."

"You do?" Maggie searched his face to see if he was joking.

"Especially the compass." He stood and crossed the room to kneel beside the ottoman and hug her. "If it always leads me back to you." Those eyes again.

Her heart whirled like a wind vane in a tornado. "Maybe so." Yes. "I'm glad you don't hate it."

"I hope you don't hate my gift either."

~~~

Would Maggie like the armoire? And what it held inside? Josh plopped down on the floor beside her. Having her next to him after so many years was more than enough, but it was cute how she'd given him half-weather, half-nautical equipment. A slight shift to middle ground. Would she move the rest of the way and give him her heart?

"Hey, hey. We're here," a man's voice called from the kitchen.

"Kyle and Cammie." Maggie jumped to her feet.

A wheelchair pushed through the archway with Cammie. Her sister's smile shone like a lighthouse through a dark night. "I've never been so happy to be home. At least for the day."

"You'll be out soon." Kyle patted Cammie's shoulder. His daughter stood at his side.

Dahlia ran to greet them. "Merry Christmas, Mama." Cautiously, she planted a kiss on her mother's cheek.

"Merry Christmas, baby." Cammie glanced at the littered room. "Y'all started without me?"

"Only our gifts from Aunt Maggie," Dahlia said. "Nothing big."

Maggie huffed. "Excuse me? I'm standing right here."

Cammie laughed strong and loud. "Another weather kit?"

"There were other things, too." Maggie grabbed a package from under the tree. "Here, I didn't get you anything weather-related."

"First, I have something for all of you." Cammie looked up at Kyle, who nodded and bent down to lift up the footrests.

Then she slid forward in her chair. Her feet touched the ground, and with Kyle's help, she stood and took a few steps.

Maggie pressed one hand over her mouth, and her chest shook. "Thank you, Lord." Tears streamed down her cheeks. "So many miracles and answered prayers."

Kyle helped Cammie turn around and return to the chair. "God is good."

After more presents were opened, Josh caught Maggie's arm. "Let's go next door so you can open the gift I have for you."

"Next door? Why don't you bring it over?" Her dark eyes roamed his face.

"You'll understand when we get there. Trust me." And he didn't want everyone to see her freak out. Or say no, thanks.

Inside his house, he took her hand and headed down the hall. "This way."

"Um, okay." One brow lifted as she glanced at him. "You're lucky I trust you. At least I used to."

When he reached the bedroom, he stopped at the door. "Okay, I guess this does seem kind of weird, but your present is in my bathroom."

"A plumber or an old toilet?"

"Ha. Neither. I could never afford a plumber on Christmas."

"Very funny."

"I couldn't put your present anywhere else without you seeing it."

"Are you saying I nose around your home?"

"Have you?" He studied her for a reaction, but all she did was cross her arms. Finally, he smiled as he swung open the door and held his breath. "This is part of it."

Maggie's mouth gaped as she took in the armoire. "When?

How? Aunt Ruth said she sold it."

"Wasn't easy, but do you want it? I know it's not exactly the same one you had before the storm."

She stepped closer and ran her fingers over the intricately carved wood. "Not exactly the same, no." Her glistening eyes blazed into his. "But maybe better, and I'll appreciate it more."

Could the same be said for their relationship? "Open the door."

Her gaze held his a second longer before she moved her hand to pull the latch. The diamond ring on the shelf caught the light and sparkled. Her hand trembled as she reached for it. "What is this?"

Josh dropped to one knee. *Here goes. Lord, help me.* "Maggie, sort of like this armoire, I'm not exactly the same boy you knew and grew up with either. There's some wear and tear on my heart, a lot of water under the bridge. But I love you more than ever, and maybe this time, we can make it. Our love could be more mature, stronger…better. I'll give up whatever I have to for you, me, and J.D. to be a family. Will you marry me, Magnolia Marovich?"

Dropping to her knees with him, Maggie took his hand. "You are who you are, Josh. I won't ask you to give up anything. But you better be careful out there in the Gulf. And don't knock the meteorology career path I'm trying to sell J.D."

Was she saying what he thought she was? "I will. I mean, I won't—"

"Put this ring on me, Joshua David Bergeron, and then kiss me like a happy fiancé should."

Yes. She'd said yes.

He took her hand, which was so warm as he singled out her ring finger. Maggie stared at the sparkling facets while he slipped the cool platinum band over her finger. It snagged on her knuckle, then slid into place as if it had always belonged there. A perfect fit. His hands moved to caress her face, followed her cheekbone to wade through the mass of dark curls that had haunted him for so long. His gaze moved to her mouth and his lips found Maggie's for the kind of kiss he'd waited over a decade to give.

She tasted of powdered sugar, sunny days of the past, and sunny days of the future. Visions flashed through his mind—sailing and the beach and star-filled skies. She kissed him back, soft and sweet at first, and then stronger, moving him with more force than any current or wind or sea. Maggie would always be his perfect storm.

Chapter 29

Maggie stroked her infant daughter's hair once more. With the wind blowing in from the Gulf, the wild mass of dark curls would not be tamed, but on Lilly Ruth, the ringlets were adorable.

Their stocky black dog nudged its wet nose on the back of Maggie's leg and whined.

"Sit, Matey. You'll be on the boat soon enough."

The mixed breed complied, tail wagging and ears flopping in the wind. About like the first day they'd met him here with the owner. Only much larger than they'd expected. At least he was a smart one.

Josh and J.D. set up lounge chairs and a playpen next to the largest rolling cooler they could find at Walmart. Who knew babies required so much equipment?

"Josh, take Lilly Ruth while I put sunscreen on y'all."

"Mama, I did it already." J.D. sighed.

"Sailor, you know better than to argue with your mama." Flashing a grin, Josh tousled their son's hair, then marched over, slipped his shirt off, and held his arms out for Lilly Ruth.

"Yes, ma'am, I mean, and sir." J.D. smiled up at his daddy with those big blue eyes. "Both of you."

Her guys stood before her, excited to take out the *Cajun Princess II*. As she slathered them with sunscreen, Maggie's heart swelled with warmth. She'd never known so much love was possible. Only a year after their marriage, they'd become a family of four, five if you counted Matey, but her love had more than multiplied. It had exploded. Thankful for each day they had together, she strived to be a humble servant of the Lord and a good wife and mother. Nothing fulfilled her more. She'd learned to worry less when Josh was out, and to count her blessings all the time. The blessings of a normal day—and they were too many to count.

The horn of an SUV honked. Maggie turned to find Kyle and Cammie striding toward them, Dahlia and Anna chattering behind. Maggie couldn't help but grin. "Hey, don't Dr. and Mrs. Castro look tanned. Must've been good weather in the Caribbean for the honeymoon."

A smile lit up Cammie's face, and she took a seat in one of the chairs. "Couldn't have been more perfect."

"Amen." Kyle's grin was even larger, if that were possible.

"You girls need sunscreen?" Maggie held up the bottle.

Josh turned to shake hands with Kyle. "Watch out. She's armed."

"Mama took care of all that before we left." Dahlia ran to where the boat was anchored near the shore, Anna right behind her. "Come, Matey, I can't wait to ride out to Deer Island."

Maggie leveled a hard stare at her husband. "You guys be careful with J.D. and the girls. And Matey."

"We promise." Winking, Josh placed the baby back into Maggie's arms and brushed a kiss across her lips. "Relax and enjoy the beach."

His kisses still fluttered her heart. Every. Single. Time.

After she adjusted Lilly Ruth against her shoulder, Maggie settled into a chair beside her sister. She couldn't wait to cross-examine her about the honeymoon, the way Cammie had done to her when she and Josh had returned from their mountain retreat.

Once the guys cast off with the kids, she rotated Cammie's way. "So, tell me all about it."

"We ate, drank, and made merry. Shopped one day. Most of the time, we were on the beach." One side of her lips lifted. "Well, not all of the time exactly, but the rest is private."

"Think y'all will ever have a child together?"

"We have children together already. We're happy with our lives now." Cammie gave a carefree shrug. "Kyle and I want to relish our time as a couple. Plus, he's a super overprotective doctor-husband. He worries about my health, and I love having someone take care of me for a change."

Her sister was positively glowing, and tears sprung to Maggie's eyes. "Who knew God could use a spinal injury to put all of our lives together like this? And now we're both stay-at-home moms while Aunt Ruth and Kyle's mother are setting sail on yet another cruise. Mrs. Daigle enjoys owning the store."

"Like Aunt Ruth says, God isn't taken by surprise."

A chuckle burst through Maggie's lips. "But I sure am, though I'm learning to trust, too. Even in the darkest storms and the deepest waters, I know He's there with us."

August 29, 2005, Mississippi

Though I've written this novel and blogged about Katrina's devastation on my webpage, I wanted to share a few actual Katrina stories.

~~~

Everything that was our lives was destroyed in one morning; my parents' house, my house, which was our grandparents' home (where my family spent every holiday until my grandmother passed away in the mid-90s and where we rode out hurricane Camille in 69), every school we all attended, our church, our kids' school. The fabric of our lives was ripped to shreds. Everyone was scattered all over for months and months. The loss of so many old beautiful historic homes is incalculable. Though we've come a long way in almost twelve years, in my opinion, the Pass will never be what it was before August 29, 2005. Much of our history was erased that day.

Pass Christian Resident

My brother rode out the storm with my eighty-year-old father in our parents' home across from the beach. They went upstairs when water started coming in, then at some point the house started shaking and sailing back. Water came bursting through the front of the house. The whole place started collapsing and disintegrating below them. A line of trees in our backyard stopped the house. There was a dormer window in the back hall of the second story. They climbed out of that window and stayed on the roof at the back of the house. Water pushed through around them in rolling waves. They waited for hours under a small roof section that provided a little alcove while the wind blew projectile boards, debris, etc. around. It was during those hours that the Bible floated up as well as an old suitcase that had been in the attic for years. They found an old feather quilt in it that had been my mother's as a child. They used it to stay warm, and it kept my father from getting hypothermia.

Pass Christian resident

(From the brother in the story above) At some point during the storm, as I looked around, I noticed down below us right at the edge of the roof, a green book had fetched up. As I focused on it and considered what it could be and how it could have gotten there, it occurred to me that it looked just like one of the pocket Bibles that the Gideons distribute in hotel rooms. At first, I just left it where it was. I had no interest in going out into the wind unless it was necessary. But as I sat there and rolled this around in my mind, it began to seem like a minor miracle, some sort of sign, if it really was a Bible. I have subsequently joked that maybe God was telling me that I wasn't praying enough, that I better step it up a notch or two if I wanted us to make it through. And, in fact, I did continue to pray. All I know is that I thought something very important and meaningful had happened with the Bible somehow landing right at our feet. I knew I had to get the Bible before it blew away because it had become very important to me and I didn't want to lose it. So I crawled down and grabbed it and put it in my pocket for safekeeping. When I later asked Mama if we had such a book anywhere in the house, she couldn't think of any. So where could it have come from? There is really no logical explanation that comes to mind, so maybe it really was a miracle, sent by God.

Pass Christian resident

Me, my husband and children and grandchildren lived on Caspian Street in Bay St. Louis, Mississippi. When Katrina hit, we left the day before and came back home the day after, to no home at all. Our neighbors lost everything also. All we could do was stare and cry. There were houses, cars, boats, trailers, sheds, everything you could imagine all over Hwy 90 and 60. After my husband and children saw the damage we stayed in Lil Ray's Restaurant parking lot for about a week and a half, then we went to stay in Robert, Louisiana, about two to three months, until my husband, son, and son-in-law went and cleaned up some by our house. We put up tents to stay in until we could get some help. We got food from Salvation Army trucks and clothes from people donating, I'm very thankful for everything we received!

Melody Bourgeois

Although my house was the only one left standing on my street in Pass Christian, it had to be gutted to the studs. I'd had ten feet of storm surge inside. We had to live in Baton Rouge for one year. I had to enroll my son in kindergarten there. My daughter, Jordan, was ill with metachromatic leukodystrophy and had been receiving 24/7 nursing care at our house. She was the only patient left with this disease in our state that had this type of in-home care. We had fought for it. If I took her out of the state of Mississippi, she would lose it. So one of her nurses who owned an assisted living house in D'Iberville made a little corner for Jordan, so she could be taken care of. It was rough times. I was going back and forth from D'Iberville to Louisiana because this was at a time that Jordan was on death's steps. Actually, during that time is when she ended up receiving an experimental treatment in Mexico. She was about to die, so we had nothing to lose. Because of that she actually lived four more years.

Charlotte Logan, Pass Christian

We evacuated to Brandon for Katrina; but we had three families that stayed in our house because it was stronger than what they were staying in at the time. God knew what he was doing. During the first half of the storm, our chimney came through the roof, and many trees were on top of the house. The friends who stayed in our home went up on the roof during the eye of the storm to tarp the hole, and they punched holes in our ceiling to let the water drain from the attic. Without them doing these things we would have lost everything in the house. When we came back a month later, it looked like a war zone, but everyone was there to help each other pick up the pieces and move on. That is what Southerners do in times of crisis. My son's swing set was like a cork screw drilled into the ground up to the cross bars. I just thank God we were not in the house during the storm and that our friends were safe.

Michele Murray Ergle

As many would colloquially say, "Katrina weren't no lady." No sir. No ma'am. When she roared ashore, she brought the whole gang with her—and they were gang-busters. The aftermath is still with me today. I no longer live on the Coast. I no longer worry much about hurricanes. But gasoline and antiperspirant? Those are a different story. Both were hard to come by in the first weeks or more after the storm. I rarely ever let my truck get below half a tank of gas. And in my bathroom cabinet, you will seldom find only one stick of antiperspirant. Silly? I'm sure. At least until you are doing relief work in temps hotter than hades—and have no gas to get where you need to be and stink in the process! It's best to be a Boy Scout and always be prepared!

Les Ferguson, Jr.

When I went there right after the hurricane and walked through places where I grew up in, I couldn't recognize anything. I didn't know where I was in a place that had been so familiar. It was a haunting feeling. Family and friends' homes were gone, all the landmarks were gone, washed out into the water with the storm surge. I had no context. In the tall pines, there were grocery bags and trash stuck in the upper branches. That was the three-story-high water line. Ocean Springs had been home, but it no longer looks like the home I knew. Such an eerie feeling, such a loss. People don't realize the impact.

Angie Renner, Ocean Springs

My mother was an eighty-year-old lunch lady at the school with no savings. Her home was one house away from the beach in Pass Christian. We arrived after the storm to find the bottom floor had well over ten feet of storm surge, but it was still standing, unlike the house in front, which was gone, along with most of the rest of town—places that formed my memories of growing up. The insurance company was saying it wasn't hurricane damage, but flood, and flood damage wouldn't be covered. But the blessing was that our family came together, removed the debris, found termite damage, and were able to collect money for that. Churches from Pennsylvania hung sheetrock and put in Mama's floors. We recognize that our salvaged home is a miracle, and we have a story of coming together, a story of hope.

Terry Hunt, Pass Christian

In all of our experiences—from delivering relief supplies to rebuilding homes—the threads that resonate throughout the years are the reality of how quickly your life perspective can be radically changed, the very real presence of a loving God Who cares greatly for us—often in surprising ways, and how tragedy can unexpectedly weave lifelong friendships into our lives that otherwise would not have been formed.

Cindy Cheeks

Don't miss the next book by Janet W. Ferguson.

The Art of Rivers

Have you read the Southern Hearts Series by Janet W. Ferguson?

Dear Reader

Thank you for trusting me with your time and resources. I struggle at times when it seems my prayers are going unanswered, despite the fact that I am pounding on the doors of heaven. I wanted, perhaps needed, to write a story that explored this disappointment. I believe God's there. But what do we do with the hurt and sadness when life spirals out of our control? What Maggie learned, and I did, too, is that God is still there with us through the storm. He's still in control. He's with us in the pain. He's there to lean on, or He carries us when we can no longer stand. He's with us through other people, a touch, a meal, a phone call. Blessings rain down on us every minute of every day in the little things, like a soft mattress, a rainbow, a sunset, or a Bible rescued from a storm.

Blessings in Him who is able!

Did you enjoy this book? I hope so! **Would you take a quick minute to leave a review online?** It doesn't have to be long. Just a sentence or two telling what you liked about the book.

I love to hear from readers! You can connect with me on Facebook, Twitter, Pinterest, the contact page on my website, or subscribe to my newsletter "Under the Southern Sun" for exclusive book news and giveaways.

https://www.facebook.com/Janet.Ferguson.author
http://www.janetfergusonauthor.com/under-the-southern-sun
https://www.pinterest.com/janetwferguson/
https://twitter.com/JanetwFerguson

About the Author

Faith, Humor, Romance
Southern Style

Janet W. Ferguson grew up in Mississippi and received a degree in Banking and Finance from the University of Mississippi. She has served as a children's minister and a church youth volunteer. An avid reader, she worked as a librarian at a large public high school. She writes humorous inspirational fiction for people with real lives and real problems. Janet and her husband have two grown children, one really smart dog, and a few cats that allow them to share the space.

Publisher's Note: This book is a work of fiction. Names, characters, any resemblance to persons, living or dead, or events is purely coincidental. The characters and incidents are the product of the author's imagination and used fictitiously. Locales and public names are sometimes used for atmospheric purposes.

Ocean Springs, Mississippi, is a real town, but other than the name, the events in the location are fictional. None of the events are based on actual people. The charming city made the perfect backdrop for my novel.

Made in the USA
Columbia, SC
18 May 2020